" .... watching people cry".

Nigel White

"You can turn round and open your eyes now Roger", she said.

Roger turned .... and stood staring at her. He had wondered if she would be wearing a nightdress .... and he had even thought that she might be naked .... because she wasn't a shy girl. He'd discovered that last night ....

But Debbie's appearance left him virtually speechless ....

ISBN 978-1-9161749-0-0

First published in Great Britain: April 2018
by www.sugarcubepublishing.co.uk
This second (revised) edition published August 2019.
Reprinted January 2020.

Front Cover:
"Roger", said Debs, " ....we might have to ....".   *Page 145*

Printed and Bound in Great Britain by
Sarsen Press, 22 Hyde Street, Winchester, Hampshire SO23 7DR

By the same author:
"get Him out"   published 2017
                  second edn. 2019

DEDICATION

To Jeanida.

Who told me the Truth .... as though it was the most natural thing in the World.

Nine o'clock saw her sitting on her bed, in a pair of new pants, painting her toe nails. *Page 298*

PROLOGUE

Judge Gerald Milburn de Courcy raised his eyes, and surveyed the packed courtroom. There had been the usual flurry of comment following the delivery of the verdict. The Court Usher had quickly called for silence.

Judge Milburn de Courcy allowed the silence to become absolute. This was his last case. In a few days time he would be seventy five years old. He had decided upon retirement. He knew that his family were planning a surprise party. He had every intention of being surprised.

The Court waited for him to speak. There would be just a few more moments before the silence would be spoilt by the first stirrings of puzzlement.

In those moments, Judge Milburn de Courcy reflected sadly .... as had become his habit over the years .... that whilst it was now within his power to pronounce sentence upon the accused .... to prescribe appropriate punishment for the crime .... he had no power at all, to compensate those most immediately affected by the actions of the perpetrator.

He could do nothing for those who suffered .... beyond allowing them to see that the crime had been judged .... and that the punishment, allowed by law, would be administered.

Judge Milburn de Courcy took a breath. He turned his gaze upon the young man standing in the Dock.

He was about to deliver his last judgement

"You have heard the verdict of the Jury", he said. "And that verdict cannot be a surprise to you. Indeed .... you have never denied responsibility for the crime of which you have now been convicted. This court is well aware of your contention that your actions were justifiable .... that you were acting on God's behalf to punish those who transgressed against His laws".

The man in the Dock looked towards the Jury.

"It now falls upon me to pronounce sentence", said Judge Milburn. "Is there anything you wish to say".

"This court has no power over me", said the young man. " Al-lah .... and Al-lah only .... shall be my judge".

Judge Milburn de Courcy nodded.

"It is certainly my personal hope that your actions will, in due course, be judged by God", he said. "But at this moment, you are to be sentenced by an English Court of Law, over which I preside. Much of this assembly will be aware that this is my final case .... it will be the last time that I sit in judgement".

Judge Milburn paused.

"Young man", he said. "I have this to say to you. You came to this country as a guest .... to further your education. This country has a long history of welcoming those of foreign nationality to it's shores. Often as simple visitors, sometimes as refuge for those escaping tyranny and persecution, and frequently, as in your case, those who seek education. We make them welcome .... but we ask that they respect and obey our laws. We understand that occasionally, there will be transgressions. That such trangressions will often be committed, unintentionally, by those in ignorance of our laws. And under those circumstances, the law can, where appropriate, show understanding.

I must emphasise that ignorance of the Law can never be used as a defence .... but it can occasionally be used in mitigation.

However .... the crime of which you have been convicted is governed by one of our primary laws .... indeed .... one of the foundation stones of human behavioural law in any civilised society.

There can be no mitigation in this case. Your actions were criminal actions. You have been found guilty of the most serious of all criminal offences. This court views you as a criminal. It will judge you as a criminal.

You have attempted to justify your actions. Such attempted justification can not .... and will not .... be recognised by this court .... or by any other court in this land.

There was a stir in the gallery.

A disapproving glance from the Court Usher was sufficient to restore silence.

Judge Milburn de Courcy allowed a pause for his words to take effect .... and for those doing "shorthand" to catch up.

"Your legal team will have informed you that Capital Punishment .... the death sentence .... is no longer extant in this country. Were it still part of our statute .... then my duty would be a clear path before me".

There was a buzz from the gallery. The Court Usher turned his head slowly, and looked upwards. There was silence.

"This is my last case", said Judge Milburn. "It is also a case that is attracting much legal .... and popular interest. And it is attracting that heightened level of interest for a simple reason. It is attracting that interest, because there are those who are saying that if we invite people of other cultures to our shores .... then we must expect more crime of the nature of that with which this trial has concerned itself.

They are saying, "We told you so".

I will say to those people, "It can never be the function of this Court to judge freedom of movement of person or persons. It is not the function, or duty, of this Court to judge cultural differences.

But it is the function of this Court to judge accusations of criminal behaviour. Therefore .... the sentence that I decide upon will be a response to a criminal action.

It will be a response to that criminal action .... and only to that criminal action. It will not be a response to any other factor".

The Court Usher eyed the gallery warily. There was silence.

"I was asked to sit on this case", said Judge Milburn. "No doubt, those who asked me, had their reasons for doing so. And I intend to presume upon their good will, by doing something that I have never had reason to do before ....

I will trust that those who set me in authority over this case will indulge my wishes for two reasons. First …. that this will be my last judgement …. and secondly …. that any sentence that I pronounce, in this case, will have lasting effect in two distinct areas. The country as a whole …. and the small group of people most affected by this crime".

The Court Usher viewed the gallery with deep mistrust.

"Before I pass sentence", said Judge Milburn de Courcy. "I intend to offer those people who have suffered most directly, as a result of this crime, the opportunity to meet with me in private. I wish to listen to anything that they might have to say. That they have suffered …. and will continue to suffer for years to come …. has been in my mind throughout the course of this case. I do not say that their opinions will neccessarily influence me in my decision. That decision must always be my responsibility …. and my responsibility alone.

But at the least …. it will give me opportunity to explain to those who suffer that my decisions, and any subsequent actions, are constrained by the law of this land.

I must make it clear that the people I mention are in no way under any obligation to meet with me …. but I hope that they will accept the invitation in the spirit with which it is offered …. because I believe that it is the very least I can do for them.

This Court will adjourn for seven days".

Judge Gerald Milburn de Courcy stood. He bowed to the Court …. and left the room.

ONE

Nobody really knew Roger's surname. He had a driving licence that said Roger Davies .... but it wasn't very convincing. There was, however, no doubt about his girlfriend's identity.

Miss Deborah Anne Wintersham's name appeared very regularly in the pages of "Horse and Hound". She was frequently mentioned in "Country Life", and she could often be seen featured in the society pages of the better newspapers .... smiling happily for the photographers, as she left an engagement party, or arrived at a wedding.

Roger and Debbie were an unlikely couple. A very unlikely couple, and by all that's right and sensible, they should never have met at all. But meet they did, and if many people expected Lord Wintersham to intervene, and call time on this curious liason .... well he never did. And he never did, because he knew, without a shadow of doubt, that his daughter Deborah was totally and utterly, truly madly deeply, head over heels in love, with Mr Roger Davies .... if that was indeed his name.

Was it "Love at first sight". Total bafflement at first sight is nearer to the truth. Mr Roger Davies had never met anyone like Miss Deborah Wintersham. And Miss Deborah Wintersham had certainly never met anyone like Mr Roger Davies.

They met at a wedding. An awfully posh sort of wedding. The sort of wedding where Miss Deborah Wintersham's presence was natural, and very much to be expected, and where Mr Roger Davies' presence was very unexpected indeed.

Deborah was very well brought up. She was very polite, very considerate to others, and had never, in her life, broken the slightest rule. Even at school, she had always assumed that the school rules were made by those much more experienced than herself, and therefore those rules must be intended for her welfare. She was in every way, a thoroughly good girl. She liked being good, and would view her friends misdemeanours with wide eyed disbelief.

And yet it never occured to her not to make love to Roger, that very first evening. Yes .... the rules said that "Making Love" was strictly for when you were married, but Debbie knew immediately that she was married to Roger, simply because she could not possibly imagine, in her wildest dreams, ever being married to anyone else.

So .... that evening, when her obligations to the Bride were completed .... Deborah had been Head Bridesmaid .... she had asked Roger to take her back to her hotel .... and then she invited him to her room. It was a Premier Travel Inn .... not too expensive .... due to her having done something very silly with her credit card .... and it not seeming to work at the moment. So Daddy had given her some cash for the weekend .... while he sorted out that little problem with her card.

Roger sat on the edge of her bed, and she made him a fiddlesome cup of coffee, which he didn't bother to drink, and then, without a single maidenly blush, and because it was simply, and obviously, going to be the next thing to do, she undressed completely .... and melted into Roger. And even if it was against all the rules, well it was nobody else's business in the whole wide world, other than hers, and Roger's.

In any case .... she wasn't sure that Roger knew the rules.

She was , in fact, quite wrong about this. Roger did know all the rules. He even knew some rules that "Debs" didn't .... mainly because he'd made them up himself.

And number one rule, on his new, fresh off the print, rule list, was that he was never going to let "Debs" out of his sight, ever again...........

The next morning, Debbie, and Roger started living together. Not in the sense that they bought a house together. More that they were, from now on, in each others lives. If it took a while for Roger to understand Debbie's life .... it took a whole lot longer for Debbie to understand Roger's.

There was, for instance, Uncle John..............

Deborah met Uncle John the next morning, at breakfast. As is usual, at a Travel Inn, breakfast was served in the pub restaurant next door.

Roger had woken first. He very quietly, and gently, eased himself up, until he could sit against the headboard .... and he sat there .... watching Debs sleeping. She stirred in her sleep, turning towards him. He brushed a whisp of blonde hair from her cheek .... and she woke. And as she woke, she looked up, and as she looked up, she opened her eyes. And as she opened her eyes, she smiled at him. And it was such a smile...........

It was better than the Sun coming out. It was like the Sun coming out and telling you it is taking you to the seaside today, and yes, there will be sandcastles, and paddling, and a picnic, and ice creams .... with a Flake on the top. Roger fell in love at that exact moment.

Yes .... he'd loved her, when he first met her, and he'd loved her quite a lot during the night, but it was at this moment that he truly fell in love with her.

"Hello Debs", he said.

Her second smile had two flakes on the top.

"Gosh, Roger", she said, "I feel frightfully tousled".

She grimaced.

"And I really think I need a shower".

Roger kissed her full on the lips.

"I do too", he said, "and the sheets need some attention too".

Debbie lifted the top sheet............

"Oh dear", she said, and giggled.

In fact, it hadn't been the best day of the month for Debbie to marry herself to Roger. She had been a little surprised, and much relieved, to discover that Roger didn't seem to find this any sort of a problem. She was also delighted to find that he seemed to know ever so much about girls. Ever so, ever so much, about girls .... even some things about girls that Debbie didn't know.

There was just the teensiest part of her that wondered how he could possibly know quite so much about girls, but he was so jolly and lovely, that she soon stopped wondering.

In the restaurant, Roger watched, with some amusement, as Debs buttered her toast. spreading the butter as thinly as a war time housewife. He had expected her to choose a natural nut and goatsmilk yoghurt sort of breakfast. But not a bit of it. Debs had gone for the full English, with all the trimmings, and then she finished it off with a natural nut and goatsmilk yoghurt.

Of course, Debbie had only booked breakfast for one, but this had easily been sorted out with their waitress. As he handed the waitress his card, Roger had told her that there might be a third person for breakfast.

"Debs", he said, as they collected their tea and orange juice from the buffet. "I've I asked a friend to join us".

"Oh Gosh" said Debs,"Am I going to meet one of your friends already .... how awfully exciting !"

"Well", said Roger,"Some people have found meeting Uncle John very exciting indeed".

"Gosh", said Debs, "Is he really your Uncle, Roger".

"Not quite", said Roger. "I call him Uncle John, because he looks after me".

"Oh you're so lucky to have an Uncle to look after you Roger", said Debs."I haven't got any Uncles to look after me".

She frowned at the thought. Then she smiled with relief,

"But I have got Daddy", she said. "And he looks after me ever so well."

She thought for a moment .

"But an Uncle would be jolly nice too", she added.

Roger smiled.

"Well Debs", he said, "If you like, we'll ask Uncle John if he could be your Uncle too".

"Oh that would be super, Roger", said Debs."I'm sure if he likes looking after you, he'll like looking after me".

Roger seemed to find this amusing. He laughed, and shook his head.

"Do you need lots of looking after then Debs", he asked.

Debbie didn't get to answer .... because, at that very moment .... Uncle John himself arrived.

"John", said Roger, smiling broadly. "How's things .... but before you answer .... this is Miss Deborah Wintersham, a friend of mine. Are we friends Debs".

Debs laughed, and stretched her hand to John. John took it .... and looked straight into her eyes. Then he leant forward and kissed her on the cheek.

"Miss Wintersham", he said, "I have seen you in the newspapers many times, but you are even more gorgeous in person".

It was John's turn to be surprised. Debs put her arms around him, hugged him for exactly the correct amount of time, and said:

"I'm so excited to meet you .... may I call you Uncle John. Roger says I can ask you if you'd be my Uncle too."

John smiled.

"Provided I don't have to give you ten shillings every time I see you".

Debbie looked crestfallen.

"Gosh .... aren't I worth ten shillings".

Roger laughed.

"You've got yourself into a hole there John .... how are you going to get out of it".

John reached into his jacket pocket, and placed a fifty pence coin in front of Debbie. She opened her purse, and stored the coin away carefully.

"Oh", she breathed, "This is just so exciting .... you're going to be just like a real Uncle for me".

John looked helplessly at Roger..............

"John". said Roger. "Go and get yourself some orange juice whilst the going is still good".

They watched him go. Debs was thinking...............

"Roger", she said. "Has Uncle John got a girlfriend".

"Not at the moment", said Roger. "Why .... have you got somebody in mind for him".

"Actually, I have ", said Debs. She sipped the last of her tea, thoughtfully.

"My friend Mellissa, would find him ever so attractive . Mellissa is so sad at the moment", she added."Her boyfriend Tarquin went bungee jumping in Malaysia".

"Well .... he'll be back". said Roger.

"No he won't", said Debbie. "The bungee thing was too long.....".

Roger winced. There was a pause. Debbie looked sad.

"Ok", said Roger, "Shall we all have an evening out .... a foursome sort of thing".

"Oh definitely yes", said Debbie. "It would be so nice to cheer Mellissa up. She used to be such a jolly friend. Can we do it next Friday".

Roger shook his head.

"Sorry Debs", he said, "John and I can't do Fridays, but Saturday would be good".

"Ok .... Saturday then", said Debbie. She paused.........

"Roger .... what do you and Uncle John do on Fridays".

"Fridays are a Church night", said Roger.

Debbie looked at him closely.

"Roger", she said. "Don't fib .... it's really naughty to fib .... especially about Church".

Roger reached over and took her hand.

"I'm not fibbing", he said. "John and I go to Church every Friday night. Sometimes we go on Wednesdays, and Sundays, as well. But definitely always on Fridays .... especially the third Friday of every month, because that's a big night for the Choir".

Debbie sat and stared at him. She believed him .... almost. Eventually she took a deep breath..........

"Can I come with you", she said.

"Of course you can", said Roger. "That would be fun".

John arrived with orange juice and coffee. Roger caught the eye of their waitress. Debbie had noticed that he seemed very clever at catching the eye of the waitress. She herself, always seemed to have the most awful difficulty with this very important life skill.

In fact .... it wasn't that Roger had any particular skill in this direction. It was just that the waitress had hardly taken her eyes off Roger, since he had walked in.

John loosened his jacket, and sat opposite Roger, and next to Debbie. The waitress took his order. She seemed a little flustered. Roger went to fetch more tea for himself and Debs.

"It is so exciting to meet you John", said Debbie, "I'm coming to Church with you and Roger on Friday".

She watched him carefully.

"Wow", said John, "Has he turned you into a church goer already".

Debbie was speechless. John spotted her discomfort, and laughed.

"I see ", he said. "Roger told you about going to Church, and you didn't believe him , did you. Oh ye of little faith".

"Actually", he said, "I suppose we might not be the most obvious of Church goers .... but yes it's true .... we really do go to Church. And you will be very welcome there, I promise you".

Roger returned with teas, and milk, and blueberry muffins. The waitress arrived with John's breakfast. John went to pick up his knife and fork, then seemed to remember something. He reached into his jacket, and produced a fat brown envelope, which he passed to Roger.

Roger raised his eyebrows.

"Yup", said John, "It'.all there".

"Any problems John", asked Roger.

"No, not really", said John. "He'd already gone to bed when I arrived .... and I thought it would be a shame if he had to get up again. So I said to his wife that I would go on up. Of course I couldn't leave Tyson in the car. You're not allowed to leave a dog in the car any more. So I took Tyson up with me. It wasn't a very big house. So to make a bit more room, Tyson layed on the bed next to him. I think Tyson must have that sore tooth again, because he kept growling. It was a bit difficult to hold a conversation, with all the growling going on, but in the end, he told me to look in the bottom drawer. That's where the envelope was. There were other envelopes there too .... but that one suited us. So I took it .... and let him get back to some rest".

"No harm done then", said Roger.

"No .... no harm done", said John, "but he's probably going to need to change his sheets".

Roger smiled. Debbie blushed. John looked puzzled.

Then John laughed.

"They'll wash", he said.

TWO

Roger, Debbie, and John finished breakfast. It was warm in the restaurant. They didn't hurry.

Outside .... a biting North East wind blew beneath a metallic grey sky.

"Looks cold out there John", said Roger.

" It's only just above freezing", said John. "There was some snow last night .... not enough to cause any problems though".

Roger nodded.

"Which car did you bring", he asked.

"The XJ", said John.

Roger smiled. He and John both loved the XJ6 Jaguars .... Roger kept promising himself that he would keep one. A nice powder blue one perhaps.

There was a long silence at the table.

"Must be twenty to, or twenty past the hour", said John.

Debbie smiled....

"I know what you mean", she said. "It's an Angel passing over. If it suddenly goes quiet at a table .... it's always twenty minutes to, or twenty minutes past the hour. My Grandmother always said it at Christmas".

"Mine too", said Roger, "and its really amazing, because it always works".

Roger and Debbie smiled at each other. It was the morning after the night before .... and breakfast together was nearly over.

They both knew that what they did in the next few minutes could change their lives forever. Roger knew what had to be done ....

He looked long and thoughtfully at Debbie. She lowered her eyes and blushed. He took a deep breath.

"Debs", he said. "Will you marry me".

Debbie looked at Roger, and then she looked at John. They were both waiting to see what she would say.

The people on the next table seemed to have gone awfully quiet as well.

Debbie felt tingles in all sorts of strange places. She plucked a croissant crumb from her plate. No need for a girl to hurry ....

Roger and John sat .... waiting.

The people on the next table seemed to be waiting too ....

"I take ever so much looking after, Roger", she said, "But there isn't anybody else in the whole wide world that I'd rather have to look after me. Yes .... I will marry you Roger".

The round of applause that followed from the surrounding tables astonished them. Eveybody wanted "in" on this moment. Debbie blushed as she looked around.

John stood. He picked up his glass .... there was still a little orange juice in the bottom.

"Ladies and gentlemen", he said, smiling broadly. "I give you the Happy Couple".

There was much laughter .... another round of applause.

Several people called out their congratulations. Debbie pretended to hide her head under the corner of the table cloth. Roger grabbed her .... they laughed .... and waved .... and ran for the door.

John sat .... with the last of his coffee. Things began to settle. He smiled around him. The waitress appeared. She looked puzzled.

"Did I miss something", she said.

John laughed. He fished for his credit cards.

"Just my boss getting engaged", he said. "Oh what a day it's going to be".

"No need to pay here", said the waitess. "I tabbed it to the room number. You can pay it all together".

John's phone rang.

"John .... we'll meet you in the Travel Inn reception", said Roger. "Is the car here somewhere".

"It's in a little car park in the town", said John. "Shall I fetch it round".

"Is it far to walk", said Roger.

"Five minutes", said John.

"No .... we'll walk round together", said Roger. "You can help carry the bags. Just come over here to reception".

John put the phone back in his pocket. He found a ten pound note for the waitress, checked the chairs, and table, for anything that Roger and Debbie might have left behind, and headed for the door.

....

John had never seen his boss looking quite so happy. The Travel Inn receptionist had heard about the proposal. She had even found a greetings card for Roger and Debbie. John took Debbie's two bags .... well actually one suitcase, and one cabin size holdhall. Roger picked up his own bag .... and Deb's very girly looking makeup case. Debbie slipped her arm into Roger's .... and they headed for the car.

"Roger", she said. "I need to pop into Boots for some things. I'll see you in the car park. What colour is your Jaguar".

"Blue", said Roger.

"The car park is end of this street, and turn right .... then it's on the left", said John.

"I know it", said Debbie. "It's opposite the auction room, and it slopes up from the road. I've been here quite often with Tallulah".

"The bride at the wedding yesterday", Roger explained to John.

Debs headed across the street to Boots. Roger and John walked on. It was bitterly cold. There were ice patches on the pavement. The wind blew little flurries of dusty snow around their heels.

"Strange time of year for a wedding", said John.

"They're honeymooning in Barbados", said Roger.

"Aha", said John.

They rounded the corner of the car park entrance .... and stopped .... bemused at the scene before them.

The car park was packed with people .... and with estate cars, and four by fours, all with their boots open.

"Must be a car boot sale", said John, looking around.

"Very posh for a car boot sale", said Roger.

He was right. All the cars were late model .... and the people with them expensively dressed against the cold. Fur lined jackets, brogue shoes, Barbour shooting attire.

Roger and John eased their way through the crowd to the Jaguar. They squeezed round to the boot, and stowed the luggage. They stood .... taking in the scene.

"Let's have a look round then", said Roger.

They moved up two cars, and after a few moments wait, were able to stand, and look into the back of a Mercedes estate car. The floor had been covered in green baize .... and displayed on the baize were at least two dozen guns of various types. Antique guns, they realised. They glanced through the side windows of the Range Rover next door. That was similarly loaded .... but with a collection of swords amongst the pistols and rifles.

"Quite a car boot sale", said John, to the owner, who was showing a sword to a potential customer .... a chap in a Bogart style hat, and black woolcloth overcoat.

The man nodded.

"It's sale day at Wallis and Wallis auction rooms across the street", he said. "But we always do some trading over here first, while we wait for them to open up. They're the specialist auctioneers for antique guns, swords, militaria .... that sort of thing. But if we can make some sales in the car park .... well there are no commission fees to pay".

"So would you need a licence to buy a gun here", said John.

"No licences required", said the man in the overcoat. "All antique muzzle loading guns here .... and they don't need a licence. Have a walk round .... all sorts to see".

John could see that negotiations over the sword were about to commence. He and Roger moved to yet another Range Rover next door.

The dealer here was younger. John asked his permission, then picked up a gun displayed on the flat tail gate. Roger was no expert on guns .... but even he could recognise a blunderbuss.

John examined the weapon closely.

"It's as good as they come, that one", said the dealer. Brass cannon type barrel, banana shaped lock, acorn finials on the brass butt plate, brass trigger guard .... acorn finials on that too. Safety bolt on the cock .... that's very unusual on a blunderbuss. And it's never been played with. Everything as it should be. Even the ramrod is the original. And the weirdest thing of all .... considering the quality .... is that there is no makers name anywhere on it. It's just possible it's marked on the inside of the lock .... but I don't want to take it appart. I don't think that gun has been appart since the day it was made".

John continued to examine the blunderbuss.

"When would you date it to", he asked.

"Without a name .... you can only go by the style", said the dealer. "I would put it about 1770 .... that wouldn't be too far off".

John nodded.

"Cigarette", asked the dealer, producing a case.

John smiled, and shook his head.

"No thanks", he said. "I don't smoke".

"Have a mint then", said the dealer. He offered the packet to John, and then to Roger.

They both took mints, and unwrapped them.

"Roger", said John. "Perhaps you ought to go and meet Debbie at the car park entrance ....".

Roger looked closely at John. He smiled.

"Good idea John", he said. "We don't want her missing us in the crowd".

....

Roger went down to the edge of the road. He looked back along the street .... but there was no sign of Debs. He decided to walk to the corner of the main road, and meet her there.

He arrived at the corner just a couple of seconds ahead of Debbie. She smiled and threw her arms round him.

"Sorry to be so long", she said. "Their tills stopped working .... they had to get the manager to sort it all out. People were getting ever so cross about it".

Roger put his arm around Debs. They started to walk back to join John.

"It was ever so kind of you to come and meet me Roger", said Debbie. "It's such a cold morning isn't it".

She snuggled agaist Roger.

"Is Uncle John with the car", she asked.

Roger laughed.

"Last time I saw John .... he was buying a blunderbuss", he said.

"A what ....", said Debs.

"Long story", said Roger. "I'll let John tell you".

As they rounded the corner into the car park .... Roger was surprised for the second time. The cars were still there .... but their boots were closed .... and half of the people were gone. Roger glanced at the sale room. People were filing in through the entrance doors. He checked his watch. It was ten o'clock.

As they walked up the slope to the Jaguar, Roger noticed an old Vauxhall Cavalier just a couple of spaces above them. For its age .... it was tidy enough .... even polished, but a stream of pale blue fluid had run from beneath its front end. The thin river of liquid ran across the slope of the car park, spread across the gritted pavement, and dribbled into the icy gutter. The stream ended at the drain, dripping slowly into the depths.

"That car is leaking something", said Debbie.

"Antifreeze", said Roger. "It wasn't strong enough to stand the frost last night. I think the engine block is cracked".

John saw them coming. Roger wondered if he'd bought the blunderbuss. He guessed it was in the boot.

They got into the Jaguar. John driving. Roger and Debbie in the back seat.

"Did you see the Cavalier, Rog", said John.

Roger nodded.

"Frost got it last night", he said.

John was just about to start the engine when Roger drew his attention to the car park entrance.

"Wait a second, John", he said.

A family had just come round the corner.

"It's their Cavalier isn't it", said John.

Roger nodded. He sort of hoped that it wasn't .... but he knew that it was.

Mum and Dad .... and three children. Roger initially thought that the children were triplet girls .... but one was a little taller .... so it was probably twins with their older sister. The children were all very smartly dressed. Shiny black shoes, wool stockings, grey school skirts, and nice blue toggle buttoned overcoats with hoods.

"Oh look at the little girls .... they're just so sweet", said Debbie.

Roger looked at their mother. She had a red winter coat pulled tightly around her. It looked too thin. She looked cold. He looked at her face. She was shepherding her daughters carefully, holding the hands of the two younger ones.

Roger looked at the Father. He had no coat. His thin brown polyester suit gave him no protection from the wind. It was the sort of suit a friend of Rogers had once bought for his first job interview .... Junior Trainee Sales Manager at Rumbelows. He didn't get the job.

"They spend all their money on their daughters don't they", said Debbie.

The girls reached the car first .... their Father had stopped when he saw the stream of liquid running across the car park. Roger saw his eyes trace it's course back to the Cavalier.

He unlocked the car doors, and saw his daughters into the rear seat. The car was too old to have rear belts. He opened the passenger door for his wife .... gave her the seat belt .... and went round to the drivers door.

"Flick the ignition switch John", said Roger.

John turned the key a notch. Roger powered his window down a couple of inches.

They saw the Cavalier owner put his seat belt on. They saw him put his key into the ignition.

Roger and John listened. They held their breath .... and listened.

The engine turned just half a revolution. Then they heard a loud click. Then another click. And then silence.

They saw the driver look at the situation. They saw him looking at the car park sloping down to the road. It was steep enough to try roll starting the engine. The driver looked at the expensive cars around him. The Mercedes estates .... the Range Rovers .... and he looked at the smart people in their expensive winter coats .... and he looked at the slope down to the road.

"Please please don't try it", said Roger.

He and John knew the car wouldn't start. And they knew what would happen if the driver tried to roll the car down the slope .... he would end up blocking the car park entrance .... in a narrow street.

"Roger", said Debbie. "Please don't let him try to start the car down the car park .... not with his wife and children there".

Roger and John looked at Debbie..............

"I'll get it", said John.

"Wait", said Roger. "Just a second".

The Cavalier driver had changed his mind. He unbuckled his seat belt. He took a final look at that oh-so-tempting slope .... shook his head .... and opened his door.

Roger and John breathed sighs of relief.

"That's good", said Debbie.

They watched the Father help his wife and three daughters from the car. He locked up .... and checked the doors. He shivered in the biting wind. He took his eldest daughter's hand. His wife took the hands of the twins. They walked back to the pavement .... turned right onto the street... and they disappeared from view.

John started the Jaguar's big six cylinder engine.

"Ok", he asked Roger.

Roger nodded thoughtfully. He glanced at the saleroom.

It was warm inside. The auctioneer had just sold an antique display case of Ely cartridges. The buyer had paid twelve thousand pounds .... plus buyers premium.

The Jaguar slipped out into the traffic.

And a family .... Mother, Father, and their three daughters walked to the bus station. The girls were promised baked beans on toast for lunch.

"Can you fix the car Dad", said Jemima .... the eldest.

"Of course your Dad will fix it", said her Mother. "Your Dad is good at fixing things".

Her husband looked at Jemima .... and her twin sisters. And he smiled at his wife.

He was cold .... but they were warm.

And that was what really mattered.

THREE

Motorway Services. An oasis for travellers. A break from the three lane tedium.

Parking. Being still. Toilets. Hot food. Coffee.

But the bright lights, and the polished floors, and the corporate glitz, all serve to hide the skanky grey loneliness. The bleak inhuman void from which your only protection is your credit card. The shelves of temptingly wrapped snacks promise comfort. But it is a comfort based only in materialism. There is no spiritual comfort to be found here.

And yet, this is a sort of Heaven. A Heaven of instant gratification .... but only for credit card holders. And it is a Heaven that will cost you dear. Is a simple bread roll really worth one pound. Is a Coffee really worth three pounds. On a credit card it is. What's a pound .... or three pounds .... on a credit card.

....

We're all rich on a summer day. Everybody can be comfortable in just a T shirt, and shorts .... rich and poor alike.

But the bitter East wind of a January morning sorts the haves from the have nots. It seeks out the poor. It skims the heat from their cheeks. It cuts through their cheap clothing, and it whistles through the cracked plastic wheel trims on their faded Ford Mondeos.

Ah yes ..... the East wind knows how to find the poor ....

It knows how to find the poor .... as they walk across the services forecourt .... to pay cash for their ten pounds worth of economy unleaded.

They look with longing stares at the fortunate ones. Those carrying supersize steaming coffees back to their four by fours. They look at the boxed sandwiches, and the grab bags of doritoes. And they would like to have those. But even a coffee to share is three litres of unleaded, and a coffee each is a whole gallon. You need credit cards to buy coffee and sandwiches.

Cash hurts too much. Cash is for the poor. Cash won't even scrape the ice from your windscreen, in the half dark of a frosty morning.

....

John brought the Jaguar onto the pumps. He came in behind a faded blue Nissan Micra.

"Do you want it filled up", he said to Roger.

Roger leaned forwards, and looked at the fuel gauges.

"Just fill the right hand tank, John", he said. "I've got somebody coming to see this car tomorrow. It might be off to Sweden .... if we do a deal".

"I need the ladies room", said Debbie.

Roger stretched across, and showed Debs how to open the door.

"Put your jacket on Debs", he said. "It's really cold out there".

He helped Debbie into her little duffle coat. It reminded Roger of the one worn by Paddington Bear.

"My name is Debbie .... please look after me ...."

Debs climbed out, and had started across the forecourt, before Roger called her back.

"You'll need your handbag", Debs", he said.

Debbie blushed. It was strange to be with a man who knew she would need her handbag.

They left John filling the tank, and walked to the shop. There was a hint of rain in the biting wind.

Roger stopped at a silver BMW. The young woman was just placing the filler nozzle into the tank.

"Not your usual car then", Roger said to her.

"Pardon", she said .... not entirely politely.

"You're just about to fill a diesel BMW with unleaded petrol", said Roger.

The young woman looked in confusion at the filler nozzle in her hand.

"It's my husband's car", she said. "I had no idea it was a diesel".

Roger smiled. He took the nozzle from her hand, replaced it on the pump, and handed her the diesel nozzle.

"Try that one", he said.

She looked at him.

"Are you sure", she asked.

"It's got D for diesel on the bootlid", said Roger. He smiled and turned away.

She hesitated.

"Excuse me", she called after Roger. "I'm so sorry if I was rude to you. It was kind of you to stop me. Would it have damaged the car".

" Definitely", said Roger, "But Hey .... no harm done .... drive carefully".

He looked round for Debs, but she had gone inside. He could see her heading for the rear of the store. He watched her. She was the loveliest thing on the whole planet. He remembered back to last night ....

To his surprise, he saw Debs suddenly turn towards the till area. He saw a look of alarm .... of consternation .... on her face. Then, at the corner of a shelving unit, he saw her bend down . She disappeared from view.

John had come up behind Roger.

"I think something's happened in there Rog", he said.

The two of them quickened their pace towards the entrance. The doors slid open, and they stepped into the warmth, and bright lights. Roger hurried down the first aisle. On the corner, in the open space before the tills, Debbie was kneeling. She was holding the hand of an elderly lady, who lay unconscious on the polished floor. She had fallen against the corner of a shelf of chocolate bars. She was surrounded by a confusion of KitKats, Bounty Bars, and Twixes. Her faded blue winter coat had ridden up above her knees. The stained hem of her petticoat was visible below her tired grey dress. Varicose veins showed through her rumpled stockings.

John looked at the situation.

"Rog", he said. "Get the blanket from the Jag. I'll help Debbie".

As Roger headed for the door, a young manager appeared, summoned by the checkout staff.

He too looked at the situation.

John looked up at him.

"Call for an ambulance", he said. "Ask for one from Chichester .... we're on the westbound side of the road .... so it will be quicker than one from Portsmouth".

"Got you", said the young manager. He disappeared into his office behind the tills.

"Is she breathing Ok, Debs", said John.

Debbie bent her head to listen.

"Yes", she said. "She's breathing".

"Do you know how to check her pulse", said John.

"I've done that already", said Debbie. "It's Ok at the moment".

John stood, looked around, and went to a shelf of travel goods. He took a travel cushion from the shelf, and tore off the packaging.

"Lift her head very gently for me", he said to Debbie.

Debbie slipped her fingers beneath the old lady's head, and lifted slowly .... just enough for John to slip the cushion into place.

"Still breathing Ok", said John.

Debbie listened again.

"Ok", she said.

"Debbie .... just open her mouth gently, and make sure her tongue isn't at the back of her throat", said John.

As Debbie's fingers touched her pale skin, the old lady's eyes flickered, and then opened. She looked at Debbie, and tried to speak. Debs took her hand again, and bent and whispered to her. She relaxed back onto the cushion.

Roger arrived with the blanket. John covered the old lady's legs, gently untangling her feet, as he did so.

"Roger .... hold her hand for me", said Debs. "I'm desperate for the loo ...."

Roger took Debs place.

"Handbag Debs", he said.

Debbie bent down and kissed him on the top of his head.

"I'll be quick as I can", she said. "Just keep holding her hand for me".

The manager appeared.

"Ambulance is on its way", he said. "Can I do anything to help".

As Roger looked up, he saw the old man for the first time. A tiny frail old man in a crumpled tweed suit, with collar and tie.

"Is this lady with you", Roger said to him.

The old man nodded. He was shaking .... confused .... scared of the attention. He stared down at his wife. He didn't know what to do. He closed his eyes. Tears formed in the corners.

Roger looked to the manager. He checked for a name badge.

" Stephen .... can you get him a chair please .... and a hot coffee", he said.

"John", said Roger. "Look to the old chap .... he's a bit upset".

John put a supporting arm around the old man's shoulders. The manager arrived with a chair. They got him seated, and Stephen went for the coffee.

Debbie came back.

"I'll take over again Roger", she said.

Roger stood to one side. Debs knelt again and spoke softly to the old lady, gently stroking her brow. Roger watched Debbie. He tried to catch some of what she was saying .... but the words eluded him. He wasn't even sure that Debbie was speaking English. He looked around him.

People had continued to come in to pay for their fuel. They all managed not to see what was happening. Human things weren't meant to happen in a sterile place like this. These people had stopped for fuel. They would give the girl on the till their pump number. She would ask them if they wanted hot drinks. They would buy sweets. That was what they expected to happen. Anything beyond that just wasn't their business. They paid .... and they left .... and they didn't see an old lady on the floor, and they didn't see an old man who was crying, and they didn't see Debbie, and Roger, and John, doing what they could.

Roger looked at John, who was standing protectively by the old man. He looked at Debbie .... who still held the old lady's hand .... softly speaking words to her that Roger couldn't understand.

And Roger looked out across the forecourt .... at the old faded blue Nissan Micra .... and he hoped that the Ambulance would come soon.

FOUR

It was nearly two in the afternoon, when Roger, and Debs, and John returned to the Jaguar. The car had cooled while it waited for them. John started the engine, and they sat for a moment, watching the recovery driver loading the Nissan Micra. The car was going to be taken to the old couple's home .... the keys put through their letter box. Roger had been really lucky when he phoned to organise this. The recovery company he used had a truck that had just unloaded a car, in Chichester. It would take the Nissan to Portsmouth on a return load basis. No payment arrangement was needed. Roger was well known to the bosses.

The paramedics had been the real thing. A young woman who seemed to be the team leader, accompanied by a down to earth chap in his early forties. They had summed up the situation with a speed born of experience .... realising that they had two problems .... not just one.

They had immense patience. Roger had offered to get the Nissan home. Gradually everything was sorted out. Debbie stayed with the old lady until she was lifted into the ambulance. Her husband was doing his best to be helpful. Debs held his hand as he was helped up to join his wife.

They had all watched the ambulance away.

Roger put his arm around Debbie.

"I love you for what you did there", he said.

John took Debs hands in his own. He nodded slowly at her.

"You're OK Debs", he said.

Debbie smiled at them.

"She was so lonely", she said. "I tried to take some of her loneliness away".

....

"Well", said John. "That little fuel stop took longer than expected. What do you want to do now Rog".

33

Roger looked at Debbie.

"Want to go to my place for the night Debs", he said.

Debbie giggled.

"I'll have to let Daddy know where I am", she said.

Debbie fished in her handbag for her mobile phone. She checked the time against the clock on the Jaguar's dashboard.

"I'll send him a text", she said. "He's probably in a meeting at the moment".

Roger watched her compose the message.

"So what does your Dad do for a living then, Debs", he asked.

Debs finished her message .... pressed send .... and smiled at Roger.

"Daddy is ever so clever", she said. "He gets payed lots of money to be chairman of other people's companies. He's ever so good at being a chairman .... and the share price of a company always goes up when he starts working for it".

"Is he like a trouble shooter then", said John.

"I suppose so", said Debbie. "He always looks at what the company does .... and suggests ways to do things more easily. He's frightfully good with money too".

She sighed.

"I'm not very good with money", she said. "I do try and be good with money. Daddy has to be ever so patient with me".

"Am I going to meet your Dad soon Debs", said Roger.

"Roger .... don't be silly. Of course you're going to meet him soon. You've got to ask him if you can marry me".

John laughed. Roger looked serious.

"Are you sure he'll say yes, Debs", said Roger.

Debbie leaned over and kissed him on the cheek.

"Of course Daddy will say yes". she said. "I'll talk to him first. You'll really like him, Roger. He's ever so lovely".

John smiled to himself. Roger watched an Audi R8 overtaking.

Debbie leaned forwards,

"John", she said. "Would you like a chocolate".

"I'd love one Debs", said John.

Debbie went into her Boots carrier bag, and brought out the box of chocolates that the service station manager had given her".

"Gosh", she said. "They're ever such posh chocolates. I thought he was such a nice young man. It's just a shame that he wasn't quite old enough to know what to do".

They all had two chocolates each .... then Debbie put the box carefully back into the Boots bag.

"Debbie", said Roger. "When you were talking to the lady on the floor back there .... were you speaking English".

Debbie seemed embarassed.

"No", she said. "Not all the time, I wasn't".

"What language was it", said Roger.

Debbie stayed Silent. She seemed to be considering something.

"Where are we John", she said.

"Almost Southampton", said John.

Debbie took one of Roger's hands in her own.

"Roger", she said. "Would you mind very much if we went to my flat in Southampton. Could you stay there tonight with me".

"Can we do that John", said Roger. "It will mean you taking the Jag back to our place, to meet the chaps from Sweden tomorrow".

John nodded.

"Fine by me", he said. "What time are they coming".

"About ten o'clock", said Roger.

"I'll get the car washed before they arrive", said John. "I'll go to that Romanian car wash up the road. They do a nice job".

John un-clipped the sat-nav and passed it back to Debs.

"Put your address and post code in Debs", he said.

"No need", said Debs. "It's really easy to get to. Just one left turn off Bassett Avenue".

John nodded.

"Bassett Avenue then", he said.

There were one or two minor traffic holdups. It was nearly four thirty when John, directed by Debbie, brought the Jaguar to a stand-still outside a very stylish block of flats, five hundred yards off the Avenue.

"Nice area Debs", said Roger.

The block was well maintained .... in its own garden. A row of mature trees ran between the entrance and exit roads.

The temperature had dropped. As the daylight faded, the street lights came on, and coloured the light dusting of snow on the lawn. It had been warm and comfortable in the Jaguar. As they stepped out of the car, their breath steamed in the cold. The wind had eased. There would be a frost later.

John helped them to the entrance with their luggage. Debbie keyed in a number on a pad next to the double glass doors. They heard the lock click .... and Debbie pushed the doors open.

She told John to put the luggage in the hall .... then she embraced him fondly.

John raised his eyebrows at Roger. Roger laughed.

"Will I see you again soon Uncle John", Debbie said.

John laughed.

"Course you will", he said. "We're a team now Debs".

"And you won't forget to bring ten shillings for me", said Debbie.

Roger laughed.

"John won't forget your ten shillings Debbie", he said. "He's your Uncle now".

John kissed Debbie on the cheek. He nodded at Roger.

"I'll phone you with the news on the Jag", he said. "Are you willing to do a deal on the price".

"Maybe", said Roger. "Phone me .... ".

John slipped back through the glass doors, and they watched him drive away.

"OK Miss Wintersham", said Roger, lifting their bags, "Lead the way please".

"It's on the third floor". said Debbie.

"I thought it might be", said Roger."Any chance of a cup of tea when we get there, Debs".

Debs kissed his cheek.

"This is so exciting", she said. "I'm engaged .... I'm actually engaged".

"But does your fiance get some tea Debs", said Roger.

"Of course he does", said Debbie. "Tea .... and lots of lovely things".

Debbie took the remaining luggage.

"Lift or stairs", she said.

"Stairs", said Roger.

Debbie turned to the right, and started up the first flight of stairs. Everything was very smart. The stairs themselves appeared to be oak. The handrails were metal .... painted forest green .... and the walls were decorated in a colour flecked rich cream matt paint. There wasn't a speck of dust or dirt anywhere.

Roger reflected that it was the first block of flats he'd ever been in, where the stairs didn't smell of ammonia.

They did the six short flights to the third floor. They went along the wooden floored corridor to the left. Debbie stopped at a door, put down her bags, and hunted in her handbag for the key. Roger was astonished when she produced the keys almost immediately. She unlocked, reached in, flicked the light switch, and turned to Roger.

"Shouldn't you be carrying me over the threshold, or something", she said.

"That's after we're married, I think", said Roger.

Debs looked disappointed ....

"Come here then", said Roger.

Debbie allowed herself to be picked up .... putting her arms round Roger's neck. Roger turned to her. They kissed.

"Are you going to carry me in, and throw me onto the bed", said Debbie.

"No, I'm not", said Roger. "I'm going to carry you in, and throw you into the kitchen, so you can make the tea",

Debbie giggled.

"I love you", she said.

"Quite right too", said Roger. "Now where's the kitchen Debs".

Debbie kissed his ear.

"Down the hall .... on the left", she said.

Roger opened the kitchen door, and still in his arms, Debbie flicked the light switch.

Roger had guessed that the flats dated from the nineteen thirties. There were hints of art deco style in the entrance .... but Debbie's kitchen was pure nineteen fifties. Roger looked around. It was all genuine nineteen fifties gear.

"Do you like it", said Debbie.

"It's amazing", said Roger. "It's an absolutely original nineteen fifties kitchen isn't it".

"Every bit of it", said Debbie. "Daddy had it all cleaned, and renovated for me .... and I've found some of the bits and pieces to go with it, on ebay".

She filled a correct period Swan electric kettle at the cream enamelled sink .... and set it to boil.

"Come and see the lounge", she said .

"I'd better get the luggage in first Debs", he said.

"Bring it into the hallway for now", said Debbie.

She joined him in bringing the cases and bags into her flat.

Roger followed her back down the hall. Debbie opened the door opposite the kitchen, and switched on the lights.

Roger laughed. The lounge was nineteen sixties .... every tiny detail of it. Roger wandered around examining the furniture. He stopped at the coffee table. Glass topped, tapered black legs, gold button feet, with a big colourful picture of Spanish Flamenco dancers, in full costume, beneath the glass.

"I love the coffee table", he said.

"I found that on an antique stall, at an event", said Debs.

"Nigel's Interesting Things", it was called. "I've bought several things for the flat from Nigel. He always seems to have old things in amazing condition. Some of his things are even in their original boxes. It's always nice buying things from him, because he has such a sense of humour".

"So may I ask what period the bedroom dates to", said Roger.

"No you may not", said Debs. "You are on the sofa tonight, Mr Davies".

"But ....", said Roger.

"Tea", said Debs.

They went back to the kitchen. The kettle was steaming. Debbie opened the big refrigerator.

"Now that fridge has to be a reproduction", said Roger.

"It's not", said Debs. "It's the one that was here when Daddy bought the flat .... but it has been resprayed".

Debbie pulled out a modern plastic container of milk.

"Oh no", she said. "The milk has gone off ..... I haven't been here for four days I suppose".

Debbie put the carton to one side of the work surface, and came over to Roger.

"Sweetheart ....", she said.

"You want me to go out for some milk", he said, smiling at her.

"That would be so kind of you Roger", she said. "I'll get you some money".

"Don't worry about cash Debs", said Roger. "I'll use my card".

"I'll give you some cash", said Debbie. "They don't take cards at the shop".

"They don't ....!!!" said Roger.

"No", said Debbie.

She handed Roger her purse.

"While you're there", she said. "Can you bring some eggs, and some bread .....and some marmalade .... and bacon .... and some sausages, if they have any. I want to cook breakfast for us.

"Milk, eggs, bread, bacon, sausages, marmalade .... got it" said Roger.

Debbie handed him a key.

"When you get to the entrance hall", she said, "Don't go out the door we came in by. Go along the corridor to the entrance at the other side of the flats. You'll need this key to open the doors half way along the corridor. Be very careful to lock those doors again behind you. Mr Smethwick, the caretaker, gets ever so cross if those doors are left unlocked".

"I could just go round", said Roger.

"Ever so much quicker if you go through",said Debbie.

"Ok Miss Wintersham", said Roger.

He took the key

"Posh looking key Debs", he said.

"It's a jolly posh lock", said Debbie. "Don't forget the milk. Oh .... and Roger .... please bring a newspaper".

"How will I get back in", he asked.

"Buzz me on the intercom", she said. "I can let you in from up here".

Roger kissed her on the cheek.

"I'm going to phone Daddy", she said. "I'm longing to tell him about you .... and us being engaged .... and everything .... it's just so exciting isn't it".

Roger kissed her on the cheek again.

"Will your Dad be excited", he said to her.

"He'll be ever so excited .... I promise you", said Debbie. "Just wait till you meet him".

"I'm looking forward to it", said Roger."See you in a minute, Debs. By the way …. where's the shop".

"Out of the flats …. turn right …. go to the end of the road …. turn right again …. and you'll see it, about a hundred yards up on your left", said Debbie. "Roger …. can I borrow your phone to call Daddy …. my battery has gone flat …. and there's no landline here …. we never got round to putting one in".

Roger pulled his mobile phone from his inside pocket, and handed it to Debbie.

"There you go", he said. "It's on a contract …. so you can talk as long as you like".

Debbie smiled.

"I'll try to have finished by the time you come back", she said.

....

So Mr Roger Davies left his fiancee …. and went out for some milk.

And Miss Deborah Wintersham placed his phone carefully on the formica topped kitchen table.

Then she opened a cupboard, and took out another phone …. a much bigger one.

Roger would have recognised it as the famous Motorola "house brick" phone, from the nineteen ninetys.

If, of course, he had been there to see it.

Debbie punched numbers. She held the phone to her ear ….

"Daddy", she said. "It's Debbie …….".

FIVE

Farhad al Zubaidy stood looking at the flat front tyre on his Nissan Skyline. He pulled a mobile phone from his pocket. He scrolled for a number .... and pressed dial.

His friend Ali Salah Javadi answered after four rings. Ali listened to Farhad .... and promised to be with him in fifteen minutes. Ali was a mechanic. A very good mechanic.

Farhad was at University. Studying business and commerce. He funded his extra curricular activities by bringing "grey import" cars into Britain, from Japan. Usually high performance models. They were easy to sell to a particular type of young English man. The Skyline had been a "grey import". It was just one year old. Farhad liked the car. He had decided to keep it.

Farhad was twenty years old, Iranian, very good looking, with olive skin, dark hair, and a carefully trimmed beard. He caught the eye of many young ladies on the university campus. One or two had even tried a smile .... or a few words of greeting.

But Farhad hated them. He hated their tight jeans, and their short skirts, and the way they were prepared to display their breasts. He hated the way they talked and laughed in public .... and expected to be able to join a discussion when men were talking. They could have nothing useful to say .... they were women. They were an embarassment.

In Farhad's culture women were not educated .... in fact they did not attend school beyond nine years of age .... because at that age their bodies began to change .... their sexual allure began to be visible.

Women were an embarrassment to God, and to men. Preferably never allowed outside the home .... women were a neccessity .... but an embarassment.

Farad hated women. He hated the lustful feelings they raised within him. He kept himself to himself .... and he kept his hatred .... and his lustful desires .... hidden.

Just once .... he had made the mistake of displaying the hatred. It had been a very hot day in July last year. One of his "grey imports" .... a Toyota .... had broken down, just two miles from the docks at Southampton. He had called out a local recovery company to take him and the car back to his home in Bracknell.

Farhad was amazed when the truck had arrived in little more than twenty minutes .... he had expected to be waiting for hours. The driver was very careful with his car. He was very polite to Farhad.

On the trip back to Bracknell they had chatted about the vehicles they had both owned.

It was midweek. They had a clear run up the motorway. Within ninety minutes of Farhad having broken down, they were just a mile from his home.

They had turned a corner, and the driver had stopped to let two girls cross the road. One of them looked up at the cab, and gave them a shy smile. She was about nineteen. She took her companion's hand as they ran across the road. It was a pretty enough site. They were attractive girls .... both with long blonde hair. They were wearing light summer frocks .... bare legs .... flip flop shoes.

As they turned onto the pavement they slipped their arms around each other's waists.

Farhad hated them. He hated the lust that welled up inside him.

He turned to the driver .... unable to let the moment pass.

"Your women are sluts", he said.

The driver didn't look at him. There was a long silence .... broken only by the sat. nav. .... as it guided them to Farhad's street. Farhad pointed out his house. The driver nodded .... and brought the truck neatly into the kerb.

"Let's get your car off then", he said.

Farhad watched as his car was unloaded. He watched as the truck's hydraulic body slid back up into position, and he watched as the retaining straps were carefully returned to their places, ready for the next job.

The driver removed his gloves. Farhad paid him cash. He looked at the driver .... then extended his hand.

The driver looked at him. He seemed not to notice the offered hand. Farhad expected him to speak. He didn't.

Farhad watched the truck move away.

He had been stupid .... very stupid .... he regretted it.

But his hatred was still there. The girls were sluts.

....

Ali arrived. He was driving a Toyota pickup truck. He jumped out.

"Farhad", he said "You are lazy .... you know how to change a wheel".

He laughed. The two men embraced. They were cousins.

Ali shared Farhad's good looks. He also shared his attitude to life .... to business .... to religion .... and to women.

They had grown up in a small community .... little more than a village .... ruled over by the local Imam. In any other culture the Imam would have been seen for what he really was. An insane and sadistic pervert.

But there .... in that community .... his word was law .... and he knew the law he enforced was the Word of God. He hated women. He spent his time watching them in every detail of their lives .... lest they should bring disgrace upon their families.

Women were hidden from men. Farhad and Ali would see their mothers hair when she took off her hijab, in the house .... they would see their sisters hair. That was all. In the street .... women were covered from head to foot .... lest they cause offence.

....

The two young men's education in Britain was funded by Ali's Grandfather. He was a wealthy man .... very wealthy. When he had decided to send Ali to be educated .... Farhad's Father had come to him. He had told him of Farhad's achievements in school.

The old man had agreed .... The boys were sent to Britain together. It had been an easy decision. He could afford it.

He looked to the future..... One day, these young men would repay him.

....

So Ali and Farhad had come to Britain .... to be educated. They were ill prepared for modern Western culture.. They had been told stories of this country of the infidel. Where few went to worship. Where women were as visible as men. Where women were educated. Where their sexual allure was celebrated rather than concealed. Where young women studied, on equal terms, with men. Where they sat in the same classes .... with hair displayed across bare shoulders .... with bare legs .... apparently knowing no shame for their condition. Unaware that they sinned before God.

After his first morning at University .... Farhad had gone to his Tutor to ask that women be banned from the lecture rooms. That they be returned to their families, to their Imams .... to face the punishment they deserved.

His Tutor had smiled at him. He explained that Farhad had chosen to be educated in a different land to his own.

He explained that Farhad must learn to accept different cultures. That this encounter with different cultures .... and different values .... was an important part of his education. He suggested that Farhad might be surprised. That he should attempt to enter into discussion with the famale students. He might discover that they were quite the equal of men in learning and understanding.

Farhad was disgusted by his Tutor's advice.

As the weeks passed. he watched as these young women formed relationships with the men they studied with. And even these relationships went unpunished. Surely the girls Father's should punish them .... their

Imams should oversee the punishment. But the girls went unpunished. Their sexual allures ran unchecked in a culture that had plainly turned it's back to God.

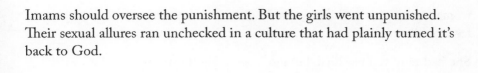

Farhad and Ali became closer. They sought out each other's company. They had grown up in a culture where women, beyond their own immediate family, were untouchable .... a mystery.

Their inability to relate to the opposite sex became a problem. It would inevitably have become a problem in their own community .... but in the culture they found themselves in .... the problem was intensified. It prevented their becoming part of student society. It began to isolate them from their fellow students

They were not unattractive to girls .... but the few who tried to approach them were quickly rebuffed. And Farhad, and Ali, soon began to be seen as "odd". To be avoided.

Farhad had flown home at the end of his first year of studies. Ali stayed. He had mastered the English language to the point where he had felt confident to apply for a summer job as a mechanic at a local garage. The garage boss had been doubtful. Ali had offered to work for three days for nothing. He would show his skills as a mechanic. The garage hired him at the end of the second day. A month later he was workshop foreman. Ali was a natural mechanic. Natural mechanics are very hard to find. The Garage liked Ali.

Ali liked his job.

Back in his home community Farhad felt safe once more. He spent his time among men. He discussed the affairs of men .... with men. But there was a part of him that was not to be denied indefinitely.

One afternoon he had left the village to visit an elderly friend of his Father's. Whilst returning, in the early evening, he had encountered a young woman on the path. She was standing there .... her head bare .... her hair free for all to see.

She had removed her hijab because a wasp had flown into it. She was shaking the insect from the material when Farhad came across her.

She saw him .... and frantically tried to cover herself from his gaze.

But it was too late. Farhad had no control over his reactions. He grabbed her .... cupped his hand over her mouth .... and dragged her from the path into the seclusion of the bushes. She scratched his face with her nails, and screamed. Farhad responded by knocking her semi - conscious. He tore away her clothing.

He had done little more than expose her breasts .... when the lust building inside him became too strong to be denied.

He ejaculated into his underwear.

Farhad looked at the girl laying before him. He turned away in disgust at the sight of her body.

He went to the Imam and told of the incident.

Three days later Sashi paid the penalty for the crime of adultery.

In the baking heat of the midday sun, she was buried to her waist on a piece of ground beyond the village boundary. Her hands were tied behind her back .... a loose sack was placed over her head and shoulders. She was to be stoned to death.

There were twenty or so people there ... all men.

The Imam listed her crimes .... and pronounced that the sentence be carried out. The stoning began.

When the sacking was saturated with blood .... and they could see no more movement .... the Imam smashed in the side of her skull with a pointed rock he had kept aside for the purpose.

Sashi had died bravely. She never made a sound.

She had been drugged .... and her mouth stuffed with cotton cloth .... her hijab. She was just sixteen years old .... the only child of a widowed seamstress.

The Imam had casually reprimanded Farhad.... for allowing the wanton guile of a young female to overcome his masculine self control.

Farhad flew back to Britain. He heard about the stoning. He was not disturbed. The girl had been a slut.

Only Farhad knew that Sashi had died a virgin. He was incapable of normal sexual intercourse with a woman. His ancestors had been desert dwellers. A thousand years of blistering heat had withered their extremities. Farhads erect penis was barely two inches long.

His inadequacy had instigated his hatred.

SIX

Roger ran down the stairs to the entrance hall .... turned right into the corridor .... and walked along to the set of doors that Debbie had described to him. They were painted a rich dark green .... no windows .... which Roger thought was odd.

"Fire doors I suppose", he said to himself.

He put the key into the lock. It turned so smoothly .... well he just had to operate the lock twice .... because it was so smooth. He examined the key under the art deco stye wall light.

"Seriously expensive lock", he thought.

He went through .... and remembering Debbie's instructions .... locked the doors behind him. It seemed a long way to the entrance at this side of the flats. Buttoning his overcoat against the cold, he pulled open the doors, which again, had no windows, and stepped out into the garden.

And he stopped .... astonished .... because everything was different.

It was light .... the soft light of a Spring evening .... he was bathed in warmth. There was no snow on the lawn. He could see flowers. He could hear crickets chirping in the bushes. This wasn't a cold dark January night. It was a balmy Spring evening.

Roger stood perfectly still .... looking around him .... and thinking. Trying to make some sense out of what had happened.

After a while .... he reached into his pocket for his mobile phone.

It wasn't in his pocket .... then he remembered that he had lent it to Debs.

He stayed very still .... then he looked back round at the entrance to the flats. He considered buzzing Debs ... but then he thought that she would be talking to her Dad. Better if he didn't interrupt that particular Father and Daughter conversation .....

He loosened his coat .... then took it off .... and put it over his arm.

It really was a very warm evening. He looked at the flowers. Roger was no horticulturalist .... but he was fairly certain of one thing.... if it was January at the other end of the block of flats .... then it wasn't January at this end.

He stepped out into the street. It was a wide tree lined road, surfaced with dusty yellow paving blocks.

He looked up .... and down .... the road. The trees were in full leaf. He could hear birds up above him, in the foilage.

He couldn't see a single car .... and he couldn't hear any traffic noise .... none at all. He thought that vehicles might be prohibited from using this road .... but the lack of traffic noise, in a City the size of Southampton, puzzled him.

He spotted a bench, set into the wall, just a few yards away on his right. Roger went and sat down. He wanted to work out just what had happened.

Whatever had happened .... It was really nice to be warm. The last month had been a very cold one .... a bitterly cold north-east wind had blown consistently for nearly three weeks. Roger loosened his shirt collar. For the moment he was very happy to enjoy this lovely evening .... but he wanted to think about the last twenty four hours.

He understood now why Debbie had insisted that he lock the doors in the corridor behind him. He also suspected that she had her reasons for borrowing his phone. He began to go back over the time since he had met Debs. Had there been any other "odd" moments ....

Well .... yes .... there had been a particular moment last night in the hotel .... He thought about it ....

And then there was Debbie's appreciation of the situation with that old Cavalier, in the car park, at Lewis. And just what language had she been speaking to that old lady in the service station ....

He wondered about her kitchen .... and her lounge. You could create that look .... with a lot of effort .... but that fridge was just too good to be true .... wasn't it.

He looked around him again. He was quite happy that he was sitting on a bench in Southampton .... and quite certain that Debbie had sent him out deliberately .... and that he wasn't in any sort of danger .... however strange things might feel. But this felt like May or June .... maybe even July. It wasn't January.

Then he remembered that Debs had added a final item to his shopping list .... a newspaper.

Roger smiled, and went to stand up. He was suddenly very keen to buy a newspaper ....

And then he had a second big surprise. All the more astonishing because of the strange peace and quiet he had been puzzled by, since he left the building.

It started very suddenly .... coming to him clearly across the balmy evening air.

It was the Muslim call to prayer, coming from an electric loudspeaker system, mounted on a Mosque. Roger knew the sound well enough. He had once holidayed in Turkey for three weeks. The amplified call to prayer from the Mosques .... five times a day .... was startling. Until you became used to it's rhythm. After three weeks there .... he had become so used to it .... that he had missed it when he came home.

And here it was again .... and Roger knew perfectly well that this means of broadcasting the call to prayer was not legal in Britain ....

He smiled .... remembering a conversation with the Turkish proprietor of a kebab van.

"Why are we not allowed to broadcast our call to prayer when your Christian Churches have all that "Ding Dong- Ding Dong .... Ding Dong- Ding Dong", on Sunday mornings ....".

Roger had thought it was a quite a sensible question .... but he hadn't been able to answer it.

The call to prayer ended as suddenly as it had begun.

Roger stood up. Time to collect the groceries.

Following Debbie's directions, he walked to the end of the road and turned right. He thought he could see the awning of a shop front about three hundred yards up on his left. He had just crossed the road .... when he was surprised to hear a car approaching from behind him. He looked round .... and shook his head ....

Roger knew cars .... he was, after all, a car dealer.

The approaching vehicle was a Ford model B four door saloon, dating from the early nineteen thirties. The watery throb from its old fashioned long stroke four cylinder petrol engine was very different to the sound made by modern cars. Roger watched it go by. He tentatively raised his hand to the driver. He received a nod in return. The car .... in amazing condition for it's age .... continued on it's way to the end of the street. It turned to the left .... and disappeared from view.

Roger walked on to the shop. It was a small local grocery store. A "One Stop". No surprises there. Roger went in .... and went to find the cold drinks cabinet. The cabinet .... when he found it .... proved very interesting. He picked out a can of Coca Cola .... changed his mind .... and swapped it for an orange Tango. He looked at the can in his hand. The Tango logo had an e on the end. Tangoe. Roger looked closely at the other drinks in the cabinet. Some he recognised .... some he didn't. What, he wondered, was "Pirate". He smiled. He picked out a can of "Pirate", blueberry flavour, for Debbie.

As he collected together his grocery list, he looked at the other products on the shelves. As with the canned drinks .... some products he recognised .... and some he didn't. When he arrived at the till .... the confectionary display was especially strange. The only things Roger recognised were "Bounty" bars, and "Kit Kats". He selected a "Montezuma". Another present for Debs.

He placed his purchases on the counter. There was an oldish man on the till. There was no credit card machine. Roger pulled out Debbie's purse. The man on the till looked at it, and smiled at him.

"Your lady sent you out shopping then", he said.

"How did you guess", said Roger.

He pulled out a ten pound note, He looked at it closely .... but it was a perfectly ordinary ten pound note. He handed it over. The shopkeeper looked at it.

"Have you anything smaller", he asked.

Roger looked at his intended purchases, and did some rapid mental arithmetic. He'd expected to have to add some coins to the note. He looked in Debbie's purse.

"Sorry .... nothing smaller", he said.

"Ok .... no real problem", said the man on the till. "It will have to be coins though".

Roger nodded. He received a substantial amount of change .... which he poured into Debbie's purse.

"Thankyou .... and have a good evening Sir", said the shopkeeper.

"It's certainly a lovely evening out there", said Roger.

Then he remembered the newspaper.

"Sorry", he said. "I forgot to get a paper".

The paper rack was just to his left. Roger wasn't too surprised, when once again, some of the names were familiar to him, and some were not. He chose a "Times", and payed for it. He picked up the carrier bag .... it was brown paper, not plastic, and left the shop. Outside, he put the bag down for a moment, and checked the date on the front of the paper. It was the sixteenth of May. He breathed a sigh of relief. The year was the same. Then he laughed.

The sixteenth of May was his birthday. He laughed again .... and turned back into the shop.

It was his Birthday.

He was going to buy a cake .... and some candles.

SEVEN

Roger walked back the way he'd come. It had been a nice surprise to discover that it was his birthday today .... and it had been especially nice to find a ready made chocolate birthday cake in the shop .... complete with icing, and candles.

He was looking forward to having tea, with a slice of his bithday cake .... and he was particularly looking forward to a long .... and interesting .... conversation with his new fiancee . The lovely Miss Deborah Wintersham.

Roger arrived back at the entrance to the flats, and buzzed Debbie on the intercom. She answered almost immediately.

"Is that you, Roger", said Debbie.

"It's me Debs", said Roger.

"Hello Roger", said Debbie .... "I expect that there are some things you'd like to ask me about ....".

"Just a few", said Roger. He heard the lock release.

"Roger .... you're not cross with me are you", said Debbie.

Roger laughed.

"Of course I'm not cross with you", he said. "But I really really want to know what's happening".

He pushed his way in with his shoulder, and walked along to the double doors. He had to put the groceries down to find the key in his pocket. He unlocked the doors, slid the bags through with his feet, stepped through himself, turned, and locked the doors again. He put his overcoat back on, and buttoned it up.

When he reached the end of the corridor, he didn't go straight to the foot of the stairs. He put the bags down in the corner, and went to the entrance doors. He pushed them open .... and stood, looking out.

It was dark .... and it was snowing steadily. Roger nodded. He collected his bags .... and started up the stairs.

At Debbie's door, he put his bags down again, pulled her purse from his pocket, and fished out her door keys. He let himself into the flat.

"I'm back Debs", he called.

"Hi Roger. I'm in the bedroom getting changed", Debbie called back. "Go through to the kitchen and make the tea .... I'll be with you in a minute or two".

Roger took his purchases through to the kitchen, and stowed the breakfast things in the fifties fridge. He looked at it closely. It wasn't a repro.

He made the tea, and opened cupboards until he found the cups and saucers.

There was a tap at the kitchen door .... which Roger, for some reason, had pulled closed behind him.

"Roger", Debbie called. "I've got a surprise for you. Can you face the opposite way and close your eyes while I come in".

It had been a day of surprises. One more couldn't possibly hurt. Roger sighed, turned to the opposite wall, and closed his eyes.

"Ready Debs". he called.

He heard the door open, and then Debbie's steps on the chequered linoleum flooring.

"You can turn round and open your eyes now Roger", she said.

Roger turned .... and stood staring at her. He had wondered if she would be wearing a nightdress .... and he had even thought that she might be naked .... because she wasn't a shy girl. He'd discovered that last night ....

But Debbie's appearance left him virtually speechless .... and you really do have to go some .... to turn a car dealer speechless.

Debbie was dressed as a Muslim girl.

Curiously .... Roger knew the correct names for her costume. Her long black dress was called an Abaya. It fell in soft folds to the floor.

The bodice was richly embroidered with geometric patterns in pink and pale green. On her head .... arranged carefully, to conceal her hair, her neck, and most importantly, her forehead .... she wore a simple pale pink scarf . The front piece fell nearly to her waist. Roger knew it was called the hijab.

He stood staring .... still speechless.

Debbie smiled at him.

"Are you going to say something to me Roger", she said.

Roger took a deep breath. He wanted to hold Debbie in his arms .... but he was suddenly very shy of her.

"Debbie", he said. "I'm not sure what to do. Can I hug you or what ....." .

Debbie laughed.

"Of course you can still hug me Roger", she said. "I'm the same girl you slept with last night".

She opened her arms .... but she waited for Roger to come to her.

Roger saw the invitation for what it was. It was her way of saying "I'm yours" .... but you have to come to me .... to what I am".

Roger stepped towards her. He put his hands on her shoulders .... then moved them down to her waist. She cupped her hands under his elbows, and they stood looking at each other.

Debbie waited patiently for him to make a decision.

Roger looked thoughtfully into her eyes.

"You have a lot of explaining to do, Miss Wintersham", he said.

Then he took the last step towards her, taking her fully into his arms. Debbie relaxed against him, laying her cheek against his shoulder, She held him .... keeping perfectly still .... allowing him time to become used to her.

Eventually Roger raised his right hand, and caressed the back of her head.

Debbie giggled against him.

"Roger …. be careful with my hijab", she said.

Roger held her at arms length again.

"I'm waiting for you to kiss me", she said

Roger took her hands in his own. He leaned forwards and kissed her lips …. and felt the soft material of her hijab against his forehead.

Roger knew just about everything about girls. He loved their company …. and they, in turn, loved his company …. sensing that he understood them far more than was normal for any man.

But Roger was lost here. These folds of cloth concealing Debbie had created a situation that he had never experienced …. that he was completely unprepared for.

He held her at arms length again.

"Debs", he said. "I just don't feel it's quite right to hug you while you're dressed like that".

"I knew you wouldn't", said Debbie.

"Just watch me for a moment".

She turned, and walked over to the door, and closed it. She returned to the sink, emptied the kettle, refilled it, and reached up to take a tea pot from the shelf above. She set it on the work surface, turned, and came back to Roger.

And as Roger watched her make all these simple everyday movements, her abaya, and hijab, gave Debbie such a feminine quality …. such a mysterious elegance …. that Roger realised that he knew almost nothing about girls.

Just perhaps the little that they had been prepared to reveal to him ….

Roger gave Debbie a final squeeze, and sat down at the kitchen table. He watched her make tea in a red polka dot Suzie Cooper tea pot, which matched the cups and saucers he'd found earlier. She passed him a cup of tea.

"I've got biscuits", she said, "but they'd spoil our dinner. Daddy has invited us to have dinner with him. He wasn't expecting me .... let alone me with my Fiance .... but he's got a chicken he can roast, and he's always got vegetables, so he says we won't leave hungry".

"We haven't got the car Debs", Roger reminded her.

"That's Ok .... it's not far to go", said Debbie.

Roger nodded.

"Debbie", he said. "Before we do anything else .... well , I'd just like to get my bearings if I can".

Debbie smiled at him and nodded excitedly.

"Ok", said Roger. "If I pick up my mobile phone there, and call John, would he receive my call, and if I asked him to, could he come back here, and pick me up in the Jaguar, and take me back to my place".

Debbie reached across the table, and took Roger's hand.

"Oh dear", she said. "I've made you feel really insecure, haven't I".

"I'm not sure that insecure is quite the right word", said Roger. "But we're sitting here at this table, and I just need to know .... are we in Southampton in Great Britain .... and if we go outside .... is it snowing because it's a January evening .... like it was when we arrived here".

Debbie laughed.

"I promise you everything is just the same as when we arrived .... apart from me having changed my clothes. Yes we are in Southampton in Britain, and it's January, and you're right .... it's snowing out there".

Roger nodded. He felt more comfortable with things.

"But where are we if we go through those doors in the corridor, Debbie", he said. "Are we still in Southampton .... in Britain".

"Yes". said Debbie. We are still in Southampton .... in the same street .... but it's a Southampton .... in fact a Great Britain .... with a different history to the Great Britain you are used to".

Roger nodded. He'd worked that out when he was there.

"What would have happened if I'd gone out of the entrance we came in by .... and walked round the block of flats to go to the shop", he asked.

Debbie smiled.

"You wouldn't have found the shop", she said. "It doesn't exist in this Southampton".

"So the doors in the corridor are the way through from this Southampton .... to the other Southampton."

"Yes". said Debbie.

"Are there other doors like that", asked Roger.

Debbie looked at him thoughtfully.

"There probably are other doorways", she said. "But that one is the only one we know of at the moment".

"We ". said Roger.

"The group of people who have keys to the doors", said Debbie.

"How many keys are there", said Roger.

"Seven", said Debbie.

Roger fell silent .... considering what Debbie had told him.

"It's going to be ever so much better if you ask Daddy about all this", she said. "I'm not really very clever about it all".

Roger nodded. He remembered the call to prayer that he'd heard.

"One last thing", he said."Would I be right in assuming that the other Great Britain .... that you've introduced me to this evening .... the one through those doors .... is not primarily a Christian country".

Debbie blushed. She nodded.

"The Great Britain through those doors is an Islamic country. Roger", she said. "And it has been for a very very long time".

EIGHT

"Perhaps we could have a biscuit", said Debbie. "Just one each ....".

"No", said Roger. "No biscuits Debbie".

"Oh gosh .... you're ever so assertive sometimes", said Debs.

She made a very pretty job of fluttering her eyelashes at Roger .... folding her hands over her heart as she did so.

"I think I'm going to swoon away .... I'm quite overcome with girlish confusion", she said.

"Little Women .... Louisa M. Alcott", said Roger.

Debbie looked at him with astonishment.

"How did you know that Roger", she said.

He laughed.

"If you're going to swoon, Miss Wintersham, can you pour me a second cup of tea first", he said.

Debbie poured the tea.

"No biscuits then", she said wistfully.

"No biscuits", said Roger.

He looked up suddenly.

"Hey Debs", he said. "I forgot the cake".

"Cake ....", said Debbie.

"You asked me to buy a newspaper at the shop", said Roger. I checked the date. Same year as here .... but it was the sixteenth of May there. That's my birthday .... so I bought a cake. It's even got candles on it".

"That's super", said Debbie. "We can have it for dessert after Daddy's roast chicken. He always forgets to do dessert".

"Except it's not my birthday here", said Roger. "It's January here".

"It'll be your birthday at Daddy's", said Debs enthusiastically.

"So we're going through the special doors to get to your Dad's place", said Roger.

"Yes", said Debbie. "It's not far to go. His flat is the same one as this .... but it's at the other end of the block".

"Ah", said Roger. He thought for a moment.

"Debs .... why is it May there, when it's January here".

"We don't know", said Debbie. "Daddy has a theory .... you can ask him later".

Debbie stood up. She came around the table, stood next to Roger, and ruffled his hair.

"Go and have a quick shower Sweetheart", she said. "Daddy is expecting us at eight o'clock .... and it's nearly seven already".

Roger looked up at the cream and red plastic Smiths electric clock on the wall.

"I've got a clean shirt", he said, "but the jacket and trousers will be the ones I was wearing for the wedding. Will that be Ok ....".

"You'll look great", said Debbie. "You mustn't worry about Daddy, Roger. I promise you .... he's really lovely".

"Does he know anything about cars, Debs", he said.

Debbie laughed.

"He knows lots, and lots about cars, Roger", she said.

"Now be good and go and have your shower".

"Lead me to it then", said Roger.

Debbie led him to the bathroom. She showed him how to operate the shower, and said she would put his clothes outside the door. The bathroom was super modern. The shower was super hot .... and super powerful. Roger had seen less powerful pressure washers. He undressed, adjusted the shower temperature, and stepped into the cabinet. He closed his eyes. The hot water streamed over him. In a moment he would shampoo his hair .... but not just yet.

It really had been an extraordinary day .... and it wasn't over yet. He had an invitation to dinner.

With his future Father in law.

In a parallel universe ....

....

Debbie and Roger arrived at her Father's door on the stroke of eight o'clock. Roger had wanted to be early .... but just as they had been about to leave .... Debbie had needed a last minute visit to the bathroom.

"Oh it's such an awful nuisance being a girl sometimes", she said.

"Handbag Debs", said Roger.

They knocked at the polished oak door .... and waited.

There was the briefest of delays, before the door opened.

Lord Wintersham had a seat in The House of Lords. Such was the strength and force of his personality .... that even in The House of Lords .... he was missed if he wasn't in that day.

He stepped out of his flat, threw open his arms and embraced his daughter.

"Daddy", said Debs.

"Debbie", said her Father. He held her at arms length.

"And just what scrape have you got yourself into now", he laughed.

"Daddy .... this is Roger", said Debs, disentangling herself from her Father's arms.

Roger stepped forward.

"Sir .... you are most welcome to my house", said Lord Wintersham.

He embraced Roger.

"Well Debbie", he said, releasing Roger, so that he could inspect him properly, "Just what have you done now".

Roger took the opportunity to inspect Lord Wintersham .... who was not quite what he had expected.

Debbie's Father was in his mid forties. He looked very fit .... almost athletic in his disposition. He had a full head of dark hair .... and the shadow of a beard around his chin. He was dressed casually in light blue jeans, and a popper fastened American collared shirt. His brown leather lace up shoes were polished to perfection.

"Well this is all most exciting", said Lord Wintersham. "But we must go in".

He shepherded them into the flat, and closed the door. Roger could smell roasting chicken. It reminded him of his Grandmother's house on Christmas morning.

He led them into the lounge.

"I must attend to matters in the kitchen", he said.

He looked at Roger and Debbie standing there.

"Roger", he said smiling. "For the sake of our digestive systems .... and that we might have a convivial evening .... might I take the opportunity to say here and now, that if Debbie has chosen you as her future Husband .... then I am absolutely and unreservedly happy to give the union my consent .... and my blessing".

Roger reached out his hand. The two men shook.

"There you are", said Debs. "I told you Daddy is absolutely lovely". She hugged her father.

"I really must away to the kitchen", said Lord Wintersham, "Or the unfortunate fowl will be little more than cinders".

They watched him go.

"Daddy is a superb cook", said Debbie. "He's only joking about the cinders".

....

Roger looked round the room .... and again had that feeling that things were a little "off kilter". The furniture was fairly conventional .... but the design of the dining chairs seemed a little strange. The patterns on the soft furnishings and curtains were also something he had not seen before.

"Roger .... come and see Daddy's model cars", said Debbie. "I think you'll like them".

Debbie led him to the other end of the room .... the end with the dining table already set. Roger noticed that it was layed for four .... and wondered who would be joining them. Debbie pointed to an alcove on the left. Standing, one at each end, of the side table, were two glass display cabinets, about 60cm long. Each case contained a model car. Roger recognised the cars immediately. The one on the left was a 1933 Model Y Ford two door saloon. The famous £100 Ford that made motoring affordable for a lot of people in nineteen thirties Britain. The car at the other end of the side table was very different. A 1959 Buick convertible .... arguably one of the most elegant of the chrome laden fifties American automobiles.

Roger approached for a closer look.

"I'll switch on the lights for you", said Debs.

She flicked a switch on the wall above the table, and both cases lit up. Roger couldn't see how this was achieved, because he couldn't see any electicity cables .... and there seemed to be no source for the light that was now illuminating both cars.

Roger went to the Model Y Ford first. He was astounded. The model appeared to have been built at one inch to one foot scale. The saloon body was a very dark blue, and the wire wheels pale yellow. The detail was absolutely extraordinary. The bonnet was open, allowing Roger to study the engine. He could see the four miniature spark plugs screwed into the flat cylinder head of the little side valve engine. He studied the wiring loom, clipped to the bulkhead, and looked at the tiny dynamo atop the engine. It was all absoutely perfect.

Roger had seen the exquisite work of the legendary car modeller, Gerald Wingrove, but this little Ford was even better. As Roger continued to study the car in detail .... he realised something quite extraordinary.

Most car models represent a car in new condition, but this car had been used. He could see petrol stains on the tiny alloy carburettor. The dynamo and crankshaft pullies were polished bright steel, where the fan belt ran on them. There were traces of oil leaks on the side of the engine, and when Roger looked through the side windows at the interior, he could actually see wear on the seats.

"This is an amazing model", he said to Debbie.

"Have a look at the Buick", she said.

Roger went to the other case. The Buick was much bigger than the Ford. The original car was over twenty feet long. The bodywork was in powder blue, the retractable hood in pale cream. And the model was fabulous. Again the bonnet was open, allowing Roger to study the V8 engine .... or as much of it as you could see below the big round "pancake" air filter. This Buick wasn't a "new" car either. The cream hood showed signs of weathering, the tyres were actually part worn, and Roger even thought he could see minute peices of gravel caught in the treads.

He turned his attention to the interior. American car interiors of this period were a mass of chrome and general "glitz". This one was no exception. The long bench seats were co-ordinated to the exterior colours, with cream pleated centre panels set in blue leather surrounds. And laying on the rear seat was a tiny duffle coat. Identical to the one Debbie had been wearing in Roger's Jaguar, but yellow instead of fawn.

"Hey Debs", said Roger. "You left your coat in the car".

"Oh that's where ...."

Debbie stopped as her Father came back into the room.

"Dinner in ten minutes", he said. " Ah .... I see you are admiring my cars".

"They're just unbelievable", said Roger.

Lord Wintersham smiled.

"I'll tell you more about them", he said. "But we are just coming up to the time for our evening prayer session. Debbie tells me you are a Church goer .... so I wondered if you might be willing to join us".

"No problem with praying", said Roger. "I'm happy to join you .... but you might have to forgive me for not being familiar with your customs".

Debbie smiled at him.

"We just face the right direction. and kneel", she said.

"Do you do the bit where you press your forehead to the floor", said Roger.

"We do", said Debbie.

"Are you Ok with me kneeling .... and then laying on the floor", said Roger. "That's the normal way for me".

"Roger", said Lord Wintersham. "We are so happy that you feel able to pray with us. Please adopt the methods which you feel are most appropriate".

He sighed.

"These matters of detail can cause such rifts", he said sadly.

Lord Wintersham moved the coffee table to one side of the room. The circular rug beneath it was patterned as a compass .... with one very prominent arrow, pointing to the corner of the room.

"The arrow points to Mecca", said Debbie.

She and her Father removed their footware, and knelt on the rug .... it was just large enough for Roger to join them. They all began the prayers in the manner to which they were accustomed .... Lord Wintersham, and his daughter, touching their foreheads to the floor .... Roger initially kneeling, with his eyes closed .... then lying down fully as the prayer progressed.

He supposed his companions were using Arabic for their prayers. After beginning in English .... he changed to his personal prayer language .... but speaking softly .... not wanting to disturb the others.

The session was short. It was just seven or eight minutes by Roger's reckoning, when Lord Wintersham and Debbie rose. They stood quietly, and patiently waiting for Roger.

Roger finished by asking that God should cast His blessing upon the evening .... returned to his feet .... and smiled at Debbie.

"All good", he asked.

"Splendid", said Lord Wintersham. "Now did anyone remember to pray for my cooking........".

NINE

Lord Wintersham had just asked Debbie to help him carry through from the kitchen, when there was a tap on the door.

"Ah .... excellent", he said. "I do believe that Isobel has returned in time. I was hoping that she might".

"Oh it will be super to have Isobel with us", said Debbie

The living room door opened, and Roger was surprised to see a girl, perhaps just a little older than Debbie, enter the room. She was dresssed as though she had come from the office .... white blouse, black pleated skirt, black tights, black shoes, and had her long dark hair tied back in a pony tail. Her hair was slightly damp, and Roger guessed she had come in from the snow.

"Debbie", she said .... astonished .... and obviously delighted. "I didn't know you were going to be here".

"Hi Isobel", said Debs."It's super to see you".

The two girls embraced fondly, and kissed each other's cheeks. Then Debbie stepped to one side.

"Isobel", she said. "I'd like you to meet my Fiance .... Mr Roger Davies".

Isobel looked at Roger .... and back to Debbie .... then at Roger again ....

"Debbie ....", she said. She looked at Roger again .... as though trying to establish that what she'd just heard was true.

"Debbie ....", she said. And she embraced Debbie again .... and the two girls hugged each other with delight and excitement.

Roger waited patiently until the excitement had subsided a little.

Debs unwrapped herself from the embrace, and pulled Isobel in front of Roger.

Isobel held out her hand.

"It's lovely to meet you Roger", she said.

Roger took her hand.

"And I'm very pleased to meet you, Isobel", he said .... looking to Lord Wintersham for some help.

"Oh .... I'm so sorry Roger", he said. "Isobel is my personal assistant for all my business activities. She is worth her weight in Gold .... aren't you Isobel".

Isobel blushed.

"I'm very blessed to have the opportunity to work with Lord Wintersham", she said. "I couldn't imagine a more interesting job".

"Yes .... we do have some exciting moments", said her employer, smiling at her. "But just for the next hour or so let us relax, and enjoy each other's company, shall we".

Isobel excused herself. She looked at Debbie.

"Lord Wintersham", she said. "Would you prefer me to change".

"No Isobel .... as you are will be splendid", he said

"Then, I'll just be a few moments", she said.

Debbie and her Father brought dishes through from the kitchen .... and Lord Wintersham carved the chicken, and placed four portions on the plates.

"Help yourself to the vegetables", he said.

Isobel looked at Roger .... and then at Lord Wintersham.

"May I say a Christian Grace for the meal", she asked.

"Of course you may, Isobel", said Lord Wintersham.

They all bowed their heads.

"Awesome God ....", began Isobel.

It was as pretty a Grace as Roger had ever heard. Isobel seemed assured and confident, in her role.

Although it was, on the face of it, a simpe enough meal, it was lifted to unexpected heights by Lord Wintersham's own speciality .... a spicy sauce for chicken. He also knew how to do superb roast potatoes .... and the potato tureen was soon emptied. There was no wine, but they each had a chilled bottle of sparkling water.

"It's chocolate birthday cake for afterwards", said Debbie. "It's Roger's Birthday today, isn't it sweetheart".

Roger smiled, and shook his head.

"Well", he said. "It's not my birthday in your flat Debbie ... but it seems that it is my birthday here".

Isobel smiled at him.

"Confusing isn't it". she said. "But you'll get the hang of it. I did".

"Then you are from the same Britain as I am", said Roger.

"I am", said Isobel.

"So are you Christian .... or Muslim", asked Roger. "If you don't mind me asking ....".

Isobel laughed.

"I go to a Christian Church", she said. "But things aren't quite as simple as you might think .... particularly if this is your first visit through the doors".

"How do you mean", asked Roger.

Isobel looked at Lord Wintersham .... but he signalled that she should continue.

Isobel thought for a moment.

"The word Muslim doesn't mean quite the same here, as it does for us", she said. "It's really complicated .... but I suppose you could say that there isn't so much difference between the two faiths here .... not as much difference as there might be in our Britain".

She thought again.

"Very simply put", she said. "I'm just as happy to go to "Church" in this Britain .... as I am in our Britain .... even if I am expected to dress "modestly", here".

"It's strange the difference the "modest" clothing makes", said Roger. "I was quite shy of Debs when I first saw her in the abaya and hijab".

"It feels different too", said Isobel. "What do you think Debs".

Debbie smiled at them both.

"It is different", she said, "But I think it would be very difficult for a man to understand why it's so different".

"Do you feel safer if you're dressed more modestly", said Roger.

Debbie and Isobel looked at each other.

"Perhaps you feel less "exposed"", said Isobel. "But it's more about feeling you are making just this little effort to be closer to God. As a woman .... you don't need to dress to attract attention .... because the only attention you crave is from God".

Debbie nodded.

"That's how I feel", she said. "I want to be noticed by God .... not by lots of men".

"I noticed you", said Roger.

Debbie blushed.

"Well you have to let one man notice you", she said.

"The one God chose for you", said Isobel, smiling. "Did somebody mention chocolate birthday cake earlier .....".

Roger unpacked the cake whilst the others cleared the table. He set up the ten candles that came in the box, and placed the cake on a glass cake stand that Debbie found in the kitchen.

"Can I light the candles for you please", said Debbie.

They watched as she used a match to set the cake aglow .... and Lord Wintersham dimmed the lights a little.

Roger stood. They sang "Happy Birthday" to him, and Roger successfully extinguished the candles with one puff.

"Speech", said Isobel, smiling at Debbie.

Roger took a deep breath, and looked round at his companions.

"I have had the most incredible .... the most extraordinary day", he said. "It began at breakfast, when I proposed to Debs .... and it has ended at my birthday party .... in a parallel universe. Could a man wish for a better birthday .... or better people to share it with. I think not. So I ask you to raise your glasses to an exciting year ahead for all at this table.

As Charles Dickens' Tiny Tim said:

"God bless us every one".

Lord Wintersham, Debbie, and Isobel applauded enthusiastically. Debbie went for plates and a knife.

The birthday cake was rich in chocolate. It was, they all agreed, a very special cake.

Debbie asked if they might have tea rather than coffee. Lord Wintersham made a large pot of Earl Grey, served without milk, and they sat on for a while. Isobel was keen to hear about how Debbie had met Roger.

Eventually Isobel asked if she might be excused. She had, she said, a busy day tomorrow. She asked Lord Wintersham if he would run through some of the details for tomorrow, before she left in the morning. They agreed on a chat over breakfast.

Isobel stood to go to her room. She "lived in".

Debbie kissed her goodnight.

Isobel came to Roger.

"Goodnight kiss please", she instructed him.

He obliged.

"Goodnight everyone", said Isobel .... and she went from the room.

"I'm going to share with Isobel tonight", said Debbie. She looked at her Father and Roger.

"You two have lots, and lots, to talk about".

Roger went to speak.

"Daddy will put you in the spare room tonight, Roger", she said. "I'll see you in the morning".

Roger fell silent .... and kissed his Fiancee good night.

They watched her follow Isobel

"Well", said Lord Wintersham. "We have been given our instructions . Brandy and cigars in the study for us Sir".

Roger laughed.

"I neither smoke or drink", he said.

"Neither do I", said Lord Wintersham. "I'll make some more tea ....".

TEN

Roger, at Lord Wintersham's invitation, returned to the lounge area. Roger put the coffee table back centrally between the sofas, and the two men made themselves comfortable. Lord Wintersham poured fresh tea .... and produced a cheese board with Blue Stiton, and Stilton with Cranberries. He opened a new packet of wholemeal cheese biscuits.

"I'm not allowed cheese", he said. "It's not good for me .... but I just cannot resist the occasional piece of Stilton. But please don't mention it to my Daughter".

Roger promised to forget he'd seen the cheese board .... and helped himself to biscuits, and a piece of Stilton with Cranberries. He too was very fond of Stilton.

"So my Daughter tells me that you are a car dealer .... and something of a car enthusiast", said Lord Wintersham.

"I am", said Roger. "I've done quite well from cars .... I've always been able to spot the best .... and if you want to sell successfully, it's always easiest if you have the best cars to offer your customers. Even if the price is higher than it might be for ordinary examples".

Lord Wintersham nodded.

"Do you have any other business interests", he asked. "Many car dealers are also into some sort of "financial services".

Roger laughed.

"Yes", he said. "I do lend money to people".

"Do you get it back", said Lord Wintersham.

"That's Uncle John's department", said Roger."If somebody forgets that they have a repayment date coming up .... well John reminds them .... and all is well".

"Always", asked Lord Wintersham.

"Always", said Roger. "Uncle John is kind, and caring, and considerate .... and very persuasive .... very persuasive indeed".

Lord Wintersham smiled.

"Is borrowing money acceptable here", said Roger.

"With interest .... no it isn't", said Lord Wintersham. "But there are ways around that problem .... as there have to be".

"But there are no credit cards here", said Roger.

"No", said Lord Wintersham."No credit cards".

The two men sat and ate Stilton cheese and biscuits .... and reflected on the difficulties caused by lack of instant credit facilities.

"I want to understand some of the basics about this parallel Britain", said Roger. "Has it always existed as a separate entity .... or did it branch off from my Britain at some point in history .... or did my Britain branch off from this one. In fact which is the original Britain".

Lord Wintersham poured two more teas.

"We simply do not know for sure", he said. "We have records of our seven key holders all the way back to the reign of Henry the Eighth. But we do not know if that represents the discovery of the door between the two worlds .... or whether a schism occured to create a parallel world, at that time".

"Are there distinct points where the history of this world diverges from the history of my world", said Roger.

"Oh very much so", said Lord Wintersham "For Britain .... and for everwhere else".

"Can you give me an example", said Roger.

Lord Wintersham stared thoughtfully at the ceiling.

"The Second World War", he said. "It never happened here".

Roger sat staring at Lord Wintersham.

"It never happened at all .....".

"Not at all .... and for the simplest of reasons. One sunny morning in Austria, a little boy ran out in front of a truck. The driver did his very best .... but truck brakes then were not what they are now. The little boy was killed outright. The lady from the nearby Post Office identified the boy .... as Mr and Mrs Hitler's little boy .... Adolf".

Roger shook his head in disbelief.

"That simple ....", he said.

"That simple", agreed Lord Wintersham. "There is an old theory that a butterfly flapping it's wings can alter world events".

Roger cut himself another piece of cheese .... he would be dreaming tonight .... if he wasn't already ....

"Debbie has told me this is primarily a Muslim country", he said. "How long has that been the case".

Lord Wintersham smiled.

"It happened gradually", he said "It seems to have started when Henry the Eighth wanted to separate from Rome. Now, as you probably remember from school history lessons .... that separation was because Henry wanted to divorce and re-marry. That's a nice "easy to remember" reason for schoolboys .... but the real reasons are much more complex .... and much more interesting".

Roger decided on one last biscuit .... with one last piece of Stilton.

"So are there still operating Christian Churches in this Britain", he asked.

"Oh good gracious yes", said Lord Wintersham.

"And the Muslims tolerate them", asked Roger.

"Oh dear", said Lord Wintersham. "I can see that you are viewing the situation here from a perspective of events in your world .... but that's not really fair, or appropriate".

He took a deep breath .... and closed his eyes to consider.

"There is so much to explain", he said, "that it really is difficult to know where to begin. There are so many historical differences between the two worlds, that we could talk all night, and still only have skimmed the surface".

"Could you just give me some of the key moments then", said Roger.

Lord Wintersham sat back on the sofa. He nodded.

"I'll try", he said.

Roger sat back. He and Lord Wintersham eyed the remaining Stilton thoughtfully.

"I'm going to put the cheese back in the kitchen", said Roger. "Before you yield to temptation".

Lord Wintersham laughed.

"Agreed", he said. "And while you do that .... I'll collect my thoughts into some sort of coherent order".

Roger put the cheese into the very modern refrigerator, the biscuits into an air-tight container that was standing on the work surface .... and returned to the lounge.

"Ok", said Lord Wintersham."Some very simplified key moments.

We'll start with the conquest of Constantinople in 1453. Constantinople had been a Roman Catholic City since the fourth century .... named, of course, after Emperor Constantine, who was the first Roman leader to impose the new 'Christian faith' onto his empire".

"Impose", said Roger.

"Yes .... impose", said Lord Wintersham. "But leaving that aside for the moment .... the Muslim conquest of the city had an interesting resultant effect.

The Christian scholars who lived and studied there, fled to Europe .... many to France, and England. And they brought with them something that scholars in those countries had never had access to before. They brought the earliest existing manuscripts of the Holy Bible New Testament with them .... and those early manuscripts of The New Testament were written in the Greek language. The language that was originally used, for instance, to write the four Gospels".

Roger nodded.

"Was anyone in Britain, at that time, able to read Greek", he asked.

"Very few", said Lord Wintersham. "But they soon learned, because those who did learn could read those four Gospels in their original form. They could see what those Gospels said, before the Romans translated them into Latin".

"Let me guess", said Roger. " Did they discover some differences".

"They certainly did", said Lord Wintersham. "Probably the most famous quote from that period, is from Thomas Linacre, a scholar, at Oxford":

"Either this is not The Gospel .... or we are not Christians".

"The Catholics had altered the scripture to suit their own agenda .... to the degree that prompted Linacre to doubt the Christian nature of the content".

"So the Bible we use now ....", Roger started ....

Lord Wintersham raised his hand.

"All in good time", he said. "Whilst Linacre and his fellow scholars were translating Greek scripture at Oxford .... a young man was growing up .... being educated .... being prepared for his future. Henry Tudor. Henry the eighth of England.

Henry was crowned in 1509. He was seventeen years old. He was intelligent .... with an enquiring mind. And he soon became aware of the work that was being done to translate the Bible from those early Greek manuscripts".

"Ah", said Roger. "And did he become unhappy with the Catholic Bible that was being used in what was now "his" Britain".

"He did indeed", said Lord Wintersham, "and by separating from Rome, he was able to take his new Church of England closer to those teachings of the Gospels .... translated from the original Greek ....".

"And he could annull his marriage to Catherine of Aragon, enabling him to marry Anne Boleyn", said Roger.

Lord Wintersham laughed.

"It all worked out rather well for young Henry", he said. "And now things begin to become interesting".

"Let me guess", said Roger. "England has separated from Rome. Did the Muslims spot an opportunity to spread the faith".

Lord Wintersham nodded.

"Initially .... the "first contact", as we might call it, was due to trade .... to business. The age old Catholic ban on trade with Islamic countries no longer applied to Britain. It didn't take long for Islamic traders to see the potential".

"Kebab vans on every street corner", said Roger.

Lord Wintersham laughed.

"What an attractive idea", he said, "And who knows: Those first Islamic merchants may indeed have brought the kebab with them .... but what they definitely brought to Britain was their Faith.

They brought Muhammad .... and his teachings. They brought news of Muhammad into a country blessed with a young Monarch ....a young Monarch with an enquiring mind .... and an insatiable thirst for knowledge".

"So are you saying that Henry the Eighth studied Islam", said Roger.

"Yes he did", said Lord Wintersham, "But this is where we begin to see signs of a schism between your world, and mine".

"You say "your world", said Roger. "Were you born here then".

"Yes", said Lord Wintersham."I am of this world".

"But you have a seat in the House of Lords in my world", said Roger.

"Yes", said Lord Wintersham. "All seven key holders have roles in both worlds .... but we must stay with Henry".

"May I make fresh tea", said Roger.

"A very good plan", said Lord Wintersham. He waved Roger in the direction of his kitchen, sat back, closed his eyes, and composed his thoughts.

Roger returned bearing tea .... and a packet of digestive biscuits.

"I found some biscuits", he said.

"Be my guest", said Lord Wintersham.

Roger proffered the packet, but Lord Wintersham was not to be tempted.

"A schism ....", Roger prompted him.

"Indeed yes", said Lord Wintersham. "Although Henry studied the Muslim faith in your world, and in mine .... well you know what happened in yours. He established the Church of England .... becoming Supreme Head in 1536.

But here .... things went differently. Our Henry wanted to make a very clear statement to Rome. He wanted to say: "Go away .... and don't bother us again".

He converted to Islam .... and took his country with him".

"Solved the wife problem", said Roger. "He could have as many as he wanted".

Lord Wintersham laughed.

"Roger", he said. "You have a knack of expressing yourself that I find very endearing. Henry had twelve wives here …. six at one time".

Roger sat back thoughtfully with his fresh tea.

"I might have to move here", he said.

"Roger", said Lord Wintersham. "I do believe that if you marry my daughter, Deborah, you will find just the one wife to be, in every way, sufficient".

ELEVEN

"You were going to tell me about the Bible we use now", said Roger.

"You're correct .... I was", said Lord Wintersham. "In your Britain, the first complete Bible .... a translation into English .... from the early Greek manuscripts .... was published in 1535. It became known to historians as The "Coverdale" Bible. Miles Coverdale, and John Rogers, were the leading lights in its creation .... but they leaned heavily on translation work done much earlier by William Tyndale, for his English translation of The New Testament, published in 1526.

The Catholic Church sentenced Tyndale to be burned at the stake for this translation. He was executed at Vilvoorde, in Belgium, in 1536".

Roger shook his head in disbelief.

"So Britain had a Holy Bible .... as close to the original Geek manuscripts, as could be achieved .... and a Holy Bible in their mother tongue .... English", said Lord Wintersham. "But there was one problem they all simply ignored .... they stayed with the same content that the Roman Catholic Church had selected, way back in the fourth century".

"How do you mean .... selected", said Roger.

"It's back to our old friend Emperor Constantine, I'm afraid", said Lord Wintersham. "He ordered the first compilation of the Bible that you are most familiar with. Let me explain .... I'll take the four Gospels as an example. Would it surprise you to know that Constantine's editors had forty possible Gospels to choose from".

"Forty", said Roger.

"Forty", said Lord Wintersham. "And that team of editors made some choices that appear very strange to us now.

There is, for instance, a lot of writing in The New Testament from Paul .... who never knew, or even met Jesus. But the Gospel of Thomas .... the 114 sayings of Jesus .... written down by the Disciple Thomas, who was with

Jesus during His Ministry, were thrown out as unsuitable material".

"So although we have an English Bible .... it's still really a Catholic Bible", said Roger.

"In selection of it's content .... certainly", said Lord Wintersham.

"So what happened here .... in your world", said Roger.

"Henry couldn't resist one final gesture to the Church of Rome", said Lord Wintersham. "He sanctioned research and assembly of a Holy Bible that would choose it's content from every surviving source. It was a stupendously difficult task. There were enormous difficulties in tracking down ancient material .... and they recognised that much had simply been lost over time".

"Did they manage it", said Roger.

"I'm pleased to tell you that they did", said Lord Wintersham. "It was called the "True" Bible .... after Joshua True, who had led the project for Henry.

The "True" Bible was published just a month before Henry died, in 1547. They say he was holding a copy in his hand on his death bed. He had managed to see Rome embarassed one last time".

"And that's the Bible the Christians use here", asked Roger.

"It is", said Lord Wintersham. "Would you like to see a copy".

"Did Thomas get in", said Roger.

"Oh he most definitely did", said Lord Wintersham.

"What about Paul's letters", asked Roger.

"Out", said Lord Wintersham.

"I'd love to have a copy", said Roger.

"I'll acquire one for you tomorrow", said Lord Wintersham.

"So how did Henry the Eighth manage to convert his Kingdom to Islam", said Roger. "Surely there must have been tremendous resistance".

"Again …. you are seeing the situation from your world's perspective", said Lord Wintersham. "In fact …. here …. there was little if any resistance. But to explain why …. we have to go back to the seventh century, and Muhammad himself".

Roger nodded.

"If I remember correctly", he said,"the Muslims agree that Jesus was sent, by God, as a Prophet …. but they believe that God sent a second prophet …. Muhammad, six centuries later. So Muhammud's teachings supersede those from Jesus".

"Well …. if you want to put it very simply …. yes that will do". said Lord Wintersham. "But there is a very important difference in the life of Muhammud, if we compare his activities in your world, to his activities in my world".

"In my world", said Roger, "Muhammud began his teachings in Mecca …. and then moved to Medina. But in Medina his teachings changed, and became much more radical. It's those later teachings that cause the ongoing difficulties".

Lord Wintersham looked at his future Son in Law with astonishment.

"Roger", he said. "Are you sure you're a car dealer".

"We get bad press", said Roger.

Lord Wintersham shook his head.

"In this world", he said. "Muhammud stayed in Mecca. He didn't go to Medina …. and therefore his earlier teachings were the basis for the faith that Henry presented to his subjects".

"And those earlier teachings weren't a million miles from Jesus, were they", said Roger.

"No", said Lord Wintersham. "They were not".

Roger reflected on what he'd learned. Lord Wintersham waited silently.

"So did Henry persecute his Christian population", asked Roger.

"Good gracious no", said Lord Wintersham. "He'd just given them a new Bible to play with".

"And what happened to the Catholics here", asked Roger."Did Henry dissolve the Monasteries".

"He stripped much of their wealth", said Lord Wintersham. "But there was no real persecution. With the exposure of the Latin Vulgate Bible for what it really was ....then the distribution of the "True" Bible .... and, as though that wasn't enough .... the whole new concept of Muhammud as a Prophet, the Catholic faith simply fell apart here.

 A very few of the older people stayed Catholic, but they were in such a tiny minority that Henry left them alone. He did make it very plain to them however, that if they practised their tradition of transubstantiation, they would incur the King's extreme displeasure".

"And did they", said Roger.

"I suspect that some of them did", said Lord Wintersham, but there is no history of Henry taking any punitive action".

I know of a little English village Church", said Roger, "where the priest was shot at the altar for continuing to say the Mass in Latin, when Henry had decreed that it must be done in English".

"Didn't happen here", said Lord Wintersham. "Henry was too busy praying five times a day, and his country was beginning to reap the benefits of the new trading agreements".

Roger sat silently thinking.

"So if the Muslims hadn't captured Constantinople ....", he said.

"And if that truck driver had stopped in time ....", said Lord Wintersham.

Roger thought.

"Do we know what happened to that truck driver", he said.

Lord Wintersham paused.

"We do", he said. "He committed suicide. He couldn't live with his guilt. He had killed a child ....

It's terrifying to realise that everything that happens .... every single thing we do .... every action we take .... can have far reaching consequences .... sometimes for millions of people".

....

Roger stirred in his chair.

"I'm beginning to need to call it a day", he said.

"I think we should", said Lord Wintersham. "It would be very easy to talk all night".

The two men rose. Roger took the cups back to the kitchen. They turned out the lights, and Lord Wintersham showed Roger down the hall, to the door of his room.

"Well goodnight, and sleep well young man", he said. "And .... of course .... congratulations upon your engagement".

Roger smiled.

"Thankyou", he said. "I promise to look after your Daughter for the rest of my life".

"And I can assure you that you could not wish for a lovelier wife", said Lord Wintersham."Until tomorrow then ....".

Roger opened his bedroom door .... fumbled for the light switch .... clicked on the lights .... and went in. The room was very pleasantly warm.

Debbie was sitting on the bed, legs folded beneath her, in a chemise, and her pants.

"Happy Birthday Roger", she said smiling at him.

"I'm not sure it is my Birthday", said Roger.

"Oh I think it is", said Debbie.

She looked to her left .... and slipped the thin strap of her chemise from her shoulder. She then looked to her right .... and slipped the strap from that shoulder. The chemise slipped downwards .... and then halted .... as though hung up on something. Roger tried very hard not to think about what it might be hung up on.

"Happy Birthday Roger ....", said Debbie.

Roger joined her on the bed. He felt a little over dressed. He put his arm around Debs, pulled her close, and kissed her.

"You're not in Hijab", he said.

"I don't need to be", she said. "I'm indoors with my Husband".

"We're not married yet", protested Roger.

Debs slipped a hand inside his shirt.

"Well Mr Davies", she said. "I don't know if you are married to me .... but I am very definitely married to you".

Roger laughed .... and kissed her again.

"Now", said Debbie. "Just suppose I was thinking of staying with you tonight .... and I'm only saying "thinking of".

Would you like to spend the night with a Muslim girl .... or would you prefer to spend the night with a Christian girl ....".

Roger smiled at her .... shaking his head.

"Oh Debbie", he said. "Which were you last night".

"Which do you think I was last night", said Debbie.

Roger closed his eyes .... and thought back.

"I think I know which you were", he said.

"So is that the one you would like to spend the night with again", said Debbie.

Roger took a deep breath.

"Yes Debbie", he said." .... again .... and again .... and again .... and again ....

TWELVE

Roger woke slowly. He should really .... if this was a novel or a film .... have stretched his arm towards Debbie .... only to discover that she wasn't there.

In fact .... he knew she wasn't there .... because he had sent her back to her own room last night.

She had made a very pretty job of pouting, and sulking, as she went .... but Roger knew perfectly well that it was what she had wanted him to do.

It was .... after all .... her Father's flat.

There was a knock on the door.

"Roger .... it's Isobel. Debbie says she is doing breakfast in the kitchen .... five minutes".

"Ok Isobel .... I'll be there", said Roger.

He got up, pulled on his trousers, and checked a likely looking door on the side of the room. It was a bathroom. Roger wahed his face, cleaned his teeth, combed his hair, finished dressing, and made it to the kitchen just as Debbie was putting breakfast onto plates.

She put down the pan and the spatula, and came to kiss Roger Good Morning.

Roger gave her a responding hug .... and smiled at Isobel.

"Good morning", he said.

"I went back to my flat for the breakfast things you bought", said Debbie. "I've done bacon, eggs, and sausages, for you and Daddy. Isobel and I are having cereal".

"I got you a couple of little presents", said Roger. "Did you find them".

"Ah .... yes", said Debbie. "A can of "Pirate", and the "Montezuma" bar. Isobel and I have eaten the "Montezuma"".

"Chocolate before breakfast". Roger shuddered.

"Girls can eat chocolate anywhen", said Debbie. "Isn't that true Isobel".

"Absolutely anywhen", agreed Isobel.

Lord Wintersham came into the room.

"Good morning all", he said, "And cooked breakfast too .... a real treat".

He and Roger sat at the table, and started on their bacon, egg, and sausages. The girls perched on stools with their bowls of Corn Flakes.

Debbie told Isobel all about Tallulah's wedding. Roger and Lord Wintersham ate quietly .... listening to Debbie.

"Have you plans for the day Roger", said Lord Wintersham.

"That will depend on talking to John", said Roger. "We have some friends from Sweden coming today to buy a Jaguar. They aren't likely to be with John until ten o'clock, so I'm not expecting him to phone until ten thirty, or so.

"He won't be able to reach you here", said Lord Wintersham. "We do have a mobile phone network here .... but it still operates on the analogue system".

"I was wondering about that", said Roger. "Are there lots of differences in the technologies between our two worlds .... no credit card machines for instance".

Lord Wintersham nodded.

"A lot of differences", he said. "We might be considered rather behind the times here in some respects .... but there are some very remarkable technological advances here, that simply haven't happened in your world yet. In fact I can show you a wonderful example in the dining room. But let's finish our breakfast first.

Debbie passed them fresh tea .... and Lord Wintersham and Isobel ran through some timings for her day.

Isobel donned her thick winter coat .... which told Roger she was to be working in January .... rather than the May here. She kissed Debbie goodbye, wished Roger, and Lord Wintersham a good day .... and left "for the office".

"If we're going through to the dining room", said Roger. "I'd love to examine those model cars again. They are unbelievable".

Debbie laughed.

"Go and show Roger your cars Daddy", she said. "I'm going to do the washing up".

Roger and Lord Wintersham returned to the dining room .... and Roger went straight to the cars.

Lord Wintersham stood watching him as he examined the little Ford Saloon.

"Roger", he said. "Bring the display cabinet onto the dining room table for me".

Roger went to oblige. He tried to slide the cabinet to the edge of the table, so he could lift it. It wouldn't budge .... not at all.

"The cabinet is fastened down", said Roger.

"I promise you the cabinet is not fastened down in any way .... it's just sitting on the table", said Lord Wintersham.

Roger tried again. He cupped his hands around the wooden base, and tried to pull the cabinet towards him. He couldn't manage the slightest movement. He looked at Lord Wintersham in complete bafflement.

"The case must be fastened down", he said.

Lord Wintersham laughed.

"Roger", he said. "How much would an original 1934 Model Y Ford saloon weigh".

Roger thought.

"About fourteen hundred weight .... about sixteen hundred English pounds", he said.

"And that is exactly what that Model Y Ford in the case weighs", said Lord Wintersham."And that is why you can't move it".

Roger leaned in close to look at the car. Suddenly the truth dawned on him. He looked up at Lord Wintersham.

"It's not a model at all, is it", he said. "It's a real car".

Lord Wintersham laughed.

"They are both real cars", he said, "And I can promise you I have driven both of them".

"But how can you do this to a real car", asked Roger, turning to examine the Buick.

"It's not as difficult as it appears", said Lord Wintersham. "It really relies on a simple concept .... which inevitably leads to the technology. In fact somebody in your world is coming very close to developing the same technology. They are currently just one step away".

"So have you brought any technology from my world into this one", said Roger. "Or have you taken any technology from this world into ours".

Lord Wintersham thought for a moment.

"You know that there are seven key holders for those doors", he said. "Our group of seven have always had a strict policy of not transferring any sort of technology from one side of the doors to the other".

"Why", said Roger.

Again Lord Wintersham paused for thought.

"The most fascinating thing about the two worlds, are the ways in which they have developed differently", he said.

"We have always been very careful to maintain the separation .... specifically to allow differing situations to develop. We know from our records that the decision to keep to that policy was taken virtually from the beginning".

"Have there been any "leaks", said Roger.

Lord Wintersham smiled.

"It is extraordinarily difficult to say for certain", he said. "It is difficult, because of the possiblity that there are other doors between the two worlds that we are not aware of.

There may be other groups .... or even individuals .... who have their own doorways".

"And they might not observe the "non transference" policy, said Roger.

"Exactly", said Lord Wintersham.

"Have you ever suspected a technology has been shared", said Roger.

"There are a couple of incidents that made us suspicious", said Lord Wintersham. "But they may simply have been due to like minds coming up with the same ideas at the same time".

"There are plenty of well known examples of that happening in my world", said Roger.

"Here too", said Lord Wintersham.

"So how do you shrink a car", said Roger.

Lord Wintersham laughed.

"I'll explain how it's done next time we have dinner together", he said. "But for the moment I must excuse myself. I have a meeting with some company directors tomorrow .... and I have some preparation work to do in my study".

"And I'd better see what Debs has planned for us", said Roger.

Lord Wintersham smiled.

"Roger .... I can see you are already thinking like a married man", he said.

Lord Wintersham went off to his study .... and Roger arrived back in the kitchen just in time to see Debbie pulling off her rubber gloves.

They embraced. Then they kissed.

"Roger .... let's go back to my place, and see if Uncle John has managed to sell your Jaguar", she said.

FOURTEEN

Ten minutes later Debbie and Roger were back in Debbie's flat .... having made sure, of course, that the doors in the corridor were carefully secured behind them.

Debbie had just made them coffee when John rang.

"I've sold the XJ", he said. "I dropped a hundred to keep it friendly".

"That's fine", said Roger. "When do they want to take it".

"It's gone already", said John. "They payed cash as usual .... and they're on their way to Harwich for the ferry".

"I want to show Debs our setup", said Roger. "Can you come and collect us".

"Which car", said John.

Roger thought for a moment.

"Bring the '74' Buick", he said.

"In this weather", said John,

Roger looked at Debs .... who was totally absorbed in painting her toenails.

"Bring the Buick John", he said. "Leave it for an hour .... so the roads dry out .... and I'll take it for an underbody wash tomorrow".

John agreed to see them at about one thirty .... and Roger turned back to Debbie.

"Would you like to see my place Debs", he said.

"Can I stay the night", she asked.

"Of course you can", said Roger.

Debbie looked up from her toe nails.

"Would you like me in hijab", she said.

Roger knelt down in front of her .... and blew on her toes.

"That tickles", said Debs.

"I want to see John's expression when he sees you in your hijab", he said.

Debbie smiled.

Well he won't see much of me at all will he", she said.

Roger laughed.

"I suppose not", he said.

"It's Thursday today", said Debbie. "Are you and Uncle John going to Church tomorrow night .... you told me you go on Fridays".

"Definitely", said Roger. "So are you going to come with us".

"Of course I'm going with you", said Debbie. "I'm married to you now".

Debbie came to Roger, and put her arms around him, and layed her head on his shoulder.

"Just think Mr Davies", she said. "You're stuck with me for ever and ever .... and ever".

Roger kissed the top of her head.

"And ever .... and ever ....", he said.

"So", said Debbie. "We'll go to your place today .... I'll stay the night with you .... and we can all go to Church tomorrow".

"Done deal", said Roger. "Let's shake on it".

They shook hands .... and laughed.

"Could Isobel come with us", said Debbie. "I think she would like to be invited".

"Fine by me", said Roger. " We'll have to come back to Southampton in the car, so we could pick her up here".

"She'll probably just meet us there", said Debbie. "She does drive .... and she's in this world today .... so I can phone her later and ask her".

Roger nodded.

"It's a third Friday of the month tomorrow", he said, "so it's the big night for the choir. The service will be nearly all music. You'll love it".

"Should I be in hijab", said Debbie, smiling.

"What will Isobel do", said Roger.

"In hijab", said Debbie. "We're going into God's presence, so we would both expect to wear hijab .... particularly because there will be men and women in Church together".

"Fine by me", said Roger. "You'll both look fantastic, I'm sure".

"I'm looking forward to seeing you and John in Church, so much ....", said Debbie.

"There's still a little bit of you that doesn't believe John and I go to Church, isn't there", said Roger.

Debbie laughed.

"Perhaps just a teeny weeny little bit", she said.

....

"Debbie's buzzer sounded just before one thirty in the afternoon.

"I think that's probably John", said Roger.

Debbie went to the intercom in the hallway.

"Hello John", she said.

"Hi Debbie", its me .... John .... and I've got ten shillings for you", he said.

"I'm going to spend it all on sweets", said Debbie.

"Pineapple chunks", said John.

"If you like", said Debbie."I've opened the door for you ....".

She returned to the kitchen.

"Roger, sweetheart", she said. Can you go and let John into the flat please. I'll be in the bedroom. Start making some coffee .... and I'll join you in a minute, when I'm ready".

Debbie went off to the bedroom .... and Roger let John in. John handed him a large envelope.

"All cash .... as usual", he said.

Roger sighed.

"Will they ever learn to trust bank transfers", he said.

He took John along the hall, and showed him into the kitchen. John stood, looking round, in amazement.

"It's all real fifties gear", he said.

"Yup", said Roger. "Wait till you see the lounge .... that's all nineteen sixties .... every detail of it. And don't forget to ask Debs where she got the coffee table .... you'll be amazed .... I promise".

"So where is Miss Wintersham", said John.

"I'm here John", said Debbie, as she came into the kitchen.

John turned to greet her .... and stood staring in amazement".

"Debs is Muslim", said Roger.

John nodded slowly.

"I should have guessed", he said. "There was something about the way you handled that situation in the service station yesterday".

He stood looking at Debs.

"You look wonderful", he said.

He handed Debs a coin.

She looked at it in her palm.

"Gosh .... it's a whole pound .... not just ten shillings", she said.

She went and kissed John on the cheek.

"You're definitely worth a whole pound", he said.

Debs made coffee, and found some biscuits. Neither she, or Roger had eaten lunch, because they were waiting for John, and hadn't been sure when he would arrive.

"Shall I do us all some lunch", Debbie said.

Roger checked his phone for the time.

"If we're quick", he said. "we might just catch our favourite cafe before it closes".

"Are you thinking of Lee's place", said John."I'll phone ahead with the order to save time".

"Three Gourmets", said Roger. "Debs .... I'm taking you out to lunch .... but you'll have to be ready in about four minutes".

"Oh Wow ....", said Debs excitedly. "I'm going out to lunch with you. Will it be a super specially delicious lunch because you love me".

"John ....tell Lee to make it a "super specially delicious" lunch", said Roger.

Debs dashed from the room .... and was back in three minutes with her travel bag.

They swallowed the last of their coffee .... and two minutes later, they stepped out of the flats entrance, into the snow.

"Wow", said Debbie. "Is that your car".

The "seventy four" Buick pillarless four door sedan never failed to impress. Twenty feet of gleaming white cellulosed bodywork .... a pale green corded interior .... and finished at front and back with the massive chromed bumpers that Americans love so much.

"Debbie's Dad has a '59' Buick 'rag top", said Roger.

"Does he use it", said John.

Roger looked at Debbie.

"Oh yes .... he uses it quite often in the summer", said Debs.

"Does he have trouble getting it out of the garage, Debs". said Roger ....
smiling at her.

"These thirties flats did tend to have smallish garages", said John.

Roger smiled.

"Yup", he said."The garage is a bit on the small side".

In the Buick, John phoned ahead, and ordered lunch for three.

"I really didn't like bringing the Buick out in the snow", he said.

"I promise you it will get steam cleaned and waxed tomorrow", said Roger.

John glanced over at Debs.

"I think somebody is trying to impress his new girl friend", he said.

Debs laughed.

"Oh gosh Roger", she said. "I'm ever so impressed by your big car .... and it
has such a huge bonnet. Is the engine really enormous".

"Absolutely enormous", said Roger.

....

They made it to the cafe well before two.

John tucked the Buick in front of a blue single decker bus that was parked
on a side road in the industrial estate.

"Here we are", he said.

" But it's a bus", said Debbie.

"It's The Breakfast Bus", said Roger.

"But it's lunchtime", said Debbie.

"And Lee is cooking our lunch right now", said Roger.

Roger pushed open the folding doors at the front of the bus, and led the way up the centre aisle, between the tables, to the counter at the rear.

"Hello Lee", he said.

Lee .... who had been washing his hands .... turned.

"Roger .... John", he said. "It's good to ....".

And he stopped short .... as he spotted Debbie. Debbie smiled at him.

"Lee", said Roger. "I'd like you to meet my very new Fiancee .... Miss Deborah Wintersham".

Lee looked at Roger .... then at John .... as though seeking confirmation that he wasn't being conned.

John nodded.

"The boss is engaged", he said.

Lee .... plainly still at a loss .... came to the counter with a broad smile on his face.

He reached out a hand to Debs .... who took it between her own .... and held it there, while she looked at him.

"Hello Lee", she said. "Your bus is amazing .... I thought these two were teasing me, when they said it was a bus".

Lee looked to Roger.

"May I kiss the bride", he said.

"Not if I kiss you first", said Debbie. She drew Lee towards her, and kissed him on the cheek.

Lee hugged her .... and returned the kiss.

"I'm very pleased to meet you", he said. He looked at her.

"I love your hijab", he said. "So can I assume that you are of the Muslim faith".

"I am", said Debs. "How do you feel about that Lee".

Lee seemed taken aback at the question. He thought for a moment.

"I'm good with it", he said.

He looked at Debbie ....

"I'm not religious at all", he said.

"Oh dear, Lee", said Debbie. "Are you going to tell me you don't believe in God".

"Sorry", he said.

Debs took his hand again.

"Lee", she said. "It doesn't matter if you don't believe in God .... it's whether He believes in you. Don't give Him a reason not to, Lee".

Lee shook his head.

"Shoudn't you be calling Him Allah", he said.

Debbie laughed.

"Lee", she said. "You should pronounce it Al - lah".

"So do you and Roger have the same God", asked Lee.

"Oh very definitely the same God", said Debbie. "Haven't we Roger".

"Same God .... different prophet", said John.

"Lee", said Roger. "Debbie and I are famished ....".

"Almost done", said Lee.

He went back to the griddle .... flipped the burgers .... and put the buns on the hot plate, to toast.

"I've done burnt onions for everyone", he said, "and a slice of bacon on the top for John".

Debbie, Roger, and John, sat at the table nearest to the counter.

Lee handed them three mugs of tea. By the time they'd taken their first sips .... the burgers were ready.

"Three Gourmet burgers to eat in", said Lee. "One with bacon".

John went to the counter and collected the order.

"Still not doing chips then, Lee", said Roger.

"No chips .... no chance", said Lee. "Too risky on the bus".

Roger sighed.

"I love a few chips with a burger", he said.

Debbie touched his cheek with her fingers.

"I'll cook some chips for you later, Sweetheart", she said.

"This is a really good burger, Lee", said Debbie, who was well into her third mouthful.

"It's why we come here", said John.

"And there was me thinking you came because you love me", said Lee.

Debbie looked up at him.

"Jesus loves you, Lee", she said.

"Don't you mean Muhammad", said Lee.

Debbie laughed.

"Muslims have Jesus as well Lee", she said.

"How does that work then", said Lee.

He came out from his kitchen .... and sat on the table across the centre aisle.

"Muhammad was born six hundred years after Jesus", said Debbie. "So we go with His teachings because they come later".

"So couldn't you just be a nice person", said Lee, "and live your life in a peaceful way .... and help other people when you can .... and try not to tell lies .... and try not to be greedy .... and all that stuff. Why can't you just be a nice person .... why do you need God".

"Yes .... that's well said, Lee", said Debbie. "And God will let you do that .... and you'll be Ok in his sight. But if you decide to invite Him into your life .... then Wow ..... amazing things start to happen .... because then it's not just you .... you're not on your own anymore. You've got God on your side. And having God with you is just the most amazing thing you could ever wish for".

"That was a Bob Dylan song", said Roger.

"What was", said Lee.

"God on your side", said Roger.

"Ok .... let's say you've convinced me", said Lee. "How does a Burger joint owner get God on his side".

Debbie laughed.

"It's just so easy Lee", she said. "Just talk to Him".

"What .... like praying, you mean", said Lee.

Debbie laughed.

"Do you think praying is boring then Lee", she said.

"Really boring", said Lee.

"So does God", said Debbie. "He's heard so much boring praying .... that He's just so excited when somebody new .... like you .... comes along, and makes it exciting for Him".

Lee looked doubtful.

"But, it's when you realise your prayers are really being heard .... and they are really getting answered .... and things are really starting to happen. That's when it gets exciting", said Roger.

"So are you seriously telling me God would answer the prayers of a car dealer", said Lee.

John and Roger laughed.

"Afraid so Lee", said Roger. "God loves an honest car dealer".

"Hmmm", said Lee. "Look .... are you three going to stop talking so much, and get those Gourmets eaten. It's nearly two o'clock .... and I should be packing up ready to go home".

"Do you take the bus home every night then Lee", said Debbie.

"Every night", said Lee. "I'm not allowed to leave it here".

They finished the last of their burgers, and stood to leave. Lee collected the plates and cups.

"Great as always Lee", said Roger.

"It really was a lovely burger Lee", said Debbie.

"I try", said Lee.

"And you succeed", said John.

"Lee", said Debbie. "Just try a prayer to God tonight .... then you can tell me all about it when we come next time".

Lee sighed.

"For you Miss Wintersham .... anything", he said .... not entirely convincingly.

"You can call me Debbie", said Debbie.

FIFTEEN

It had been warm in the Breakfast Bus. They felt the first warning chill of the coming evening as they walked back to the Buick. There was a dull calm in the air that spoke of frost to come.

The afternoon cast it's last rays of Winter sunlight across the windscreen as John turned the Buick southbound onto the Motorway. He pulled the sunvisor down, and glanced in the rear view mirror.

"There's a Nissan Skyline coming", he said to Roger. "And it's in a hurry".

They watched the Skyline go down the outside lane at a speed they estimated at over ninety miles per hour.

Chrome disc wheels. Pearlescent black paint. Side exhausts.

"Fantastic bits of engineering", said Roger. "We've had two of them. Totally reliable. Frightening performance .... but absolutely no soul. No soul at all".

"Sort of a Japanese BMW", said John. "No soul at all".

"Do cars really have a soul", said Debbie.

"Of course they do", said John.

"Jaguars have a soul", said Roger. "They're just like a girl".

"Oh please tell me", said Debbie .... rolling her eyes skyward. "Why is a Jaguar like a girl. Please do tell me, Roger".

"They're unreliable .... and they leak", said Roger.

Debs punched Roger on the arm. She drew her fist back for a second hit .... but Roger was ready this time, and caught her wrist. Debs gave him a jab in the stomach, with her other fist. Roger grabbed that wrist too. Debbie protested .... and they both went down onto the rear floor of the Buick, in a giggling, struggling, tangle of limbs.

John glanced back at them .... and sighed.

"Miss Wintersham", he said. "Might I remind you that you are the daughter of a Peer of the Realm …. and that you are in hijab. I really consider your behaviour to be most inappropriate".

Debs returned to her seat …. sat up very straight …. straightened her hijab …. and looked for all the world as though butter wouldn't melt in her mouth".

"I'm sorry Uncle John", she said. "But Roger said I'm unreliable …. and I leak".

Roger had also resumed a more conventional position for a rear seat passenger in a motor car. He ran his fingers through his hair.

"Sorry Debs", he said. "It's a joke we got from our Swedish friends".

"Think yourself lucky if I don't divorce you", said Debbie.

"We're not quite married yet are we", said Roger.

"I don't think my Daddy is seeing it quite like that", said Debbie.

John flicked the headlights on. The instruments on the dashboard lit up in a tourquoise blue green glow.

"Twenty five minutes to home", said John.

"Uncle John", said Debbie, in her best little girl voice. "When are we getting there …. when are we getting there …. when are we getting there".

Roger pulled Debs towards him. She let her head rest on his shoulder …. and began to sing quietly.

Under the bonnet the seven litre V8 engine pulled the Buick effortlessly …. using a litre of gas every two miles. It was smooth and peaceful. Debbie began to doze against Roger's shoulder.

Debs phone began to ring. Roger gave her a squeeze, and passed her handbag. Debbie rummaged in the bag, produced her phone, and checked the screen.

"It's Lorraine", she said excitedly. Roger raised his eyebrows.

"Hi Lorraine .... Wow .... it's so nice to get a call from you", Debbie said breathlessly. "Where are you .... can we get together really soon .... I'm engaged. It's just so exciting. His name is Roger. I'm in his car with him at the moment .... and I want you to meet him .... and I want you to meet his friend John, because I think you'll both really like each other .... and they're really taking me to their church tomorrow evening .... and he knows I'm a Muslim girl .... and he's OK with it .....and you should see his car because it's just so big .... and white .... and lovely".

Debbie stopped. She had run out of breath.

Lorraine .... who was well used to her friend's ways .... had waited patiently for her chance to take a part in the conversation.

Debbie listened. She smiled. She turned to Roger.

"Sweetheart", she said.

"Yes Miss Wintersham", he said .... cautiously.

"How far are we from Wimborne .... Lorraine is visiting her parents .... and it would be super to see her .... and you and Uncle John could meet her".

John glanced back at Debbie.

"We can be in Wimborne in thirty five minutes easily", he said.

"Go for it John", said Roger.

Debbie gasped with pleasure .... and went back to Lorraine.

"We can be with you in about half an hour", she said to Lorraine excitedly.

"Can you ask Lorraine for her post code please", said John. He passed the sat. nav. on it's power cord back to Roger.

Debbie said her farewells to her friend .... took the sat. nav. from Roger .... and tapped in Lorraine's address and post code.

"I'll have to direct you in for the last two miles", she said. "We don't want to go in via the narrow lanes in this car".

She returned the sat.nav. to John .... relaxed back against Roger's shoulder .... and closed her eyes.

"A penny for your thoughts Debs", said Roger, after she had been quiet for five minutes or so.

"I was thinking about Lorraine", said Debbie. "You and John are never going to forget the moment you first meet her. She has such an intense personality .... it sort of knocks you sideways until you've got used to her".

"So how did you two meet", said Roger.

"We were at school together", said Debbie. "We were in the same class, we always sat next to each other, our beds were next to each other in the dormitory. She is just the loveliest person ....".

Debbie went quiet again.

"Roger", she said eventually. "If I'm staying with you tonight .... can I invite Lorraine to stay with us .... is there a room she could have".

Roger nodded.

"No problem at all", he said. "There are two spare bedrooms".

Debbie reached up and kissed Roger on the cheek. She took one of Roger's hands in her own,

"So is Lorraine your very bestest of best friends, Debs", said Roger, smiling.

"Oh yes .... definitely", said Debbie. She thought for a moment.

"Roger .... sweetheart", she said.

"Yes Debs", said Roger.

There was a long pause.

"Actually", said Debbie. "There have been times when Lorraine and I have been just the teensiest bit more than bestest friends".

Roger turned Debs to him .... looked straight into her eyes .... and kissed her.

"How many more surprises are you going to throw at me Debs", he said.

"One more .... quite soon", said Debbie. "Lorraine is really going to surprise you. You won't have met anybody quite like her .... I promise you".

She giggled .... and snuggled up to Roger.

"I do like this car", she said. "It's so comfy .... and you and John are going to like Lorraine so much".

It was quiet in the car for a while. An endless stream of modern cars passed by in the outside lane. John held the Buick at a sedate sixty miles per hour. It wasn't a car you needed to hurry. In this car .... other people waited for you to arrive .... because you were somebody.

Debbie stirred ....and turned to Roger.

"Roger", she said. "Have you driven any of the fifties American cars with the push buttons to work the automatic gear box".

"We had a '58 Edsel with a push button auto box", said Roger. "Why do you ask".

"Those cars are like a man", said Debs. "Only four buttons to push".

"Really", said Roger. "And what would those four buttons be then, Miss Wintersham".

"Food, Sex, Toys, Cuddles", said Debbie. "Just the four buttons for a girl to press .... so she can operate her man".

"And how many buttons do girls have then", said John.

"Oh loads and loads of buttons", said Debs. "You men think we've only got three .... and sometimes you don't even seem to be able to find all of those".

Roger laughed.

"What about the other buttons", he said. "Can a man find those".

"Only if his girl decides to show him where they are", said Debs. "And that's only going to happen if he's really really loving and kind".

"So am I really really loving and kind", said Roger.

"Super especially so", sighed Debs. She lay along the back seat, cradled her head in Roger's lap, and looked up at his chin."

"You have a specially nice chin", she said.

John coughed. Debbie laughed.

"I hope you like Lorraine, John", she said. "I'm going to lay here and start planning your wedding".

"Debs", said John. "Do I have to propose to her tonight".

Debbie giggled.

"That would be so lovely", she said. "Have you ever proposed to a girl, Uncle John".

John shook his head.

"I came close once", he said.

"What happened", said Debs.

John laughed.

"I met Roger", he said.

"You're not ......", said Debbie.

"He's teasing you", said Roger. "John is a ladies man alright .... and he's very caring and kind .... aren't you John".

John laughed.

"Debbie", he said. "Joking aside .... perfectly serious now .... what do you think the chances of Lorraine and me liking each other really are".

"It's going to be "Love at First Sight", I promise you John", said Debbie.

"Ok", said John. "You have a deal. "Love at First sight", and I promise you I'll propose to Lorraine this very night".

"Oh Gosh .... this is going to be ever so exciting", said Debbie.

Following Debbie's directions, John turned the Buick off the main road not far to the west of Wimborne. Although they were now on country roads .... they seemed to have been sufficiently well used to clear them of all but the last traces of snow. Just a little remained on the verges in one or two shady places. About four miles north of the main road .... and after several left and right turns .... Debbie pointed to a long wide gravel pull in on the right hand side of the lane. John brought the car to a graceful halt in front of a large stone barn. A barn that had obviously recently been converted to a very attractive residence.

John killed the lights .... and switched off.

"Nice place", said Roger, leaning across for a better view. The gravel pull in was flooded with light . The Buick had triggered the movement sensor switch.

"Roger .... John", said Debbie. "Just before we go in .... I want to warn you that Lorraine can be a little self conscious and uncomfortable with people she hasn't met before. But once she realises you are OK with her .... then she soon gets her confidence back .... and then she's just totally gorgeous".

They left the warmth of the car. John locked it .... then immediately had to unlock it again, because Debs wanted her little duffle coat for later .... for when they left.

Debbie led them to the front door at the left hand end of the building. Everything .... including the elm wood door seemed fresh and new.

"They've only just moved in to the barn", said Debbie. "Lorraine's Father loves renovating old buildings. He's been working on this one for three years".

Debbie gave the black iron door knocker three taps. Roger examined the knocker with interest. It was a blacksmith made one-off. A stylised dragon. He nodded thoughtfully.

They stood waiting .... their breath smoking in the frosty air. Debbie took a very deep breath ... and hooshed steam at Roger.

"Roger", she said. "Let's play baby smoke dragons".

She hooshed more "smoke" at Roger. Roger hooshed her back .... and went to grab her. Debs ducked away, and hooshed a great cloud of steamy smoke over him. She laughed .... and hooshed at John.

John rolled his eyes skwards.

"Uncle John doesn't want to play baby smoke dragons". said Debbie. "He's being a grown up".

"Somebody has to be", said John.

Debs was just about to knock again, when they heard the door being unbolted from the inside.

The front door opened.

"Roger", said Debbie.

She stepped in, and threw her arms round the slightly portly figure, who immediately burst out laughing, and made a play of fighting her off.

Debbie let him win .... then turned to Roger and John.

"Roger", she said. "I'd like to introduce you to my Fiance, Mr Roger Davies".

"Another Roger", said Roger .... reaching out a hand.

"Mr Roger Makepiece at your service Sir", said Lorraine's Father.

"And this is our very special friend, John", said Debbie.

Lorraines Father shook John's hand.

"Come on in the warm", he said. "Lorraine will be so excited that you're here Debbie".

He got his guests into the hall, and closed the door.

"Debbie and Lorraine were at school together", he explained to Roger.

"I know", said Roger. "Debs has been telling me all about it".

"So how did you two meet", said Roger. "Let's get through to the kitchen. Kettle's nearly boiled".

"We met at Tallulah's wedding last weekend", said Debbie.

"And engaged already", said Lorraine's Father. "That's how you do it .... you should always take longer over choosing a meal in a restaurant, than choosing the person you're going to marry".

"I did make him a cup of coffee", said Debs.

"Did he drink it", said Roger.

"I think he forgot to", said Debs.

"I'll drink it this time", said Roger.

"I guess that's your cue to make the coffee, Roger", said Debbie.

"Let's do it", said Roger.

He turned to the kettle .... which had just started to play baby smoke dragons.

SIXTEEN

Roger Makepiece saw his guests seated around the kitchen table .... a good old pine kitchen table with plenty of battle scars.

"I'll run up and tell Lorraine you're here", he said. "She's in the shower at the moment. Would you make the coffee please Debs".

Debbie took mugs from the mug tree in the centre of the table, and found the coffee in the first cupboard she opened. The milk had her baffled for a few moments, until Roger suggested the fridge could be behind one of the lower kitchen cupboard doors.

"Try the one furthest from the cooker", he advised her.

Debbie spooned Nescafe into five mugs, and added hot water. She found a jug for the milk. She moved the mugs, with their steaming contents, to the table, filled the milk jug, and sat down again, to wait for Roger and Lorraine.

Roger came back in almost immediately.

"Good", he said. "You've made the coffee. Lorraine will be down in a few minutes. She is so pleased you're here Debbie".

He slid two of the mugs towards Roger and John, and sat down at the far end of the table. Debbie handed him his coffee, and was just about to pass the milk jug, when they heard a flurry of footsteps on wooden stairs, the latch snapped up, and a figure in a short white towelling bathrobe, with a mass of black curls, burst through the door, and threw herself into Debbie's arms.

Roger and John watched in amazement as the two girls buried themselves in each other. They spun around and around with excitement, Debbie's blonde locks, and Lorraines dark curls, tangling together on their shoulders, until Roger began to wonder if the pair of them would be knotted together for the rest of the evening.

Eventually the excitement subsided a little. Debbie took her friend's hand,

and stepped aside, allowing Roger and John, who were now both standing, to get their first proper look at Lorraine.

Roger and John were both young men .... but equally .... and very much under differing circumstances .... they had both been taught to be gentlemen .... especially in the presence of the opposite sex. And their first instinct, as gentlemen, was to avert their gaze .... because Lorraine's bathrobe was perilously close to falling undone.

But at exactly the same moment they went to obey this impulse .... they both realised that it was the one thing they really must not do .... because to have done so .... would have sent a signal to Lorraine, that neither of them, as gentlemen, could bear to contemplate.

Debbie spotted the problem with the bathrobe, and quickly put things right. She kissed Lorraine on the cheek, and turned to Roger and John.

"Lorraine", she said. "I'd like you to meet my Fiance Roger, and his very good friend John. Roger .... John ... this is my very best friend Lorraine".

Lorraine appeared to take a deep breath. She stepped towards the two men .... shook back her hair .... still damp from the shower .... and smiled .... and extended her hand.

And Roger and John both realised they had just moments to get their act together .... because their behaviour as gentlemen .... in front of Roger's Fiancee .... and Lorraine's Father .... was about to be tested .... very visibly tested.

John got there first. He simply took Lorraine's hand .... pulled her towards him .... and wrapped his arms around her. And he held her .... and he held her .... and he held her.

And never before in his whole life, had John done so precisely, the very thing that was most needed.

And Lorraine wrapped her arms around John .... and relaxed into his embrace .... and Debbie looked at Roger .... and Roger looked at Debbie .... and they waited.

And then John took Lorraine by her shoulders .... and turned her to Roger and Debbie .... and said:

"Roger, Debbie .... I'd like you to meet my very new Fiancee Miss Lorraine Makepiece".

And Mr Roger Davies smiled .... and he took The hands of Miss Lorraine Makepiece .... and he looked her full in the face .... and she looked at Roger .... and she took John's hand .... and she began to cry.

The tears streamed down her cheeks. On the right side of her face, Lorraine was blessed with an English rose complexion. But on the left side, her tears ran into the course grained skin of a livid purple birthmark that covered the whole side of her face.

This startling division of colour began under her hairline, ran down the centre of her forehead, continued down the center of her nose, and lips, through the dimple in her chin, ran down her throat, and eventually .... taking a slight turn to the left .... it disappeared under her white robe.

Fresh from the shower .... the right side of her face glowed with health and vitality. But the left side glowed an angry magenta.

Roger stood there, and imagined what it must be like to wake every morning and look in the mirror. He tried to imagine what it must be like to be this fantastic girl .... and to live every day with this disfigurement.

And she was indeed fantastic .... because nature had recognised the cruelty that it had inflicted on this lovely young woman .... and it had given her compensation in extreme measure.

Nature gives all young women their measure of sexuality .... their measure of sex appeal. Because Nature has needs.

And Nature had indeed given Lorraine sexuality .... but it had given her that sexuality in such a massive dose, that any other girl would find it a burden almost beyond endurance.

Lorraine's appeal was so intense that it was almost impossible to be with her. Every movement she made was drenched with her sexuality. To be friends with Lorraine .... to spend time with her .... you had to find a way to cope with her intense allure.

For her female friends .... it was difficult.

For men .... it was impossible. They ran from her .... because of her birth mark .... and because of her sexual intensity.

So Lorraine had learned to live with her lot in life .... and she smiled at Roger again .... and for the first time .... she performed the gesture that John would come to love so dearly .... and the gesture that was so very familiar to all her friends.

She raised her left hand, extended her little finger, and stroked that finger down the centre of her forehead. She stoked her finger down the edge of the birthmark, from her hair line to the tip of her nose .... and she repeated the action as she spoke.

And as she stroked the line that was hers .... her left hand contrived to conceal the left side of her face. And that person to whom she spoke would never be allowed to see quite all of Miss Lorraine Makepiece .... not quite all. And it was so alluring .... because there is nothing we want to see more than that which is hidden from us.

But tonight .... Lorraine took John to the other end of the kitchen .... and she folded her left hand neatly behind her .... into the small of her back .... into the soft towelling of her bathrobe .... and she shook back her hair, still damp from the shower, and she looked up into John's face .... and she laughed .... and she smiled .... and she talked.

And when she took John's hand .... and led him to that door where she had first appeared .... and when she had led John through the door .... and when those that were left behind heard their feet on the stairs .... they found that there was no need to comment .... because what had happened .... was meant to happen .... and beyond that door was now a world that belonged to John and to Lorraine.

And those that remained sipped their coffees .... and Debbie searched .... and found the biscuits.

And Debbie watched her Fiance talking with Lorraine's Father .... and she so loved them both.

And she looked at the door, where Lorraine had disappeared .... and if, perhaps .... there was just the teensiest part of her ....

Well .... wasn't it just so worth it.

SEVENTEEN

Roger Makepiece downed the last of his coffee. He glanced at the door to the stairs, raised his eyebrows, and turned to Roger and Debbie.

"Would you two like to spend the night here", he said. "The house isn't quite finished .... but there is a room you can have".

Roger laughed .

"I only thought I was going to a wedding for a few hours", he said. "This will be my third night away".

He looked at Debbie.

"Debs", he said. "I'm fine to stay .... it's up to you".

"Oh can we please Roger", said Debbie. "Breakfast will be so much fun won't it".

Roger Makepiece laughed.

"Any meal with you is fun Debs", he said. "Look at what's just happened .... and that was just coffee and biscuits !"

Debbie smiled at him.

"Roger .... do you want me to cook supper for us", she said. "Jayne is away with the choir isn't she".

Debbie turned to Roger.

"Jayne is Roger's wife", she said. "She sings in a choir .... and they are away in Birmingham at the moment".

"Debbie", said Roger. "I am not going to have you cooking for us. I was planning on going down to the carvery for supper, with Lorraine, so lets do that shall we".

"Sounds good to me", said Roger. "What shall we do about John and Lorraine".

129

"If we leave a note on the table to say where we've gone .... and we go in my car .... they could follow us in your car later .... if they wanted to", said Roger.

"Does Lorraine know where the carvery is", Roger asked.

"Yes .... we eat there two or three times a month ....it's only five minutes down the road".

Roger Makepiece went for pen and paper. He returned to the table, sat, and wrote a note for his Daughter. He left it where Lorraine would see it as she entered the room.

The two Rogers, and Debbie donned coats. They followed their host through a door at the far end of the kitchen, which led straight into a garage.

"Not as exciting as your car I'm afraid", Roger Makepiece said.

"Nothing wrong with a Ford Mondeo", said Roger. "I've owned quite a few, and they are a really well built reliable car".

He opened the rear door for Debs .... then slid in next to her.

Roger Makepiece started the engine .... and they waited for the remote controlled garage door to rattle its way into the roof. Roger looked at his Buick standing alone in the cold.

"I wonder if the others will join us", he said.

"I think they will", said Roger, "because Lorraine was looking forward to her roast dinner".

"John likes a good roast dinner", said Roger.

Debbie leaned over and kissed him.

"They'll be along soon", she said. "I just know Lorraine will want to join us".

....

"Roger and John are taking me to Church with them tomorrow night", said Debbie brightly. She sipped her orange juice and lemonade .... and smiled at Roger Makepiece.

They had found a table for five .... anticipating that Lorraine and John would join them. Roger had suggested they have the "Hand battered Cod and chips".

"They cook it for you fresh", he said, "and it's really good".

They all went with the suggestion .... which meant they had ten minutes to wait, while the fish was cooked.

"Church", said Roger Makepiece .... in a serious tone .... but with a flicker of a smile that Roger just caught in time.

"Church", he said. " I don't believe a word of it".

He looked at Debbie.

"I thought you said Roger was a car dealer".

Roger sighed, and looked to the ceiling. It wasn't the first time he'd heard this comment. He smiled at Roger .... who was just about managing to keep a straight face.

"Yeah", he said. "John and I go to Church. God loves an honest car dealer".

"In most people's minds .... that's a contradiction in terms", said Roger Makepiece.

"It's easier to be honest about the car you're selling if you only buy the very best in the first place", said Roger. "You pay too much money for the best cars .... and you sell them for too much money .... but you can look your customer in the face and tell them it's a good buy .... because you know it's the truth".

The waitress, Kirsty, called by to tell them their fish was just coming out to the serving deck. Roger made a mental note of the name on her badge. Force of habit ....

There were just two people in front of them at the servery. The carver had just handed the couple their plates of beef and gammon .... when the fish appeared. It looked superb in it's coating of puffy batter.

"I'd stay with chips and mushy peas if I were you", said Roger Makepiece. "Carrots and cauliflower, and roast potatoes, don't work too well with the Cod .... believe me .... I've tried".

There were a lot of vegetables to choose from .... and Roger did add some garden peas to his plate. He looked thoughtfully at the baked beans .... looked at Debs .... and decided against them.

They returned to their seats, after a brief stop for tartare sauce, at the sauces table in the corner.

"Can you do us a Grace please Debs", said Roger.

"Of course I will", said Debbie. She closed her eyes and bowed her head. The others followed her example.

"Awesome God", she said. "I thank You for the blessing of this food. I thank you for the blessing of my companions .... and I ask you to find a way to bestow these blessings on those less fortunate than ourselves .... Amen".

"Amen", said Roger .... and the other Roger.

Debbie began eating her Cod. Roger had been right. It was really good.

She glanced at her Fiance. He seemed lost in thought .... almost as though he had forgotten his companions.

Roger was chewing slowly .... and gazing across the restaurant floor at the other diners. It was now much busier than when they had first arrived. There were several families with children .... and what were obviously two birthday party groups on the raised section of the room. The birthday cakes would be secreted behind the scenes .... for the waitress to bring them forth, as a huge surprise, at the appropriate moment.

Roger was thinking about John and Lorraine. He was wondering if Lorraine would come to Church with them tomorrow night. He was wondering if he could persuade Debbie, and Lorraine, and John, to organise a double wedding in the Church .... in the not too distant future. Was Lorraine a Church goer .... was she a Muslim girl like Debs. He didn't know.

He looked around the restaurant and studied the faces .... and wondered how many of the people here would be in a Church tomorrow night.

And he remembered an evening in his own local carvery a few years before .... when he'd looked around at his fellow diners .... and looked at their faces .... and he'd finally understood something that had puzzled him for so long.

He'd looked around that carvery .... just two miles from his home .... and he'd realised he was sitting amongst the living dead. They that hath no life in them.

"For those who do not eat of the flesh of the Son of man .... and drink His blood .... they hath no life in them".

It was from John's Gospel .... the bit where Jesus was sorting the sheep from the goats .... not long before the end.

And why had he understood what Jesus meant .... sitting in a carvery........

Because the evening before .... he had been with his Church at their Christmas party. About a hundred and fifty people .... mainly Africans .... and he knew they had all eaten that flesh that Jesus spoke of .... and they had all drunk that blood. And they were alive. So alive. Ten times more alive than those who chose not to share what was free to all. They were simply not brave enough to come and share .... even if the opportunity was offered them.

"Let the dead bury the dead".

And that's how .... sitting in a carvery .... Mr Roger Davies had come to understand what it meant to "hath life in you".

"Roger", said Debbie."Can I give you that penny back for your thoughts".

He shook his head .... and returned his gaze to Debbie .... and laughed.

"Tell you later", he said.

"Why", said Debbie. "Is it so sad".

"No", said Roger, "..............well just the teensiest bit sad, I suppose".

"Let's not do sad tonight", said Debbie. "It's been an amazing evening .... I do so hope that Lorraine and John will be here soon".

And as though by magic .... and right on cue .... John and Lorraine appeared at the table.

Roger looked at them both.

"True happiness", he knew, was a rare and elusive commodity. But he looked at John .... and he looked at Lorraine .... and he knew that he was looking at "True happiness".

Debbie and Lorraine were hugging again .... and talking to each other at their normal frantic speed.

Roger reached out a hand to John.

"Congratulations", he said.

John smiled .... and looked at Lorraine.

"Shall we talk to John Paul about a double wedding when we see him tomorrow", he said.

Roger laughed.

"Do you know", he said. "I was planning to persuade you to do just that".

John guided Lorraine into a chair .... and sat down himself next to Debs.

Roger Makepiece beamed at everbody.

"I wish my wife was here to share all this excitement", he said.

"Obviously Sir", said John. "I shall seek your permission .... and your blessing .... upon our union".

Roger Makepiece laughed.

"My study .... brandy and cigars .... this very evening", he said.

John reached his hand over. Roger Makepiece took it.

"This very evening it shall be", John said. "I shall look forward to it".

"I insist on supplying the brandy", said Roger.

"Which is just as well", said Roger Makepiece. "Because I don't think we have any".

"Debbie", said Roger. "Back in two minutes".

Roger headed for the nearest waitress. It was Kirsty.

Debbie watched. It was that thing with Roger and waitresses again ....

Kirsty disappeared behind the scenes .... and Roger returned to the table.

One of the birthday parties began to sing "Happy Birthday". The adjacent tables joined the chorus .... and Kirsty the waitress appeared from the kitchen .... a cake alight with candles in one hand .... and a bottle of brandy for Roger in the other.

Roger kissed her on the cheek. She smiled.

Roger passed the bottle to John.

"Cigars", said John.

"Your turn", said Roger.

Lorraines Father laughed.

"I'm good for cigars", he said.

Kirsty returned.

"Two more freshly cooked cod at the servery", she said.

"Lorraine telephoned ahead to order", John said.

John escorted his Fiancee to the servery .... and Debbie leaned across and kissed Roger Makepiece.

"Wow", she said. "It's going to be the most amazing wedding in the history of everything".

She thought for a moment.

"Roger", she said. "Do you think we could ask your Church to marry us all".

Roger laughed.

"John's ahead of you on that one", he said. "We'll ask tomorrow night .... and I'm sure they'll say yes".

John and Lorraine returned with their meals .... and as they sat .... Roger took a final glance around the room.

"For My flesh is food indeed", he thought.

Debbie did a Grace for John and Lorraine.

Roger looked around the table at his companions .... and remembered that all this had happened in just three days.

But then .... he knew from experience .... that even three minutes can change your life forever.

EIGHTEEN

Roger Davies was dreaming.

He was laying on a towel on the beach. Debbie was laying next to him. She was wearing a yellow bikini.

The day had started well .... hot and sunny .... but now at three thirty in the afternoon, the sky had clouded a little. The breeze .... so pleasant at midday .... played around Roger's shoulders. He shivered slightly .... just as Debs rolled over and layed on top of him.

"Oh you're so lovely and warm Roger", she said.

She snuggled down into Roger .... and kissed him on the lips.

Roger reached for her towel .... and drew it over her shoulders.

"Oh thank you .... that's ever so much warmer", she said.

She wiggled.

It was nice when she wiggled.

"Debbie ......". said Roger.

Debbie giggled.

"I'm going to roll off you now", she said. "And I bet I know exactly what you will do next...........".

She rolled off.

Roger rolled over onto his stomach

Debbie giggled again.

"Told you", she said. "Shall we walk down to the cafe at the other end of the beach for our tea now Roger".

"Just a minute or two Debs", said Roger.

"Poor Roger", said Debbie. "Isn't it just so awfully uncomfortable laying like that".

"You did it deliberately", said Roger.

"Gosh Roger", said Debbie. "What did I do. Can you whisper it to me .... so I'll know not to do it again".

She lay down again .... and put her ear to Rogers mouth.

Roger blew gently in her ear.

"Come on Roger", she said. "It's tea time .... and I think it might be going to rain soon. We'll try and get to the cafe before it starts".

They left their towels. Roger pulled on a T shirt and shorts .... and Debs slipped on her beach dress.

It was a good ten minutes walk to the other end of the beach .... and the cafe. They were just a minute away .... when the first drops of rain started. They made a dash for the doors.

Other people had anticipated the rain. The place was busy. Very busy.

Debbie and Roger queued for their tea .... and Danish pastries. It was an expensive cafe .... but then Sandbanks in Dorset is just generally expensive.

The cafe was populated by the young and trendy. Girls with sun bleached blonde hair .... transparent beach wraps over very expensive bikinis. When you spend that much money on a bikini .... it fits .... it fits exactly.

The cafe didn't have a licence .... so the girls were drinking Coke floats .... or fruit smoothies. Their companions sipped Red Bulls .... from the can. You don't put Red Bull in a glass. It's just not cool.

The couples tended to avoid the two large round tables in the center of the room .... leaving them for the very few families who came in. The families with Range Rover Vogues, who could afford the "ten pounds for seven hours" car parking fee, behind the cafe. Families who could afford the "double what it should be" prices for their tea and cake .... and their smoothies.

Roger and Debbie got a table for two towards the center of the room. Roger was just pouring the tea .... when a family came in from the rain.

Roger had been poor once. He knew poor when he saw it. The head of this family was an enormous woman in her early fifties. She was dressed in a huge shapeless garment made from floral printed cotton. So faded was her dress .... that one could only imagine she had made it from old curtains. Curtains that had been hanging for years in the sun.

There was a younger woman with her .... dressed in a track suit. She suffered from acne. Her blonde hair was unwashed .... greasy ....tight to her scalp in a pony tail.

There was a small thin man who might have been her husband. His trousers had once belonged to a suit. He wore a football shirt .... with the colours virtually washed away. His face was pale and thin .... his chin unshaven .... and what was left of his dark hair was slicked back with Brylcream.

And there were five children. The oldest .... a boy. Perhaps twelve. Another boy a couple of years younger. And two girls .... one of about seven or eight .... her sister perhaps fifteen. The older was holding a baby. Roger wondered if it was hers. He had dated a scondary school teacher once, and in her class at school, she had a thirteen year old student who was pregnant. She was going to keep the baby.

The younger children were in school uniform .... white shirts and grey shorts for the boys. White blouse and grey skirt for the younger girl. Her sister .... with the baby .... was wearing a very new purple shell suit. She looked down at the baby and smiled.

Roger knew better than to feel sorry for people. He knew that money could make it easier to be happy. And he knew that you could be happy without money.

He didn't feel sorry for this family .... they reminded him of the extended family in the old Giles cartoons. Only Granny appeared to be missing.

But he was uneasy about their being in this cafe. Their clothes were damp. They had come in to escape the rain. It was now raining heavily. The temperature outside had dropped .... and the cafe windows were steaming up rapidly.

The family seated themselves around the large round table, just a few feet from Roger and Debbie. Roger glanced at Debs. She was watching the situation develop .... her Danish pastry untouched on her plate.

The Mother brought a huge carrier bag up on to her lap. It was obvious who was in control of the family. She brought out a jumbo economy size plastic bottle of orange squash, and placed it on the table. She found white plastic cups and passed them to the children. The oldest sister began to pour the watery squash. The Mother went into her bag again, and produced a huge supermarket white loaf, in a white and orange striped wrapper. It contained ready made sandwiches which she passed out to the family. Roger looked at the bread. No Mother would have shown much pride in it. It was white and limpid. Roger caught a glimpse of the Spam in the sandwiches. Bags of crisps came next. "No frills" blue and white striped bags.

Roger looked at the signs on the cafe walls. All beach cafes have them:

"Only food and drink purchased from the cafe may be consumed at the tables .... inside or outside".

Not many takers for the outside tables at the moment.

Roger picked up his Danish pastry. He felt decadent holding it. He looked at Debs. She hadn't touched hers. She was sipping her tea. She looked at Roger.

"Roger", she said. "Pray with me".

Roger nodded.

A teenage waitress appeared with a tray .... to clear tables. She looked at the table in the middle of the room. She stayed still .... looking. Roger saw the moment when she decided that dealing with the situation was beyond her job description. She disappeared back through the double swing doors to the kitchen. Roger looked around the room. Things had gone a little quieter. People were waiting.

The Manager came through the doors. He was about twenty five. Crisp white shirt .... black trousers .... shiny laced shoes. He started towards the family. The conversation in the room began to fade away. Just a baby crying in the far corner.

The manager faltered slightly as he became aware that he had centre stage. Not that anybody was actually watching him. In fact everybody had suddenly become very busy pouring tea .... or cutting cake.

He reached the table .... and looked at the Mother figure.

The room was silent.

The Mother looked up at him.

"May I help you", she said.

Roger closed his eyes. The tension in the room was palpable .... and everbody was thinking the same thought.

"Let it go .... please .... just this once .... let it go".

The manager looked at her. He looked at the orange squash, and he looked at the Spam sandwiches, and he looked at the "No frills" crisps. But he didn't look around the room, because he knew that a hundred people were waiting for him to speak. He took a breath.

"I just thought I would come and check that you have everything you need", he said.

The Mother looked at him .... her face impassive .... dignified. She looked around the table, at her family.

"Thank you for asking", she said. "But we have everything we need ....it was kind of you to enquire".

The Manager looked at her. Roger saw him connect to her for just a moment.

"If there is anything ....", he said. "Please let me know".

"Thank you", she said. "I will".

The manager turned and walked briskly back to the kitchen.

The relief in the room was unmistakable. Conversation started again. Debbie picked up her Danish pastry. She smiled at Roger.

"He was a nice young man", she said.

Roger nodded.

The waitress appeared with a tray laden with two large tea pots .... steaming gently. There were cups and saucers and milk and sugar. She went to the family .... and rested the tray on the table .... and began to place the cups and saucers.

The Mother looked at her.

"We didn't ....", she began.

"Managers compliments", said the waitress. He thought you might like a hot cup of tea".

The Mother looked at the tea. She looked at her family. She looked at the waitress.

"Please tell your manager", she said. "That I am so grateful for his kindness. Thank you".

The waitress finished unloading her tray.

"I'll bring extra hot water for you", she said. "I couldn't get it all on the tray".

The Mother smiled at her. It was the first time she had smiled.

"Enjoy your tea", said the waitress. "I don't think the rain will last much longer .... it's brightening up out there already".

She was right. A ray of sunshine hit the windows as she made her way back to the kitchen.

Roger and Debbie stood to leave.

"Hand bag , Debs", said Roger.

Debbie had been just about to forget her bag …. it was down at her feet.

Debs smiled at him.

They went out of the cafe into the watery bright sunshine, and walked to the edge of the terrace, to look across the sea.

But the tide was out …. so far out …. they couldn't see any water. Just dry sand to the horizon.

"The tide's gone out", said Debbie dreamily. "I do hope it will come back in soon".

And then they saw the tide coming. Slowly. Steadily. And they looked down from the terrace, across the water.

And it was all wrong …. because the sea should be blue …. and Roger looked at the sea …. and it was red …. bright red … and it was horribly wrong …. because the sea should be blue. The sea isn't red.

He jumped down from the terrace …. and the sea lapped around his feet …. and he lifted his right foot from the water …. and it was stained bright crimson.

....

"Roger", said Debbie, looking down into his eyes. Are you alright Sweetheart. Did you have a bad dream".

Roger looked up at her. She rolled on top of him.

"You're ever so warm Roger", she said.

Debbie snuggled down into Roger.

She wiggled.

"Debbie………………", said Roger.

She whispered in his ear.

"Am I doing that thing again Roger", she said.

"Oh Gosh", she said. "I think I am".

NINETEEN

The dream stayed with Roger. He slipped his arm around Debbie for comfort. She rolled towards him. He raised himself on one elbow, and looked down at her. She put her arms around his neck and drew him down for a kiss.

Roger's hand slid to the curve of her waist .... stroking gently. His finger traced the hem at the top of her pants. They weren't her best ones.

"Roger", said Debs. "..................we might have to.......".

"I know", said Roger. " Perhaps I'll just see how many of those push buttons I can find".

Debbie lay on her back. She giggled.

"Go on then", she said.

"Well", said Roger. "I think there's one .... just there .... We'll call that "Park", shall we. Now shall I push it .... or shall I just touch it gently .... like that ....".

His fingers brushed across her chemise.

Debbie sighed.

"And just next to "Park", said Roger .... moving his hand across. "I think that we'll find "Reverse". I'll just kiss that one though. We don't want you in reverse just yet .... do we...........".

Roger slid her chemise aside .... and kissed "Reverse".

He felt Debs press her nails gently into his shoulders

Roger's hand traced downwards .... and stopped. He heard Debbie take a breath. She lay motionless .... waiting.

"Now my lovely Deborah", he said. "I think the "Drive" button is just ....there".

He felt Deb's nails press hard into his neck.

"So have I found "Drive", Debs", he whispered.

Debbie slid her hand down .... and tangled her fingers into Roger's. She giggled.

"We mustn't Roger", she said. "It's all new bedding .... and I'm................".

Roger kissed her on the lips.

"I know", he said. "But just you wait till I get you home young lady".

"Oh Gosh Roger", said Debs. "What is a girl to do .... you are just so masterful".

Roger collapsed laughing, back onto his pillows.

"Debs", he said. "I love you".

Is that "I love you", as in : "Lay down .... I think I love you", said Debbie. She kissed Roger's ear.

"Go to sleep now Sweetheart", she said. "Breakfast with John and Lorraine will be fun".

"And Roger", said Roger.

"And Roger", said Debbie.

....

In the next room John watched Lorraine sleeping. She had wanted John to lay on her right in the bed .... but that meant he was on the side furthest from the door.

The man always sleeps nearest to the door. John knew that. He knew that it has always been that way .... since we lived in caves. He slipped out of bed .... went round .... and slid gently back under the covers on Lorraines left. Without waking .... Lorraine moved across to make room for him. Even asleep .... her sexual intensity was almost suffocating.

John layed back and stared up at the ceiling .... then he turned and kissed

Lorraine. She opened her eyes and looked up at him.

John looked at the dark hue of her cheek. He kissed her. The skin felt different. He saw a tear form in her eye.

"Can you really live with me John", she said.

"Where else would I go", said John.

Lorraine brought her right hand from beneath the duvet. She brushed her hair clear of the crimson left side of her face. The white of her eye glowed bright.

"Are you really sure you can live with this John", she said.

"Where else would I go", said John.

....

Debbie woke first. She gave Roger a shove .... jumped out of bed .... and dashed for the bathroom. Roger sat up just in time to watch her bottom disappear through the bathroom door.

Definitely not her Best Pants, he thought.

He needed the loo .... so he decided to get dressed, and go downstairs. He pulled on his trousers .... then went over to the window and drew the curtains. He looked down at his car. There was a very light dusting of snow across the roof. Standing behind his car was another Buick .... a 1959 convertible .... a ragtop. Roger stared at it. There was no snow on it's roof, or bonnet, or trunk. It must have arrived this morning. Roger checked the time on his phone. It was seven forty five .... early.

He looked down at the new arrival. The last time he'd seen this car .... it had been in a glass cabinet .... and it had been just twenty inches long. He shook his head.

He went to the bathroom door .... and knocked.

"Debbie .... your father is here", he said.

The door opened. Debbie had a mouth full of toothpaste.

"Daddy's here ....!!", she said.

Roger pointed to the window. Debs went to look out .... and Roger made a dash for the loo. He closed the door behind him.

"Roger .....!", said Debbie.

She sighed .... and went to the window. Roger had been right. It was her Father's car. But what on Earth was he doing here .... before breakfast.

Roger came out of the bathroom. Debbie gave him a quick jab in the ribs.

"That was very naughty, Roger", she said. "Bathrooms belong to girls. Men are only allowed in as a very special concession".

"Sorry Debs", he said. "It was desperate".

Debbie kissed him. She was topless ....with a mouth still full of toothpaste. Roger tried not to look at "Park" and "Reverse".

Debbie went to her bag.

"Bother", she said. "I've run out of clean pants .... I'll have to borrow some from Lorraine".

Roger smiled at her.

"It's sweet the way girls borrow underwear from each other", he said.

"Don't you and Uncle John lend each other your pants then", said Debbie.

"Definitely never", said Roger.

"Men are so funny", said Debbie.

Roger went to his bag .... delved to the bottom .... and passed Debbie a new boxed set of Sloggi Tai briefs.

"How on Earth ....", said Debbie.

"Girls are always running out of pants .... and things ....", said Roger.

"Have you got tampons as well", said Debbie.

"Course I have", said Roger,".....and paracetemol .... and tissues .... and lip gloss".

Debbie stood looking at him ...

"I think I've found the perfect man", she said.

"Better believe it Debs", said Roger.

"So have you got a bra in there", said Debbie .... looking at Roger's bag.

Roger brought out a Sloggi stretch halter top .... new .... and boxed .... and passed it to Debbie.

"Do I get a kiss", he said.

"Will it wait till we get to your place", said Debs. "You're going to give me a jolly good seeing-to there .... aren't you".

"Shouldn't we wait till we're married", said Roger.

"Roger .... we are married", said Debbie.

Her tone was serious. Roger looked at her questioningly .... but she was gone .... back into the bathroom. She turned back for just a moment.

"We are married Roger", she said. "My Father will explain things to you".

She closed the door.

Roger went to his bag. He sighed.

He had run out of clean pants.

....

Twenty minutes later Roger and Debbie were respectably dressed .... and ready to go down to breakfast. Roger had washed some pants .... two pairs of Debbie's .... and two pairs of his own. They were drying on the radiator.

He wanted to feel prepared. He'd gone to a wedding on Tuesday. Today was Friday. He was beginning to wonder just how long he would be away for.

In the kitchen .... Lorraine was hostess. She was wearing skin tight blue jeans .... a white blouse .... and her black hair was tied up in a red scarf.

Roger looked at her .... took a deep breath .... shook his head .... closed his eyes .... and sat down.

Lorraine was scrambling eggs and making toast. John was making the tea.

"Lorraine", said Debbie. "Where are Roger and my Father".

"How did you know ....".

"We saw his car out of the bedroom window", said Roger.

Lorraine nodded. She smiled at Debbie.

"Our respective Fathers are talking in the conservatory", she said.

Roger made a huge effort not to look at her. Her jeans were the most perfect fit he'd ever seen .... and what they were fitted to .... was even more perfect. He tried not to look. He cast a glance at John.

John caught the glance .... raised his eyebrows .... and smiled.

"John", said Roger. "What did you do with that Blunderbuss".

John laughed.

"It's in the Buick's trunk", he said. I swapped it over from the XJ's boot just before it went. I almost forgot it was in there".

"Uncle John", said Debbie. "Can I see your Blunderbuss please".

"Debbie ....",said Lorraine. "I'm not having you looking at John's Blunderbuss".

"Just a peek", said Debs.

"No", said Lorraine. "You're not old enough to appreciate it".

"Is it jolly nice", said Debs.

"Quite splendid", said Lorraine.

She gave Debbie and Roger plates of scrambled eggs on toast. John gave them mugs of tea.

Debbie had just started to ask Lorraine why her Father had come .... when the kitchen door opened, and Roger Makepiece .... and Lord Wintersham .... entered the room.

"Daddy!!", said Debbie.

She rushed round to him and gave him a hug.

"It's just so exciting", she said. "I introduced John to Lorraine .... and it was just magical .... and now they're engaged .... and it all happened so quickly .... and ....".

She stopped. She looked thoughtful. She looked at John and Lorraine. She looked back to her Father.

"That's why you're here isn't it ......", she said.

Lord Wintersham smiled at her.

"Roger phoned me late yesterday evening", he said.

He looked at John. He held out his hand.

"I don't believe we have had the pleasure of meeting Sir", he said.

John stood from the table. The two men shook hands.

"Lord Wintersham", said John. "It's a great pleasure to meet you .... I watched the television programme about your visit to that sports car factory".

Lord Wintersham laughed.

"Yes .... that was me", he said. "They weren't entirely open to new ideas were they".

"Well", said John. "You did make a difference there. You shortened the waiting list from two years to fifteen months".

"Indeed", said Lord Wintersham. " .... and talking of waiting times .... I have waited a very long time to meet the man who would make an honest woman out of this very special young lady".

He stepped towards Lorraine, and embraced her warmly.

"I am so pleased for you my dear", he said. "I came straight away".

Lorraine looked up at him. She swept the hair aside from the crimson side of her face.

Lord Wintersham understood her gesture well enough. He had seen her the day she was born. He had watched her grow up. He has seen the bond develop between the two girls.

He leaned forward and kissed Lorraine on her forehead.

"Very well done Lorraine", he said.

She hugged him.

"Can I cook you some breakfast", she said. "We're having scrambled eggs on toast".

"Splendid", said Lord Wintersham. "I would love to have scrambled eggs on toast".

"Tea or Coffee Sir", said John.

"Actually .... I think I'd like a coffee please John". said Lord Wintersham. "Not too strong .... no milk .... one sugar".

He sat down and looked around him.

"Roger", he said. "Is that a '74' Electra you have out there .... I had a quick look when I arrived. It's a beauty".

Roger nodded.

"He never uses it in the Winter", said John. "He asked me to bring it to Debbie's flat. I think he wanted to show it off to her".

Roger laughed.

"It's the long bonnet", he said. "Never fails ....".

"And just how long is the bonnet", asked Debbie.

"Nearly six feet", said Roger.

"Gosh", said Debbie. "That's ever so long Roger".

Lorraine gave Lord Wintersham and her Father their plates of scrambled eggs on toast. Lord Wintersham reached for the salt and pepper.

"Thank you so much my dear", he said. "I shall enjoy this .... and then we must get down to business".

He looked at Roger and John.

"Isobel will be joining us shortly", he said. "I'm expecting her around ten o'clock".

Roger Makepiece looked around his kitchen table. He beamed. He always missed his wife when she was away with her choir. To have the company of all these young people .... and Lord Wintersham .... was an enormous pleasure. And to see his Daughter so happy ....

They heard a knock from the front door.

"Surely not Isobel already", said Lord Wintersham. He looked at his watch.

Lorraine went to answer the door.

A few moments later she ushered Isobel into the room.

They all stood to greet her. Lord Wintersham looked at her.

"Isobel", he said. "I have a feeling that you have some news for us .... that something has happened ......".

Isobel nodded. She went to speak .... spotted John .... and stopped. She looked back to Lord Wintersham.

"It's Ok to speak freely Isobel", said Lord Wintersham. "John is Lorraine's very new Fiance .... that's why I'm here".

Isobel looked at Lorraine .... Lorraine came to her.

"Wow Lorraine", said Isobel. "That's two weddings .... are you going to do a double event".

"If we can find somebody for you Isobel .... we could make it a treble", said Roger Makepiece.

Isobel blushed. She was very good at this. Lord Wintersham always enjoyed Isobel's blushes.

Isobel hugged Lorraine .... and asked to be introduced to John.

John took her hand .... and smiled at her.

"Isobel", he said.

Isobel blushed again.

Roger smiled. John was a ladies' man.

Isobel declined breakfast .... asking for just a cup of hot water.

She sat .... and looked at Lord Wintersham.

"I'm afraid I've brought bad news", she said. "Simon died last night. Sarah followed him three hours later".

Lord Wintersham looked down at his coffee.

"I thought it might be that Isobel", he said.

There was a long silence in the room.

Lord Wintersham stirred his coffee thoughtfully. The others watched .... waiting for him to speak.

Eventually he looked up.

"Thank you for coming Isobel", he said. "It seems we have a great deal to discuss".

TWENTY

Lord Wintersham looked to Isobel. They were sitting alone in the conservatory.

"This is a lot to deal with all at once", he said.

"Whatever I can do to assist", said Isobel.

She reached into her pocket.

"Sarah left this with Mrs McPherson", she said.

Lord Wintersham opened the package that Isobel had passed to him.

He layed two silver keys on the table.

He sat looking at them. He sighed. He took the keys and stored them in his brief case.

"Well .... first things first then.", he said. "Simon and Sarah have no relatives that I'm aware of. That means we have the funerals to organise".

Isobel produced her ipad .... and brought up the memo page. She looked at Lord Wintersham.

"Start with the undertakers first please Isobel", he said. "Langham Brothers in Southampton".

Isobel tapped her keyboard.

"Organise Simon and Sarah to be moved to their Chapel of Rest. I'm an executor of both wills. I'll write you a note of authority in a moment".

He thought.

"Solicitors next", he said. "Fellows and Moore .... again in Southampton. The wills are with them. Ask them to check for any special requests regarding the funerals. Burials I would think. I'd be surprised if they wanted cremations".

"Am I phoning .... or making personal visits", asked Isobel.

Lord Wintersham thought.

"It's difficult without a single surviving relative", he said. "I think you should make personal visits. I'll do you letters of authority for both the undertakers, and the solicitors. Try to get a date set for the funeral".

"There's going to be some delay", said Isobel. "Simon died at home .... so there will have to be a post mortem before the Doctor will issue a death certificate".

Lord Wintersham sighed again.

"Did Mrs Mcpherson let you know", he asked.

Isobel nodded.

"Sarah came round to her to tell her that Simon had died .... then collapsed herself. Mrs Mcpherson called for an Ambulance.

They did what they could .... but Mrs Mcpherson told me it was as though Sarah had no will to live. She died in the hospital three hours later".

Lord Wintersham sat thinking. He looked up at Isobel.

"Do you know", he said. "They were together for fifty eight years. Those three hours were probably the longest time they'd spent apart in all that time".

Isobel sat waiting.

Lord Wintersham brought his briefcase onto the table. He wrote the two letters of authority. He put the two pieces of paper into envelopes .... but left them unsealed.

"That should be enough for today Isobel", he said. "I'll see you back in the flat this evening .... if you run up against a real problem .... give me a call .... but I've got to talk to Roger and John".

"So try not to phone unless it's really neccessary". said Isobel.

Lord Wintersham smiled at her.

"It seems we have a beginning .... and an end", he said. He closed his eyes.

"For where the beginning is .... the end shall also be".

"Thomas .... saying eighteen", said Isobel.

"Well done", said Lord Wintersham. " Isobel .... you go and do what you can with the end .... and I'll make a start on the beginning".

He closed his briefcase. Isobel closed her Tablet.

"I'll see you this evening then", she said.

They went out into the snow.

Lord Wintersham saw Isobel into her Golf. He watched her drive away.

"Blessed is the one who stands at the beginning", he murmured. "For that one will know the end .... and will not taste death".

He turned back towards the front door.

....

Lord Wintersham returned to the kitchen.

"I've just sent Roger through to the conservatory with coffee for you both", said Debbie. "I know you want to talk to him".

"Thank you", said Lord Wintersham.

"It's awfully sad about Sarah and Simon", said Debbie.

Her Father nodded.

"They were together for a very long time", he said. "I'm sure their spirits will continue together".

He found Roger sitting by an ornate conservatory stove.

"Good morning again Roger", he said.

Roger stood.

"I'm sorry to hear that you have had bad news", he said.

"Yes", said Lord Wintersham. "It didn't come as a total surprise, I'm afraid. Sarah and Simon had become very frail over the last few months".

"They were old friends of yours", asked Roger.

"They were our Senior Key Holders", said Lord Wintersham.

The two men sat down. Roger poured two coffees.

"It is so strange", said Lord Wintersham,"that endings are so often accompanied by beginnings. Debbie and yourself, John and Lorraine .... you stand at the beginning. In a few days time I will stand at a burial. I will see the end".

He fell silent. He sat staring at the floor.

Then he went to the stove, opened the door, and stirred the flames. He added another log from the nearby basket.

"Lord Wintersham", said Roger. "Debbie has told me, several times, that she and I are, in fact, already married. Can you explain that to me please".

Lord Wintersham sat again. He looked at Roger and smiled.

"I can indeed", he said.

He sat sipping his coffee, as though collecting his thoughts.

"We need to go back to the seventh century ....to Mecca .... and to our old friend Muhammud".

"In your world", said Roger.

"Yes .... in my world .... and Deborah's world".

Roger nodded.

"Muhammud's ministry in Mecca was into it's fifth year. He wasn't universally loved .... but he was making steady progress in building a following.

And then calamity struck .... in the form of what we would now recognise as a virus".

"A plague", said Roger.

"Yes", said Lord Wintersham. "A plague. It seems to have started in Mecca itself .... but over the next two years, it was to spread into the entire region. It was a ruthlessly selective virus, in that it attacked only one demographic group".

Roger raised his eyebrows.

"It attacked only young women of child bearing age .... and it killed seven out of ten of those who developed the symptoms. A girl became vulnerable the moment she entered puberty. Indeed .... any woman capable of getting pregnant, was likely to contract the virus"

"What were the symptoms", asked Roger.

"Very simply a fever", said Lord Wintersham."The young woman would suffer a rising temperature, which would resist all efforts to lessen it's progress. Delirium would lead to a coma. Death usually occurred on the fourth day".

"Did anyone who contracted the symptoms ever recover", asked Roger.

"It seems not", said Lord Wintersham."All those who developed the fever died. There were no exceptions. Those few women who survived the epidemic .... did not develop any symptoms at all".

"I'm guessing that there were those who claimed the virus was an instrument of Divine Retribution upon women", said Roger

"You would be correct", said Lord Wintersham. "But Muhammud was not one of those who claimed it".

"He wasn't ....!", said Roger.

Lord Wintersham shook his head.

"Muhammud was intelligent …. much more intelligent than is sometimes supposed in your world. He was also blessed to have amongst His followers one of the most learned men of medicine of that time. One Tazzeed Ramur".

"But they could do nothing to stop the virus", said Roger.

"Nothing", said Lord Wintersham. "Nothing at all. They made one attempt. A group of women …. nearly a hundred …. were moved to an isolated village. For a month or so, all seemed well. Then the virus appeared amongst them. Within a week all but fifteen of those isolated were dead".

Roger sat deep in thought.

"Did anyone see the future consequences of all this", he said.

"Tazeed did", said Lord Wintersham."He realised that they must start to plan for the future. A future with very few young women …. and therefore a future in which new births were going to be rare events. A future with very few new babies".

"And a future with a rapidly decreasing population", said Roger.

"Exactly", said Lord Wintersham.

"So what did they do", asked Roger.

Lord Wintersham smiled.

"Aha", he said. "This is where the story becomes very interesting …. very interesting indeed. But before I begin …. I am going in search of tea. Tea …. and hopefully a biscuit or two".

He picked up the coffee pot, and the cups, and headed off for the kitchen. Roger attended to the stove. He looked out at the garden. A robin sat on a twig watching him. There was just the lightest dusting of snow on the lawn.

Lord Wintersham returned with a tray. Tea, milk, and a new packet of Digestive Biscuits. Roger picked up the packet, and looked at the label. The word "Digestive" had always amused him. A sales pitch based on Victorian dietary beliefs, he supposed.

"Now", said Lord Wintersham, pouring tea as he spoke. "Where were we".

"No new babies", said Roger.

"Yes …. well very few", said Lord Wintersham.

He passed Roger his tea.

"You perhaps have to rember that in the culture of Muhammud's time, women did not enjoy the social staus and equality that Deborah and Isobel and Lorraine are used to. They were very much second class citizens with very few real rights. In some more backward areas they were viewed almost as a farmer views his cattle".

"But suddenly everything changed for women", said Roger.

It did indeed", said Lord Wintersham. "It changed a great deal. Women of child bearing age were now a very precious commodity. A very precious commodity indeed. They became very cosseted".

"Their price was far above that of rubys", said Roger.

"It soon became so", said Lord Wintersham. "And any birth of a healthy child was much celebrated".

"But the birth of a baby girl was even more celebrated", said Roger.

"It was indeed", said Lord Wintersham. "And naturally …. Muhammud and Tazzeed began to discuss the possibility that there might be ways to increase the odds in favour of female births".

Roger smiled.

"I knew a girl who believed that if you stood on your head ………….".

Lord Wintersham laughed.

"It sounds most uncomfortable", he said.

"Are there really any methods to increase the odds", asked Roger. "I know there are lots of what you might call "Old Wives Tales".

"And you shouldn't dismiss them too readily", said Lord Wintersham. "They are often based on centuries of observation and experience".

"So did Tazzeed have any theories", asked Roger. "He was the one with medical knowledge".

"Tazzeed had always been interested in procreation", said Lord Wintersham. "He had made what we now call a "specialised study" of the subject. And what he had learned was now critical to he and Muhammud's advice to their followers".

Roger opened the biscuits. They took one each.

"It was the custom of the time for younger women to be married off to older men", said Lord Wintersham. "As much for financial reasons as anything else. An older man was more likely to have accumulated some wealth .... and therefore be able to support a wife and her children".

"Or more than one wife", said Roger.

Lord Wintersham nodded.

"But Tazzeed's studies had revealed that a girl married to a younger man ...."".

" ....was more likely to give birth to girls", said Roger.

"Yes", said Lord Wintersham. "Statistically it was so obvious that he could not ignore it".

"It takes a man to make a girl", laughed Roger.

"Yes .... well we are back to those "Old Wives Tales" there", said Lord Wintersham.

"Tazzeed also had a theory, and it was very advanced for it's time, that nature must surely favour the birth of girls .... because they are ultimately responsible for the continuation of the species. He commented to Muhammud that a village of fifty girls, and one man, would be blessed with many children. But a village of fifty men, and one woman, would be cursed".

Roger smiled.

"I would have to feel sorry for that "one man", he said.

Lord Wintersham smiled. He poured two more teas.

"Tazzeed had another theory", he said. "He believed that women were potentially very instinctive in their behaviour when it came to the opposite sex. He believed that, left to make her own choice of husband, a woman would choose a man who would give her the stongest and healthiest children .... and therefore .... give her the greatest chance of giving birth to female offspring".

"Was the marriage of young girls to older men originally started as a means of lessening the chance of female births", said Roger. "I know that male births were far preferable to female".

"There is actually no evidence for that", said Lord Wintersham. "We believe it was simply never considered. It was just a natural result of creating, what was, after all, an un-natural situation".

Roger nodded.

"So are you going to tell me that in your world .... way back in the seventh century .... young women were told they now had the right to choose their own husband", said Roger.

"I am", said Lord Wintersham.

"I'll bet that concept met with some resistance", said Roger.

"It certainly did", said Lord Wintersham. "But Muhammud and Tazzeed persevered .... and within five years the results proved that Tazzeed had been correct in his deductions. Three girls were being born for every boy .... and it was obvious that a viable population might again be possible".

"Wow", said Roger.

Lord Wintersham laughed.

"Now", he said. "To return to your original question....

Would I be correct in supposing that my darling daughter Deborah organised a situation in which she could make it very obvious to yourself that she would like you as her husband".

It was Roger's turn to laugh.

"I can almost feel myself blushing", he said. "But .... yes .... she did exactly that".

"And you .... well shall we say that you decided to accept her "proposal", said Lord Wintersham.

"I did", said Roger.

"Then I am very pleased to inform you, Roger, that according to the laws and customs of The World to which Deborah and I belong .... you are well and truly "married" to my daughter .... and I am sure that God will bless your union".

"Amen", said Roger.

"A toast then Sir", said Lord Wintersham. He held up his tea cup.

"To the Bride and Groom", he said. "May you live long and Prosper".

Roger raised his cup.

"Amen", he said.

TWENTY ONE

It was Saturday .... and Woman Police Constable Susan Witherspoon had been to the Dentist. Knowing that she was booked for a filling .... she had taken the first appointment of the day at eight am.

She had deliberately not eaten breakfast .... not even a cup of tea. On an empty stomach .... the Novocaine had hit her hard and fast .... she hadn't felt a thing.

She walked back to her car, dribbling from the right side of her mouth. That side of her face would be numb for hours .... until the early evening. She had a tissue in her hand. The dribbling was embarassing.

She pulled out her phone, and checked the time. Just after nine fifteen. She was off duty today .... and she had a hair dressing appointment booked for one thirty .... at "Thai Sing Can" on the corner of Keeling Street. It wasn't cheap there .... but they really made you feel special.

But that was this afternoon.

She intended to spend the rest of the morning on the Police firing range.

Sue Witherspoon had grown up on a farm .... her Father had taught her to shoot. She was proficient with her little twenty eight bore shotgun .... shooting clay pigeons .... by the time she was eight.

She had requested .... and was granted .... firearms training .... almost as soon as she had joined the force at eighteen.

Her instructors were quick to realise that they had a very remarkable ability on their hands.

Susan Witherspoon was recommended for advanced firearms training. If she was a little disappointed that the course seemed to concentrate mainly on how to avoid using her weapon .... unless there was no other option .... that disappointment was allayed by her instructors suggestion that she might consider training for a place on the British Olympic Team. The next Olmpics were two years away.

As the training and practise sessions would form part of her duties as a Firearms Officer, she would be funded throughout the course. The only condition was that she make herself available for inter-force competitions.

Sue had agreed readily.

On this particular morning, she and her instructor were going to concentrate on her fifty metre ability. She would use Revolving, Automatic, and single shot pistols .... the latter being for her Olympic training.

There was a light breeze blowing .... the air was chilly .... but it was dry. A perfect morning for practise, she thought.

She drove out to the range. Her instructor was parking his car as she arrived. He came over and greeted her warmly.

Sue was popular with her fellow officers. She had very good "people skills" .... as those officers who had been on duty with her when the pubs "turned out", had discovered.

Bracknell town centre on a Friday night could be a very "lively" environment.

Sue and her instructor walked to the armoury to sign out their pistols and ammunition.

The air was bright and crisp. Sue felt it was going to be a good session.

....

As Sue and her instructor were signing for their pistols .... Nobby the Dog was finishing his breakfast on Keeling street. It was Saturday morning, so he was breakfasting at number eighteen. It was a real "dog's breakfast". Leftovers from last night .... but Nobby polished it off enthusiastically.

Nobby the Dog was a thoroughbred mongrel. His Father and Mother had been mongrels .... his Grandfather and Grandmother had been mongrels.

There were rumours that his Great Great Grandmother had been a Labrador .... but that was as good as it got. He was of such mixed strain .... that he might almost have been seen as the pioneer for a new breed.

Nobby had a cheerful disposition .... and a cheerful expression. Great attributes for a dog in his position.

Everybody on Keeling Street assumed that somebody else owned Nobby the Dog.

He wore no collar.

The local dog warden .... and the RSPCA officer .... were both aware of Nobby .... and his lack of a collar. Both had tried to catch him, on numerous occasions .... but his extraordinary skill in evading their efforts, had earned him their grudging respect. They decided that Nobby appeared well groomed .... well fed .... and in control of his own destiny.

A truce was called.

....

Nobby licked the last of the leftovers from the dish. It was Saturday .... so he would be expected at number four for lunch. He looked up and saw Mrs Smith waving at him from her kitchen window. He wagged his tail .... and gave her a smile to show his appreciation. He went out through the garden gate .... turned right .... and headed for the old gas works site, at the end of the street.

He had three hours to kill. He had a bed there .... in an old water tank .... he could take a nap. And there was always the chance of a rat.

There was a bit of Terrier in Nobby's ancestry.

....

Farhad al Zubaidy stirred in his sleeping bag. He had spent the night at his Cousin Ali's flat .... in Bracknell. They had attended the Mosque yesterday lunchtime.

A visiting Imam had been the draw. He was well known for his graphic descriptions of the Rewards that would be bestowed upon his listeners. Rewards ready and waiting for those who died in the course of carrying out God's Retribution upon non believers.

Yesterday he had spoken about the Virgins of Heaven.

He had excelled himself in describing the softness of their milky white breasts .... the luscious curve of their thighs .... the moist kiss of their lips .... the welcoming curve of their bellies .... their obedience and subservience .... and their endless joy in pleasing those who had earned their favours.

Sixty-seven virgins .... waiting for those with the courage to carry out God's Work.

Farhad had come very close to ejaculating into his clothing. The furtive movements of other young men in the room, suggested to Farhad that not everybody could control their lust for these promised beauties. He grimaced. He had never approved of masturbation in the Mosque.

It was unseemly.

Those with a more practical experience, of everyday life with a member of the opposite sex, could have pointed out the downside.

They might have pointed out that if Farhad .... or Ali .... or indeed any of their fellow worshippers .... had ever experienced any sort of adult relationship with a real woman .... they would have known that sixty-seven virgins would be a punishment straight from Hell. One virgin is quite enough .... sixty-seven would be a torture designed by the Devil himself.

But Farhad and Ali .... and their fellow worshippers .... had no experience with real members of the opposite sex.

Women were a mystery .... shut away from men's gaze .... until their marriages were arranged.

Farhad, and Ali had never bought a girl a coffee. They had never felt a real warm living girl in their arms. Never been taken to her bed.

They had never experienced the realities of sex with a living .... loving .... and needful, female.

They dreamed of The Virgins of Heaven. Those were the women they lusted for. Those would be their reward.

As Farhad was padding throught to Ali's kitchen on bare feet .... Miss Deborah Wintersham was coming down the stairs, into the kitchen, at Roger Makepiece's barn. She was singing a refrain from one of the songs she had heard in Church the night before.

Debbie had been much moved by the song. After the second line of the break .... when Roger had collapsed onto his knees, head bowed .... Debbie had followed suit without the slightest self conscious thought.

"Great are You Lord .... Great are You lord .... Great are You Lord", she sang .... as she put the kettle to boil.

Within five minutes, Roger, John, Lorraine, and Isobel, had joined her in the kitchen. It was to be a busy day. They had an engagement party to organise. A very short notice engagement party. It was to be in the barn on Monday evening. There was food and drink to organise (Roger Makepiece had volunteered for that job). There was music (John knew a man). And there were clothes.

Lorraines clothes were at her flat. She wanted to fetch some of her wardrobe .... and she wanted to get her hair done. And for Lorraine, and Debbie, and Isobel .... well there was only one hairdressing salon in the whole World. It was just five minutes from Lorraine's flat. "Thai Sing Can" .... on the corner of High Street and Keeling Street. Bracknell.

"Thai Sing" wasn't cheap. But it was the ONLY place to go .... If you were Debbie, or Lorraine, or Isobel.

They had appointments for twelve o'clock.

They asked John if he would take them to Bournemouth railway station .... but John had laughed.

"If I'm doing that .... I might as well take you to Bracknell", he said.

So they were all going. Roger, and John, and the three girls. Plenty of room in the Buick.

They got away from the barn just after ten. Lorraine left her Father

169

undisturbed. His wife had got home late last night.

She left a note for her parents on the kitchen table.

....

Some seventy miles away, the "Express Parcels" van driver admitted defeat. He was Bulgarian. It was his first week as a parcel delivery driver .... and using the sat. nav. he'd been doing fairly well in finding his way around in this strange country. But this morning the sat. nav. had failed to find the destination. A post code would have helped. He didn't have a postcode. Just a street name and number. He couldn't find the street.

Stephan pulled his van in to the kerb. It was a small package. He had it on the passenger seat. He'd brought it into the cab after his last drop.

There was an old man walking his dog. Stephan spoke little English. He was learning at evening classes. He approached the old man, and showed him the address label on the package.

The old man told his dog to sit .... then took the package and examined the address.

"Killing Street", he said. "No ......".

He shook his head .... then he looked again. He thought .... then he nodded. He looked at Stephan.

"It must mean Keeling Street", he said. "But I haven't heard it called "Killing Street" for seventy years or more. Used to be an abbatoir at the bottom end .... that's why it's such a wide street .... for driving the cattle and sheep down".

Stephan looked blankly at the old man .... he wasn't understanding anything that was being said to him. He pointed back up the road .... then he pointed down the road .... and held his palms apart.

The old man understood the gesture. He pointed to the traffic lights down the street.

"Left at the lights", he said, pointing vigorously to the left. Then he held up two fingers.

"Second street on the left", he said."The wide one".

He drew his arms appart to signify width.

Stephan understood. He shook the old man's hand .... and patted the dog's head".

"Left at lights. Two at left", he said.

The old man stuck his thumb up .... and smiled. He watched the van go through a red light .... then make the turn into Keeling Street. He shook his head.

"Killing Street", he said to his dog. "Where on Earth did he get that from. Hasn't been called "Killing Street" for seventy years or more. Not since they built the houses down there. The builder called them "Keeling Street Villas". He didn't think "Killing Street" was good for sales. Then the council renewed all the signs after the war. It's been "Keeling Street" ever since.

Bit rough down there at one time. Posh street now though. All young professional couples. All the houses "done up". Bathrooms and everything".

He patted his dog .... and walked on.

"Killing Street". He hadn't heard it called that for years. It brought back some memories though.

....

In Ali's kitchen .... Farhad made two herbal teas. He returned to the bedroom, and shook Ali awake.

"Today is the day my Cousin", said Farhad. "Tonight we shall be in Heaven .... the rewards shall be ours to savour to the full".

Ali stirred and sat up .... and took the tea. He looked across the room. Leaning against the wall were the instruments of retribution .... the instruments of punishment for those who defiled God's vision.

Ali would wield a First World War bayonet. It had a tapered blade some twenty inches long. Ali had found it at a car boot sale. He had paid three pounds for it. The original wooden handle had long rotted away, but Ali had fashioned a replacement in the workshop at the garage. He had also cleaned, sharpened, and polished the long blade .... coating it lightly with grease to prevent rusting. It was, once more, an effective weapon. Ali considered his three pounds to have been well spent.

Farhad had chosen a different route. He had visited a garden centre, and bought a heavy "parang". It was a tool intended for slashing .... for chopping off branches .... and for brush clearance. It had a three inch wide flat blade nearly two feet long .... edged on one side. With Ali's help .... again in the garage .... Farhad had cleaned the flat blade of it's original black paint, polished the steel to a bright finish .... and refined the cutting edge until it was razor sharp.

He had felt rather self conscious making the purchase .... and had bought gardening gloves, and a pair of garden shears, with the parang .... to make the transaction as innocuous as possible. He had paid cash.

The two weapons indicated the two young men's differing views.

Ali felt strongly that flesh must be defiled by the penetration of the blade .... if Divine purpose was to be served.

Farhad felt that true punishment could only be delivered by severing the heads of those who failed to observe the modesty expected by The One True God.

Farhad and Ali sipped their herbal teas, and munched on cereal bars. They eyed their instruments of Divine purpose. They were both very tense .... they had been "saving themselves" for the delights soon to come. Their testicles ached. They were close to "sexual emergency".

....

172

TWENTY TWO

At two minutes past ten, on Saturday morning, Miss Deborah Wintersham, Miss Lorraine Makepiece, Miss Isobel Branson, Mr Roger Davies, and Mr John LaSalle left the Makepiece home near Wimborne Dorset, bound for Bracknell.

John was at the wheel of the Buick. Lorraine sat next to him. Debbie, Roger, and Isobel shared the rear seat.

The sat.nav. said they had a ninety minute drive ahead of them. The weather had turned brighter and drier. The roads were clear .... but stained white with the salt that the Highways Authorities had spread so liberally over the last few days.

John had suggested going back to their base for a modern car. He wasn't happy about using the Buick in the Winter conditions. But Roger felt comfortable with the Buick .... they would use it today .... and get it cleaned underneath tomorrow.

John pushed a USB stick into the front of the music system.

The Jeff Buckleigh version of "Hallelujiah" began to play.

"This is my absolutely number one favourite song", said Debbie, "...........but it's so sad".

They listened to the words.

"That line about the roof always reminds me of "Winter's Tale" by Mark Helprin", said Roger. "The bit where Peter Lake is burgling the house .... and he falls in love with Beverley. She lives on the roof, because she's dying of TB".

"Roger", said Debbie. "Have you really read "Winter's Tale". That's so amazing".

"Debs", said Roger .... interrupting her. "If you say "Thats so amazing .... for a car dealer" .... I'm divorcing you .... now".

Debbie giggled.

"But why on the roof", said Isobel.

"It's Winter", said Roger. "The air is colder up there .... so she can breathe without coughing so much".

"Is this song about religion .... or is it about sex", said Lorraine.

They listened.

"It's about both", said Isobel. "...........well the fourth verse definitely is".

"Isobel", said Debbie. "I'm shocked .... and not so much as a maidenly blush from you".

Roger looked at Isobel.

She rolled her eyes skywards .... and smiled.

"Seriously now Isobel", said Roger. "Is there anybody special in your life .... could we make it a triple wedding".

Isobel turned to him. She'd taken the question seriously.

"There is somebody", she said. "But he's a lot older than me .... and he's married. And nobody I ever met comes close to him. He always made me feel like the most special person on Earth when I was with him".

There was a silence in the car.

Roger looked at Isobel.

"I guess you don't get to choose who you fall in love with", he said.

"Hallelujiah", said Lorraine.

"Hallelujiah", said Debbie.

....

On the range .... Sue Witherspoon was struggling with her revolver shooting. She had been shooting at ninety eight and above with her automatic .... but she was down around the upper seventies with the revolver.

Eventually her instructor called a halt.

He asked her to unload. She slipped the four cartridges from the chamber into her jacket pocket .... and handed him the pistol.

"I'm wondering if it's the grip", he said. "Hold it in the shooting stance for me".

Sue took the pistol back .... and aimed it at the target fifty metres away. It was a fair distance for a pistol .... but she'd been doing fine with the auto.

The instructor examined her hands .... he gently prized her fingers from the grip .... and wrapped them back into place.

"It's the grip that's causing the problem", he said. "Take it to Wayne Jones .... the armourer. If you show him exactly as you're showing me .... he'll know how to alter the grip for you".

Sue put the revolver back into it's fitted case.

Her instructor checked his watch.

"We'll carry on with the single shot pistol", he said. "See Wayne at lunchtime".

Sue was still dribbling. The instructor handed her a bunch of tissues from the box on the table. Sue dried her mouth .... and pushed the tissues into her pocket for later.

She took the single shot pistol from it's case. It was the gun she would use at the Olympics.

"Now", said the instructor. "Remember your breathing .... that's the secret of single shot".

....

In the flat .... Farhad and Ali were getting themselves ready. They had started with a prayer session. They prayed that God would guide them on

175

this auspicious day. The day that they would give their lives in Jiihaad.

The Holy War that all true believers should fight without cease.... until the whole world was united in The One True Faith .... in the One True God.

They donned black track suits .... with crisp white training shoes. They had close fitting black woollen hats, and black leather gloves. They had no intention of covering their faces. Let the unbelievers know the name of God's Agents of Retribution.

Farhad, and Ali looked at each other. Farhad handed Ali a twist of silver foil. It contained a white powder.

Ali went to open the foil.

"No Ali .... later", said Farhad. "When we get into the car".

....

Nobby the dog stirred in his sleep. He was in his water tank at the old gas works site. He had never understood how the blanket came to be in the tank. In fact Mrs Smith at number eighteen had put it there for him. His ears twitched. Nobby was dreaming.

A young couple had just moved in at number twenty.

They had a young Labrador bitch. Ancient family memories had stirred in Nobby. He was optimistic. He had high hopes of a meaningful relationship.

Nobby woke for just a moment. Lunch at number four was always excellent. There was much to look forward to. Nobby closed his eyes .... and slept.

....

The Buick slipped into Bracknell High Street at a quarter to twelve.

"When you come to collect us", said Lorraine. "Park the car in the street that runs down the side of the salon. It's really wide .... and there are no parking restrictions".

"Keeling Street", added Isobel.

"Will do", said John. "What time will you be finished in the salon".

"We're just having a wash and cut", said Lorraine, "so we should be out at about one fifteen".

John brought the car into the kerb outside the salon. He slipped from the drivers seat .... and held the doors open for the girls to get out. They were a great looking trio, he thought. They were all dressed in the fashion of the moment with short duffle coats, short black pleated woolcloth skirts, and thick black tights. They all wore colourful berets .... and matching Doc Martin lace up boots.

John smiled at them as they stood on the pavement.

"Have fun Girls", he said. He embraced Lorraine .... and kissed her. Roger, who had got out too, followed suit with Debbie.

He and John looked at Isobel.

Isobel stood waiting.

They both embraced her .... and gave her a kiss on the cheek.

Isobel blushed.

Roger and John were going up to Staines. Roger had a mind to buy another caravan .... and he knew a dealer there who had a reputation for finding the very best vans. They wanted to check out his stock .... and they would have a chat .... and a coffee.

John spotted a gap in the traffic. The Buick pulled away. The girls waved .... and headed for the door of "Thai Sing Can".

"You two are so lucky", said Isobel. "Those are such great guys you have there".

"We are Much Blessed", said Debbie."And God will bless you too Isobel".

She looked after the Buick.

It's tail was just disappearing round the corner at the end of the High Street.

....

Sue Witherspoon and her Instructor walked back to the reception to check in the pistols.

"How did it go this morning", said the man on the desk.

"Ok Will", said Sue. "But my revolver shooting was rubbish. Mike here thinks it a problem with the grip".

"Needs Wayne Jones to do a re-profile job on it", said Mike. "Is he here".

"Sorry", said Will. "It's Saturday. He'll be working in his Father's gunsmiths on the High Street. Why don't you take the revolver in to him this afternoon. He might even get it done for you today, if they're quiet".

"Can we take it off site then", said Sue.

"I'm Ok with it", said Will. "You're a warranted firearms officer .... you're delivering it to the force armourer. Yeah .... no problem from my point of view .... as long as you sign it out .... and it's not as though you've got any ammunition for it".

"Ok", said Sue. "I'll drop it in to him before my hair dressing appointment. That's in the High Street. Then I'll pop back afterwards to see how it's going".

"He'll probably need to do two "fittings" anyway", said Mike. "But you'll be amazed at the difference it can make when it fits your hand properly".

Sue nodded.

"Look", he said, "I'd better go. The wife and kids are waiting for me to take them shopping".

He slapped Will on the shoulder .... and saluted Sue.

"Great work this morning young lady", he said.

He turned, and headed for the door.

"Sue", said Will. "You're dribbling again".

He pushed the box of tissues she'd placed on the counter, towards her.

She pulled out a wad, dried her mouth, and pushed the tissues into her jacket pocket.

"Dentist this morning", she said. "I had a filling".

Will grimaced.

"Dentist …. and then the shooting range", he said. "Tough lady".

She laughed.,

"You reckon", she said.

She liked Will. He'd watched her progress on the range with great interest.

"I'm off", she said. "More tough lady things to do. Getting my hair done".

She laughed …. and turned towards the door.

He let her take a couple of steps …. then took a deep breath.

"Sue", he said. "Any chance of a coffee with you sometime".

She looked at him. She knew he'd been building up to asking her.

She smiled at him.

"Costa's", she said. "And you can buy me a lemon zesty tart".

"Will smiled happily.

"You're on", he said.

Sue left.

Will sang a line from a song he'd been listening to on the radio.

Strange song, he thought. Like a modern hymn …. with that word Hallelujiah.

Sort of sticks in your mind.

TWENTY THREE

Debbie, Lorraine, and Isobel admired each other's new hair. They had finished their appointments a little earlier than expected .... and they were sitting in reception with cappuccinos and biscuits. They all felt a little self conscious.

Isobel looked mischievously at Debbie .... and Lorraine.

"So .... ehm .... what does it actually feel like then", she said.

"What does what feel like", said Debbie.

"You know.........................", said Isobel .... holding an expression of innocent awe.

"Isobel ....", said Lorraine, in a warning tone.

Isobel held the expression for as long as she could. Then her mouth twitched .... and she laughed.

"Horrid girl", said Lorraine. "Well ... perhaps you'll find out for yourself one day".

"You mentioned somebody earlier", said Debbie. "Did you ....".

"No", said Isobel. "No way".

"Did you want to", said Lorraine.

Isobel looked thoughtful.

"Sort of", she said. "I had a fantasy about having a baby with him".

She looked at her phone.

"Roger and John might be back by now", she said.

They stood . One of the salon juniors brought their coats .... and gave them a large chocolate lollipop each. They helped each other on with their duffles .... but left their berets off .... because of being careful with their new hair.

They moved towards the door.

Isobel hesitated.

"Actually", she said. "I think I may need the Lady's room".

Debbie and Lorraine noticed a twinge of pain cross her face. They both knew that Isobel could suffer quite badly.

"Are you Ok Isobel", said Debbie. "Do you want one of us to go with you".

Isobel smiled .... and shook her head.

"I'll catch up with you in a moment", she said.

"Do you need.............", said Lorraine .... offering Isobel her bag.

Isobel shook her head.

"It's not a total surprise" she said. "I even remembered the pain killers".

Isobel ran up the curving stair case.

Debbie and Lorraine moved towards the door. The salon junior opened it for them. They said Goodbye .... and went out into the cold bright air.

Isobel went into the Rest Room. It was very posh. A real nineteen fifties "powder room".

She drew a cup of water from the cooler in the corner and sat down on one of the pale green sofas.

"The Green Room", she thought.

She opened her handbag, and fished for her enamelled tablet box. She took two of the pills .... and washed them down with a sip of water. They would take twenty minutes or so to kick in. She wished for a moment that a certain person was there to rub the small of her back.

Isobel closed her eyes .... and began a prayer.

"Awesome God .... why do I have to suffer this pain every month. Why can't I be like other girls. Please .... Awesome God .... please please take the pain away".

She went into her bag again .... for her Lillets. Then the thought came to her .... as it always did.

Only another twenty years to go .... get with the programme .... you're a girl.............deal with it.

She began to cry softly.

Awesome God watched her cry. He hated to see Isobel cry.

It was the worst part of being an Awesome God .... watching so many people cry.

....

Outside .... Debbie and Lorraine felt the cold on their ears.

"Gosh .... my ears are cold", said Lorraine. "Imagine what it's like being a sheep when you've just been shorn".

"Or the Collie dog in the Spec-savers commercial", said Debbie".

The girls laughed.

Lorraine slipped her arm around Debbie's waist .... and they rounded the corner into Keeling Street .... to show off their new hair to their men.

....

Farhad and Ali took their weapons out to the Nissan in a black holdall. Farhad put the bag on the rear seat. He slipped behind the wheel. Ali walked round .... checking the tyres .... and then joined him in the car.

Farhad brought out his twist of foil .... and showed his Cousin how to divide the white powder into two .... and how to sniff half up each nostril.

They sat .... waiting for the cocaine to hit them.

The engine started first time. Farhad let it warm. He looked to Ali.

"Are you ready my Cousin", he said.

Ali nodded.

Farhad headed for the town centre. He knew the perfect location for what he had planned.

Fifteen minutes later he was in Bracknell High Street. He took the second left after the lights .... and turned into Keeling Street. He went to the far end .... turned the car .... and brought it into the left side kerb half way back up the street. They were about a hundred metres from the main road.

He had chosen this location because there was a famous hair dressing salon on the corner. The women who went there parked in this street. They would appear from the salon with heads uncovered .... often two or more together .... walking without shame.

They were sluts.

Farhad and Ali sat and waited. Farhad left the engine running. He put the interior heater control to max. The cocaine would be more effective if they were warm.

The Cousins watched a large white American sedan turn into the street. They heard the rumble of it's big V8 engine as it passed by.

"Buick Electra", said Ali. "About 1974 or 75. Very nice".

Farhad nodded. His mind was elsewhere.

He twisted in his seat .... and watched the Buick turn.

It came in to the kerb, about thirty metres behind them.

....

Sue Witherspoon turned her Astra into Keeling Street .... ran down to the end .... and turned. She parked ahead of a large white car .... she guessed it was American. She noticed that there were two men in it .... probably waiting for their girlfriends to come out of "Thai Sing Can".

The black Nissan in front of her also had two men in it. She noticed that the car was running .... steamy vapour coming from the exhaust. They were probably running the heater while they waited.

Sue felt herself dribbling again. She pushed her hand into her jacket pocket for her tissues. The tips of her fingers found something metallic and cold.

Sue started. She pulled out the wad of tissues .... put them on the passenger seat .... and put her hand back into her pocket. She drew out four live cartridges.

She looked at them as they lay in the palm of her hand.

"How on Earth.....................".

Then she remembered. Mike had asked her to unload .... so that he could examine her grip on the revolver. She'd slipped the four cartridges into her pocket .... and forgotten them.

She was aware that she had broken range rules.

Ah well, she thought. They'll be safe enough.

She dried her mouth .... again .... and looked at the case in the passenger side footwell. It contained her revolver.

....

Roger and John hadn't made it to Staines. They'd returned to the M3 .... but found a queue of traffic waiting to join the motorway. There was no sign that the queue was moving .... and they guessed the motorway was blocked.

John turned the Buick in a convenient side road .... and looked at Roger.

"Shall we go back up and try the old A30", he said.

Roger shook his head.

"Hadn't better risk it", he said. "If the motorway's closed .... the A30 will soon back up as well".

He thought for a moment.

"What we could do", he said. "is go back to the A30 .... but turn back towards Camberley. There's a garden centre a mile down the road with a

185

good cafe. We'll get some lunch. I've been there before. Not cheap .... but it's good food".

Twenty minutes later they were eating shepherds pie with side orders of french fries.

Roger had his Tablet with him. He asked the waitress if there was a wi-fi connection available.

She smiled at him. She picked up the menu.

"The password is down at the bottom .... just there". she said leaning close to Roger to show him.

"Thank you", said Roger.

"Everything Ok with your meals", she asked.

Roger and John smiled at her.

"Perfect", said John.

He and Roger checked the caravan stock at Staines .... on the dealers website. There was one van .... a Tabbert .... that they looked at very closely.

"I'll give Steve a ring on Monday", said Roger.

There had been a hint of sun as they'd sat in the garden centre consevatory over lunch .... but as they came out, the air had turned colder. A grey overcast promised rain, or sleet.

By five past one they were turning back into Keeling Street. John turned the car at the end, and parked.

"Did you notice the Skyline", he said to Roger.

Roger nodded. A girl in an Astra was parking in front of them.

"Might almost be the one on the M27 the other day", he said.

John nodded. He checked the time on his phone.

"How long did the girls say they'd be", said Roger.

"Should be out anytime now", said John. "In fact that might be them now".

Two girls had turned the corner .... and were walking down the right side of the road. It was Debbie and Lorraine. John saw Debbie point out the Buick.

"Where's Isobel", said Roger.

"Probably powdering her ....". John stopped.

The Nissan was moving. The engine revs had shot up .... the rear tyres screamed .... and the car shot away from the kerb.

John hurled open his drivers door.

"Rog", he said. "I don't like it .... something's going to happen".

He began to sprint towards the girls. He began to shout to them.

....

In the Astra .... Sue Witherspoon was a moment or two ahead of John in realising something was wrong.

She had reached down for the revolver case .... and brought it up on to her lap .... realising that she didn't have time before her hair appointment to take it to the gunsmiths.

As she sat up .... movement in the black Nissan caught her eye. The young men had donned black woollen hats. One of them reached over to the back seat.

Sue saw the polished blade of the "parang". She saw what looked like a bayonet. She saw the black leather gloves. She heard the engine revs rise. She saw the two girls who had just come round the corner from the salon.

She tore open the revolver case .... flipped open the chamber .... and loaded the four cartridges from her pocket. As she left the Astra .... one of the men from the American car ran by her. He was shouting a warning.

....

In the Buick the USB stick completed it's cycle. There was a slight pause

.... the opening sigh .... and Jeff Buckley's version of "Hallelujiah" started to play. The street would hear it. The Buick's doors gaped open ....

Roger was just a few yards behind John.

....

Farhad slewed the Skyline across the pavement, just ten yards short of Debbie and Lorraine. He and Ali were out of the car in seconds.

The two girls stopped in surprise. Farhad and Ali heard the warning shouts from behind them. They threw themselves at the girls.

Farhad swung the heavy parang at Debbie's neck. She screamed .... but the scream was cut short. The blade was razor sharp. It severed Debbie's neck. Her body collapsed. Her head rolled into the gutter. Blood pumped from her torso.

Farhad shouted in triumph.

Ali was a split second behind his Cousin. As Lorraine screamed .... and began to turn .... he plunged the bayonet into her chest. He would have pulled it from her .... and stabbed again .... but at that moment a bullet from Sue Witherspoon's revolver caught him in the spine, two inches below his neck. He went down. A few moments later he was dead.

Another young woman came round the corner. Farhad raised his parang .... and started towards her. Sue witherspoon screamed at him.

"Armed Police .... Stop .... throw down your weapon".

Farhad turned .... he saw Sue.

Another slut to pay the price of Divine Retribution. He ran towards her .... shouting about Aluminium bars.

Sue saw the raised parang. She saw the look on Farhad's face. There was just enough distance to risk a leg shot. If it brought the assailant down .... she would have him alive. If it didn't .... she would have no choice. She would have to kill.

She aimed. She wanted to smash the femur .... just below the knee.

And it would have been a perfectly placed shot .... if Farhad hadn't stumbled into a pothole in the road. As he fell forwards .... the parang flew from his grasp .... and Sue's shot caught him between the legs. The bullet removed his penis and testicles. His precious organs disappeared under a parked car. Farhad collapsed .... screaming in agony,

Sue desperately wanted to put her third shot into his head .... but she wanted him alive. Equally she didn't want him getting up, and finding that parang. She put her third shot into his right leg. Farhad screamed .... but he was going nowhere.

Sue rushed to the driver from the American car. He was kneeling over the girl who had suffered the bayonet stabbing. The bayonet was still in her chest. Her mouth dribbled blood.

Sue pulled her mobile phone from her pocket .... and punched in 999.

It rang just once.

"Emergency services operator", a female voice said.

"Woman Police Constable Susan Witherspoon speaking on her private mobile number", she said.

"Hi Sue .... Whats up .... it's Janet here", the voice said.

Sue could have cried with relief.

"Janet", she said. "I'm in so much trouble. Keeling Street off Bracknell High Street. I need Paramedics, really serious paramedics, Ambulances, Fire Service .... and as much police back-up as you can get me. I need the paramedics desperately urgently. Two adults with serious injuries. One adult female believed dead.

"Ok, Ok Sue .... take it steady", said Janet. "Give me thirty secs .... I'll get the ambulances organised".

During the pause .... Sue looked back. The other young man from the American car was kneeling by the girl who had been be-headed .... in a spreading pool of her blood. He was sobbing.

Sue needed to reach him.

Janet came back on the line.

"Sue", she said. "Everything you requested is on it's way. The ambulance station is only two miles away .... so you should see them in five minutes".

"Janet", said Sue. "Listen carefully. I need a senior officer to speak to .... I'm way out of my depth with this situation. Can you find out who's on duty, and get them to call me back. Janet .... use the phrase "Time at the bar". That's important Janet .... and please please be quick .... I'm in so much trouble here".

"Got it", said Janet. "Keep your line available Sue".

She was gone.

Sue looked down at the bayonet still protruding from the girls chest.

"I'm WPC Susan Witherspoon .... what's your name", she said to the man.

"John", he said. "This is my Fiancee Lorraine. She's still alive .... but I don't know whether to pull the bayonet out of her chest".

"Leave it there", said Sue. "Paramedics here in five minutes. Who's that over there please".

John looked behind him.

"That's my boss .... Roger Davies. That's his Fiancee Deborah Wintersham".

Sue was about to turn away. She span back to John.

"The Deborah Wintersham .... the society girl", she said.

"Was", said John.

Sue looked back to Roger.

"John .... try and keep Lorraine conscious .... I need to speak to Roger".

Sue looked up and down the street. To her astonishment her shots hadn't brought any of the residents out onto the pavement yet.

Sue approached Roger. She tried very hard not to look at the head in the gutter.

"Are you Roger", she said.

She layed her hand gently on the young man's shoulder.

"I'm WPC Susan Witherspoon".

He looked up at her.

"This is Debbie", he said. "We were going to get married".

"I know Roger", said Sue. "John just told me".

Roger turned back.

"Roger", said Sue. "You can't help Debbie any more .... but you can help me. I'm only a very junior police officer Roger .... and I need you to help me. Will you help me Roger".

Roger looked up at her .... as though struggling to understand what she was saying to him.

"You're a Police woman", he said.

"Yes", said Sue. "I'm off duty. I was here to get my hair done".

Roger looked at Debbie.

"Debbie just had her hair done", he said.

Sue started to cry. She wanted to use her last shot on the bastard who had done this.

"Roger", she said gently. "You can't help Debbie any more .... but you can help me. Please help me Roger".

Roger stood up .... slowly. Time would get away from Debbie now.

He looked at Sue Witherspoon.

"What do you want me to do", he said.

They heard sirens. An ambulance swung into the street.

TWENTY FOUR

Nobby the Dog had overslept. He emerged from his water tank .... and stretched. He felt better for a good sleep. He had an appetite for lunch. He came out of the gas works, and started up the right hand side of the street.

He'd only gone a few yards when he heard the squeal of vehicle tyres .... shouting .... screaming .... and a loud bang.

Nobby disappeared under the nearest vehicle .... a Ford van. He lay sniffing the air. There were strange smells. He could smell blood. There was a sweet burnt smell as well, which he knew was associated with the loud bang he'd heard. As a young dog .... he'd spent a while on a farm.

Nobby stayed where he was .... and waited for developments. Something was happening .... and it wasn't good. He could smell adrenaline. The fatty cloying aroma of fear.

He'd just decided to bolt for the safety of home .... when there was a second bang .... and to Nobby's total amazement .... a fresh, warm, and deliciously bloody snack, arrived right under his nose.

It was Farhad's penis and testicles.

Nobby decided to get out while the going was good. He grabbed the offering .... savouring the taste of fresh blood in his mouth .... and headed for home.

Farhad had his mind on his immediate problem .... otherwise he might have seen Nobby making off with his manhood .... such as it was. When Sue Witherspoon deliberately put a second shot into his leg .... Farhad realised that Jiihaad hadn't gone his way. He clutched his wounds to try and stem the flow of blood.

Even if Farhad were able to claim his sixty seven virgins .... his relationship with them would be on a purely spiritual basis. Farhad and his virgins would be "Just Good Friends".

Back in his water tank Nobby attacked his unexpected "appetiser" with gusto.

The penis was a disappointment .... it slipped down his throat in one swallow .... but the testicles were much better. Satisfyingly chewy, with a moist and flavoursome filling.

Nobby enjoyed the treat. Very pleasant .... but not so filling as to spoil his lunch. Excellent.

He headed back to the street .... but proceeded very cautiously when he spotted lots of people in bright yellow jackets .... and even more worrying .... three large white vans.

He eyed them cautiously. They seemed busy. They didn't seem to be searching for Nobby. He decided they couldn't be dog wardens. Keeping under cover as much as possible .... behind the cars on the right hand side of the street .... Nobby headed for his lunch at number four.

It was always good. He had no intention of missing it.

TWENTY FIVE

Roger stood looking at WPC Sue Witherspoon.

"What can I do.................", he said.

Sue took his hand between her own .... and looked into Roger's face. She knew he was heading into the frightening territory of deep shock trauma. If she could just keep him with her for another ten minutes.

"Roger", she said. "Do you understand how important it is to contain this area".

Roger looked at her.

Sue was horribly aware that he was struggling to stay with her.

"So what can I do ....", he said.

"Go up to the main road .... and don't allow anyone to come into this street", she said. "You won't have to do it for very long. I've got more police officers on their way .... but we absolutely must contain this area until they arrive".

Roger nodded .... and headed for the end of the street.

Sue watched him go .... and shook her head. A movement half way down the street caught her eye. An oldish lady had emerged onto the pavement.

Sue ran down to her.

"I'm WPC Susan Witherspoon", she said. "What's your name please".

"The lady looked up the street to the paramedics .... the Nissan slewed across the road .... the young man in black clothing still shouting on the ground.

"I'm Jill Saunders", she said. "What's happened .... can I help in any way".

Sue looked at her .... trying to assess her. Could she help.

"You're Susan Witherspoon", said Mrs Saunders. "I saw your picture in the Police Gazette. You're the sharp shooter".

"How..................", said Sue.

"I was in the force for twenty years", said Jill Saunders. "Retired five years ago .... but I still get the Gazette".

"Jill .... I could kiss you", said Sue. "Yes .... you can really help me. You probably know most of the people in the street. Can you stand there and watch .... and if anybody comes out .... please go and tell them to go back indoors .... to keep their family indoors .... until a uniformed officer tells them it's safe to come out".

"Got it", said Jill. "Luckily its Saturday afternoon. They're nearly all young professional people so most of them won't be home till six o'clock .... or even later".

Sue looked relieved.

"Leave it to me Sue", said Jill Saunders. "I'll watch the street for you. Get going .... you've got a lot to cope with".

Sue got half way back to where the paramedics were working on Lorraine .... when her phone rang.

It wasn't a number she recognised. She accepted the call.

"WPC Sue Witherspoon", she said.

"Sue .... it's Chief Constable John Haines here".

Janet had come good. Sue had got her senior officer.

"Sue", he said. "I've been asked to contact you on your personal mobile number. Are you able to speak freely".

Sue took a deep breath. She recognised the Chief Constable's voice. She'd seen him interviewed on local television.

"Yes Sir", she said. "Thank you so much for phoning me Sir".

"Sue", he said. "I need to understand the situation as it stands. Can you bring me up to date. Do your best to keep it concise please".

Sue looked around her.

"I'm off duty today sir" she said. "I was about to attend a hair salon appointment and parked my car in Keeling Street .... just off the High Street in Bracknell. Within moments of arriving here, I witnessed an attack by two young male armed assailants of possible Middle Eastern origin. They attacked two English girls leaving the salon. One of the girls is dead .... decapitated. The other is being treated by paramedics at the moment. She was stabbed in the chest with a bayonet. One assailant I believe to be dead. The other is severely wounded. The girls' Fiancees were waiting for them. They witnessed the attack. One of them is very severely traumatised. We'll need a councillor for him. At the moment I've had to enlist his help to stop people coming into the street. I'm also being assisted by a retired WPC who lives here. She is keeping the residents indoors for me. Sir I need help. I don't feel I have sufficient experience to handle the situation".

Sue ran out of breath.

"Sue", said the Chief Constable. "Take a big breath. You have done a fantastic job so far .... particularly in containing the area. Is it a through street Sue".

"No Sir", said Sue. "Keeling Street is a dead end".

"What sort of street is it Sue".

"Small terrraced houses. First time buyers. Mainly young professional couples .... a few older residents".

"Sue .... my message included the phrase "Time at the bar". Can you confirm that is still your opinion of the situation for me".

"Two seconds please Sir", said Sue.

She ran back to Farhad .... and turned her phone towards him. Farhad did the first useful thing he'd done that day. He shouted the cry of the Jiihaadi warrior.

"Alluah Akbhar".

Sue put the phone back to her ear.

"That was the surviving assailant Sir", she said.

"Sue .... are you .... or anyone else still at risk of further attack".

Sue looked at Farhad.

"No Sir", she said.

"Sue .... I'm on my way. I'm leaving my office now. I want you to act for me until I get to the scene. I'll end this call now Sue. They're bringing a car round for me now".

"Sir .... please .... before you go. The girl who was beheaded is Miss Deborah Wintersham .... Lord Wintersham's daughter".

There was a silence on the line.

"Sir....................".

"Is that information confirmed Sue".

"I'm afraid it is Sir. Her Fiancee saw it happen. I'm very concerned about him Sir. We'll need to get a statement from him .... we'll need a councillor for him Sir".

"Agreed Sue", said the Chief Constable. "I'll get Doctor Helen Lloyd there for you. If anybody can help .... it's Helen Lloyd".

"Thank you Sir".

"Sue .... until I get there you have my absolute authority to direct the operation. You've shown an extraordinary ability to understand the issues involved .... and you have my personal thanks".

"Thank you Sir".

"Sue .... you are now acting directly under my authority .... and I have to ask you to report only to myself .... do you understand".

"Yes Sir …. I understand".

"Sue …. I'm on my way".

He was gone.

There was a shout from the High Street end of the operation. Three marked cars had arrived with a total of ten uniformed officers. One of them was holding Roger in his arms. She ran to join them. She recognised most of them. Steve Smith had Roger in his arms. Roger was sobbing…. and holding on to Steve.

Steve looked at Sue with a bewildered expression.

"What do you want us to do Sue", he said. "We've been told you're in charge until the Chief gets here".

"I'm so pleased to see you all", said Sue.

She turned to Bill Right. He was the biggest and tallest officer amongst them.

"Bill", she said. "Just down the street there's a young man in a black track suit laying on the ground. He's bleeding from two injuries. He's guilty of murder …. and we want him alive. Find a free paramedic if he hasn't got one with him already. Keep him alive …. and keep him out of mischief for me".

Bill saluted …. and rushed off.

"Rhys", she said, to another of the new arrivals. "That's retired WPC Jill Saunders down there on the pavement. Please liaise with her …. and help her to keep people in their houses".

Sue detailed four officers to cordon off the entrance to Keeble Street …. instructing them to clear the cars for the ambulances to get away. She knew the paramedics would want to leave as soon as the injured were considered stable enough to travel.

She looked at her remaining officers. All youngish men.

"Can you start the door to door", she said. "Get the names and house numbers of anybody who witnessed what happened this afternoon. Ask if anybody got photographs or video footage. I think it's unlikely because of the speed and short duration of the incident .... but you can ask".

"May we ask what's happened", said the youngest of the men.

Sue thought for a moment. It seemed rude not to give them just a bare outline.

"Two young male assailants carried out an un-provoked attack on two females", she said. "As a result we have two dead .... and two severely injured. That's all I can say for the moment".

She looked at them.

"I'm really sorry", she said. "It's going to be a long afternoon for us".

The door to door detail moved off .

Sue looked at Steve Smith .... who was still holding Roger.

"I'll take him Steve", she said. "Go and relieve WPC Jill Saunders .... and ask her if she can get teas and coffees organised in her house. Tell her I'll be with her shortly".

Sue prised Roger from Steve Smith. She drew him close to her and pulled his head down on to her shoulder. He sobbed against her.

"I'm so grateful for your help Roger", she said. "What you did was absolutely essential until the back-up arrived".

Roger stirred against her. He stepped back and looked at Sue.

"Where's Isobel", he said. "Is she safe".

"Who is Isobel", said Sue.

"Friend of Debbie and Lorraine. She was in the hairdressers with them", said Roger.

Sue looked around.

"She must be still there then", she said. "We'll find her".

She took Roger's hand.

A garish BMW area car pulled in to the Street entrance. The rear doors opened. Sue recognised Chief Constable John Haines.

The Chief came straight to her.

"I'm Chief Constable John Haines. Are you Sue Witherspoon".

"Yes Sir"

"Sue", he said. "You've done a great job so far".

A very smartly dressed female police officer had joined them.

"Sue .... this is my Assistant CC Jayne Phipps".

"Ma'rm" said Sue.

Assistant CC Jayne Phipps winced.

"Sue", she said. "Please please call me Jayne .... Ma'rm is just a bit formal for me".

Sue smiled.

"Thank you", she said.

"John", said Jayne. "There's a cafe just across the street .... and we'll need an incident centre".

John Haines looked at the cafe. "The Adastra Coffee Shop".

"See if you can have it cleared for us in about fifteen minutes", he said. "That should give people time to finish their lunches. Tell the owners they'll be compensated for any losses .... and tell them we'll need them to stay open for us for teas and snacks all night. They might want to get extra staff in".

Jayne Phipps looked at Sue.

"Are you OK Sue", she said. "You appear to be dribbling".

"I'm Ok Ma'arm. Sorry .... dental appointment this morning. I had a filling".

Jayne looked at John Haines.

"Take care of her for me John", she said. "I'll go and commandeer that cafe for us".

She headed across the street.

Chief Constable John Haines turned to Roger Davies.

"Sir", said Sue. "This is Mr Roger Davies. Fiance to Miss Deborah Wintersham. He witnessed the attack".

John looked thoughtfully at Roger.

"Roger", he said. "I am most terribly sorry that we have to meet under such circumstances".

Roger nodded. His face was drawn. He seemed dazed.

"Can you help me find Isobel please", he said.

TWENTY SIX

Isobel came back in to the "Green Room" at "Thai Sing Can". Her period had started .... which was a relief .... because she could expect the pain to ease .... but for the moment .... she was very uncomfortable.

She sat down again .... waiting for the tablets to work.

Isobel began to pray again.

"Awesome God.........................".

The door from the stairs opened .... and a large black African lady came in to the room. She was wearing a colourful flower patterned frock. So colourful that Isobel wondered that she hadn't noticed her downstairs. Maybe she'd just arrived for her appointment.

She looked at Isobel.

"Are you Ok there little Sister", she said. "Your friends seem to have gone without you".

Isobel smiled at her

"I'm Ok", she said. "They'll be waiting round the corner in the car for me. I just had to pop up here for a moment".

"It's been a bit more than a moment sweetheart", the African lady said. "I was just thinking to myself .... Mama Kath .... you'd best get up them stairs and see if that Daughter is Ok. She must have some trouble .... she been gone so long".

"That really is so kind of you", said Isobel.

She stood and held out her hand.

"I'm Isobel", she said.

"And I'm Mama Kath", said the African lady, " .... and don't you be shaking no hands with me like I'm next President of the United States. You just come right here Isobel, and let Mama Kath give you a hug. 'Cause you is a sweetheart .... and Mama Kath can see that's true as true".

Isobel laughed, and let Mama Kath hug her.

"Now I'm guessing you're in some pain", said Mama Kath, "And I'll take a guess it's for that same old reason .... and us Sisters in the Lord just have to see our way through it".

Isobel nodded.

"Paracetamol any use to you", said Mama Kath. "Some in my bag right there if you need it".

Isobel shook her head.

"I've got some special medication from my Doctor", she said. "I took the tablets just now, and I'm waiting for them to kick in".

"Special medication", said Mama Kath. "Well I guess you got the same affliction as my younger Daughter Ella. Now my other two .... Jeanida, and Abigail .... well they're not too bothered .... but Ella. Well .... she has to suffer every month".

Isobel nodded.

"It's really bad this time", she said.

"Have you got started yet", said Mama Kath.

Isobel blushed.

"Just this afternoon", she said.

"You need ....".

Isobel blushed again.

"No", she said. "I'm sorted thank you".

"You're a pretty child when you blush like that", said Mama Kath. "But don't you feel no embarassment in front of me. I got three daughters not far off your age remember".

Isobel smiled at her.

"You're very kind to come up and see me like this", she said.

"Isobel", said Mama Kath. "If you'll just trust old Mama Kath for a moment .... well I can help you some with that pain you got. Will you trust Mama Kath Isobel".

Isobel nodded.

"Ok now", said Mama Kath. "You just lay right back there on that nice sofa and close your eyes now .... and I'll just lay my hand right there on your tummy. Now I'll be so gentle you'll hardly know that hand is there .... but you just breathe slow and easy, and let Mama Kath sing to you .... get you relaxed now".

Isobel felt Ok with this .... she didn't quite know why .... but she layed back, and closed her eyes. She felt Mama Kath sit down at her head .... and then she felt a hand layed very softly on her stomach.

"Now while I sing to you Isobel .... I want you to take yourself to Jesus .... and I want you to touch his robe, like that girl in the scriptures. You do know your scriptures don't you Isobel".

"I go to Church", said Isobel

"And Mama Kath was sure of that the moment she layed eyes on this Daughter", said Mama Kath. "Now you just lay there, and take yourself to Jesus, and touch His robe, and Mama Kath will sing a hymn .... and we'll see what Jesus can do .... cause if The Lord have a mind to .... then nothing ain't impossible for The Lord".

Isobel closed her eyes .... and Mama Kath sang softly to her .... and nobody else came in to the "Green Room" .... and Isobel remembered the story of the Woman with the Issue of Blood .... and she took herself to Jesus .... and she did as mama Kath said .... and she touched His robe.

And Isobel listened to Mama Kath sing .... and it was a voice like an Angel .... and Isobel must have slept .... because when she woke up the pain had gone .... and she felt healed in her body.

And she looked round for Mama Kath .... but Mama Kath had gone. The room was quiet .... and peaceful .... and Isobel was alone.

TWENTY SEVEN

Roger, Sue Witherspoon, and Chief Constable John Haines had just reached the door of "Thai Sing Can", when Isobel emerged .... clutching her second chocolate lollipop.

"Roger", said Isobel.

She looked at the Chief Constable's uniform .... then at the collection of Police cars in the High street.

"Roger", she said. "What's happened".

Roger looked at Isobel .... then took her in his arms. He looked to Sue Witherspoon.

Sue looked at the Chief Constable.

He nodded gently.

"Isobel .... I'm WPC Sue Witherspoon. I'm afraid I have to tell you that there has been an assault .... and, as a result, Miss Deborah Wintersham has lost her life. Miss Lorraine Makepiece has been severely injured .... but paramedics are assisting her at the moment".

Isobel was unable to speak. She looked from one to the other as though in the hope of finding some sense in what she had just been told.

She saw that it was true .... and she hugged Roger .... and she began to cry.

The Chief Constable put a protective arm around his party.

"I believe that we should all be more comfortable in the Coffee shop across the road", he said. "We have just taken it over as our incident room".

As he said this .... his phone bleeped. He read the text message.

"Yes", he said. "They're ready for us over there. We"ll all be better for a hot cup of tea".

....

The Chief Constable saw Roger, Isobel, and Sue Witherspoon across the road .... and into "The Adastra Coffee shop".

Jayne Phipps met them at the door.

As they went in .... the first of the ambulances came out of Keeling Street .... switched on it's blue lights and sirens .... and headed off up the High Street in the direction of Bracknell's Hospital. A second followed it a few moments later .... again with lights and sirens.

Roger's phone rang. It was John.

"Roger", he said. "Where are you".

"In the cafe across the street. The Police are setting it up as an incident room".

"Roger .... have you seen Isobel".

"She's here with me", said Roger.

"Thank God for that", said John.

"John", said Roger. "What's happening with Lorraine".

"The paramedics are hopeful", said John. "They don't think the bayonet hit her lung .... or anything else vital. I'm in the Ambulance with her. They've got a team waiting for her at the Hospital".

John's voice choked up.

"Rog", he said. "I'm so sorry about Debbie".

"Yeah", said Roger.

There was a silence on the line.

"Rog ... I left the keys for the Buick with the retired WPC. We parked outside her house".

"Yeah", said Roger.

There was another silence.

"Rog .... are you Ok ....".

"No", said Roger.

There was another long silence.

"Roger", said John. "We need to pray for Lorraine".

"And for Debbie", said Roger.

....

Roger looked around him. The cafe was filling with the men and women who would direct the investigation. The street outside was backing up with cars.

Roger sat down at a table.

Debbie wasn't his anymore. She belonged to all these strangers now.

Isobel sat down next to him.

Roger turned to her.

"I want her back Isobel", he said.

He collapsed onto the table .... and Isobel put her arms around him .... and held him as he cried.

She wished Mama Kath was there.

Isobel began to pray.

"Awesome God ....".

And Awesome God watched Roger cry. He hated to see Roger cry.

It was the worst part of being an Awesome God .... watching so many people cry.

TWENTY EIGHT

"Hello Isobel", a voice said quietly.

Isobel looked up in surprise. Standing next to the table was a smartly dressed, and very efficient looking lady, in her forties. She looked down at Isobel .... and reached out a hand.

"Doctor Samuels .... Verena", said Isobel in surprise. "How on Earth ....".

Doctor Samuels looked at Roger .... and turned back to Isobel.

"Isobel .... is this...............".

Isobel nodded.

"Roger", she said. "This is Doctor Verena Samuels".

Roger seemed to take some comfort from Isobels introduction. He looked up .... rose from his chair .... and took the Doctor's offered hand. His face was streaked with tears .... he made no effort to brush them away.

"Doctor Samuels", he said. "Thank you for coming".

Doctor Samuels looked at him long and thoughtfully.

"Roger", she said. "Do you think you might be able to find me a cup of tea".

Isobel was about to intervene .... when she suddenly realised that her friend Verena had just pushed Roger into taking the tiniest of steps back into normality.

Roger stared at her .... then he nodded.

"Milk and Sugar", he said.

"No sugar thank you", said Doctor Samuels.

Roger went towards the counter.

"And how are you Isobel", said the Doctor.

Isobel stood looking at her friend .... and the tears that she'd held back until now flooded from her.

"We've lost Debbie", she said. ".... and I wasn't even there to help her".

Doctor Samuels took Isobel in her arms .... and held her as she cried.

"Isobel", she said. "I am going to have to ask you for your help. I'm asking you .... because I know that you're tough enough to do the job".

Isobel looked at her friend.

"Isobel", I want you to lead Roger, and John, and Lorraine out of this .... and back into the real world. You have to be team leader for them. Helen Lloyd and I will advise you. But we can't be with them all the time .... in the way you can. And you can really help them all .... and yourself .... far far more than you could ever realise".

Isobels eyes filled with tears again .... and she clung to the Doctor for support.

The Doctor gently took her shoulders, and eased her away, until she could look into her face.

"They're all going to need your help Isobel", she said. "Do you remember that you were once told that you would be offered .... but that you could refuse".

Isobel shook her head in confusion.

"But how on Earth could you know that".

The Doctor squeezed Isobel's shoulders.

"Isobel .... will you help", she said.

Isobel nodded.

"I'm going to miss Debbie so much", she said. "She was such a kind girl".

"Isobel", said Doctor Samuels. "The Police are very keen to get a statement from Roger while the events are still fresh in his mind. I can use my influence to delay that .... but it will be much better for Roger if we can get it over and done with".

Isobel nodded .... and glanced towards the counter. Roger was being handed three mugs of tea. He had produced his wallet .... but the payment was waved away.

"Isobel",said the Doctor. " Just try to work with me for the moment. I'll offer to sit in with Roger on the statement, if he wants. After that I'll suggest a mild sedative to help him get through the first few hours. I'm hoping Helen will be here soon. All this is her speciality. But I have worked with her before .... so I'm confident I can keep things together until she arrives".

Roger came back with the teas.

"All on the house apparently", he said "Anybody want a sandwich".

"Let's have a few sips of our tea first shall we", said the Doctor. "Thank you so much for this Roger".

She smiled at him.

Roger nodded.

Doctor Verena Samuels suspected that Roger would be well aware that he was being led along a carefully scripted path .... a path designed to keep him from the worse the human mind could do.

She knew that Roger was beginning to feel surrounded. Surrounded by darkness .... and that this darkness would creep closer and closer over the next twenty four hours.

If Roger turned to face it .... then the darkess would recede a little. But the moment he took his eyes from it .... then it would exploit that lack of attention .... and creep closer again.

She watched Roger as he sipped his tea. She saw him facing the darkness .... and she saw very clearly that Roger knew only too well the horrors that lived within it.

Grief .... the unconsolable grief of loss. Despair .... hoplessness .... loneliness .... and depression.

A depression that could so easily lead to self destruction.

Verena Samuels glanced at the far corner of the room. A set of dark green screens had been set up to create a private space for statements to be taken.

Jayne Phipps came out from behind the screens .... and raised her eyebrows at the Doctor. Verena Samuels nodded to her.

"Roger", she said. "The Police would like to take a statement from you. That can only happen with my approval because you are now under my personal medical supervision. If you would like to wait for a while .... we will respect that. But it is my advice that it's better to get it over with now, if you can. I can sit in with you..................".

"Are you allowed to do that", asked Roger.

"Yes", said Doctor Samuels. "I am allowed".

Roger looked at her thoughtfully. He turned to Isobel questioningly.

Isobel looked at Roger. She felt so sorry for him. She wanted him to be done with this .... for it to be behind him.

She nodded.

Roger turned back to the Doctor.

"Let's get it done", he said. "But I would like you to sit in with me .... and I want somebody to look after Isobel while we're not with her".

Doctor Samuels took a deep breath. Roger had just given her one of the signs that Helen Lloyd had trained her to watch for. He had thought of somebody else's wefare. She looked over to Jayne Phipps .... and nodded.

ACC Phipps came over to the table.

"Jayne", said Doctor Samuels. "Roger is willing to make a statement now .... provided that I can sit in with him .... and providing that Isobel has somebody with her while we are absent".

She put the slightest of vocal emphasis on the second request.

ACC Jayne Phipps was quite experienced enough to see what the Doctor wanted.

She turned to Roger.

"Thank you for agreeing to do this", she said. "It will help us so much with the investigation. If you start .... and then feel unable to continue .... then just say .... and we'll postpone things".

Roger nodded.

"Isobel", she said. "I'll get WPC Susan Witherspoon to look after you. Please stay with her at all times until we get back here to you".

Isobel nodded. She began to cry again because she saw that she was safe enough here .... but only her total and absolute protection would satisfy Roger.

Sue Witherspoon appeared with chocolate biscuits and two teas. She sat down next to Isobel.

Roger looked at them.

"If Isobel needs the ladies room .... please go with her", he said to Sue Witherspoon.

WPC Witherspoon nodded.

"ROGER................. !!!!!!!!!!! ", said Isobel.

Roger bent down and kissed the top of her head.

"Girls always go together anyway", he said.

TWENTY NINE

Isobel looked at WPC Susan Witherspoon.

"You missed your hair dressing appointment", she said.

"How did you know that", asked Sue.

"Clive did my hair", said Isobel. "He was telling me that his next lady was going to be in the Olympics. He mentioned your name".

Sue smiled.

"There was an article in the local paper", she said.

"So how did you get into shooting", said Isobel.

"I grew up on a farm", said Sue. "My Father bought me a gun when I was seven. He showed me how to shoot clay pigeons".

"Are they really made of clay", said Isobel.

"Do you know …. I'm not sure what they're made of", said Sue. "But they turn into dust if you hit them square on".

"Can you tell me what happened this afternoon", said Isobel. "How did Debbie die".

Sue Witherspoon shook her head.

"I'm so sorry Isobel", she said. "I'm not allowed to talk about it. I was first officer on the scene …. and the Chief Constable has said I have to report to him first".

"But you saw what happened", said Isobel.

Sue Nodded.

"Yes", she said. "I saw what happened".

"Will you tell me when you can", said Isobel,

Sue Witherspoon looked at her.

"If you want me to .... then yes I will .... when I can", she said.

Isobel nodded.

Sue Witherspoon looked down at her tea.

"Isobel .... are you a close friend of Roger's", she said

"Not really", said Isobel. "I only met him on Wednesday evening. Debbie brought him to her Father's flat. He and Debbie had got engaged that morning. Debbie was so excited about it. We both were .... and you only had to see the way he looked at Debs to tell he was totally in love with her".

Sue Witherspoon nodded. She remembered Roger kneeling by Debbie's body .... and she could never forget the look of utter despair on his face when he had looked up at her and said: "This is Debbie .... we were going to get married".

"I'm worried about Roger", she said to Isobel.

Isobel looked up. There were tears on her cheeks.

"Doctor Samuels was asking me to look after Roger and John and Lorraine .... she wants me to be their "team leader".

Sue looked at Isobel carefully.

"I think Doctor Samuels made a very good choice Isobel", she said.

....

John Haines joined them at the table. He looked at Isobel.

"How is it with you lady", he asked her.

"Alright", said Isobel. "I just don't know what to do really".

CC Haines smiled at her.

"I believe you work for Lord Wintersham. He is on his way here at the moment. Lorraine's Father, Roger Makepiece, is on his way to the Hospital to join John. Lorraine is in the operating theatre at the moment. I haven't got any fresh news about her condition .... but the paramedics were fairly positive. I spoke to them just before they left".

"How is Lord Wintersham", said Isobel. "I should have told him the news about Debbie myself".

The Chief Constable shook his head.

"I told him, Isobel", he said

Isobel buried her face in her hands, and sobbed. The tears ran between her fingers onto the table cloth.

Sue Witherspoon reached over and took her hand.

"We're so sorry, Isobel", she said softly.

John Haines looked at this young WPC. He still didn't know the full story of her part in the incident this afternoon. But he did know that her presence of mind .... and her ability to see what needed to be done .... would mean that she would have promotion offers very soon. He would be lucky to keep her as a member of his force.

Chief Constable John Haines was a good man. He'd been appointed to his position because he was good at his job .... and he had the respect of everyone he worked with. And they knew that they had his respect .... he was on their side.

"Now Isobel", he said. "We would like it if you could all stay close to hand .... at least until tomorrow afternoon. I can't compel you to do that .... but it could help us with the investigation if you're all together .... and not to far away".

Isobel nodded.

"We've booked rooms for you all in a Hotel on the outskirts of town", he said. "In fact we've taken over the whole Hotel because there may be families who live in the street over there who haven't got friends or relatives to stay the night with. We've closed the street off, for the phorensic people to do their stuff".

"Is Debbie still there", asked Isobel. "Would you take me to see her please".

John Haines shook his head.

"The undertakers are going to take her to their chapel of rest, Isobel", he said. "It would be much better for you to visit her there".

Isobel looked at him.

"It's horrible isn't it", she said. "That's why you think I should wait. But Doctor Samuels asked me to look after Roger .... and I don't think I can do that unless I see what Roger had to see".

The Chief Constable reached across the table and took Isobel's hands. He examined her face. This was his decision to make .... and there was every sensible reason for him to say no.

He looked long and thoughtfully at the table. Eventually he nodded.

"I'm going to take you to see Debbie", he said.

He stood.

"Sue", he said. "I'm going to ask you to come with us".

Sue Witherspoon looked towards the screens at the other end of the room.

"Roger will be at least another twenty minutes making his statement", said the Chief Constable.

"Are you really sure about doing this Isobel", said Sue Witherspoon.

Isobel nodded.

"I have to", she said. "I have to be able to relate to where Roger is in his mind .... and I know that Debbie would want me to do what I can for Roger .... and her Father. I have to see her".

John Haines took off his coat. He came around the table .... and as Isobel stood .... he slipped the coat around her shoulders.

They left the "Adastra", and stepped out onto the pavement. It was beginning to get dark …. and a thin sleet had begun to fall. The whole area was floodlit …. the entrance to Keeling Street cordoned off.

The Chief Constable unfurled an umbrella. He escorted Isobel and Sue Witherspoon across the road. They stepped carefully over cables that ran in all directions. Flashing blue lights reflected from the falling sleet. There were three officers standing on duty by the metal barriers. They looked cold.

They saluted the Chief Constable.

The most senior officer quietly moved the barrier aside …. allowing them to pass through.

John Haines nodded to him

"Thank you Sergeant", he said.

....

Six streets away, an old man sat by the fire. He patted his dog.

"Killing Street", he said. "Where on Earth did he get that from. I haven't heard it called Killing Street for sixty years or more".

He picked up the remote control for his television set …. and pointed it at the screen. He ruffled the dog's ears.

"Well", he said. "Let's watch the news …. see what's been happening in the World shall we".

Part Two

Sandbanks

Fog on the seashore, fisherman's lights

Mist in your hair, I recall those nights

Cold our noses, hot your kiss

Beach hut alcove, that was bliss

We loved each other, we knew how

But that was then, and this is now

And so I asked you, you said yes

I meant for ever, will you confess

That you still love me, or must I allow

That that was then, and this is now.

N.S.W.   1978

ONE

Miss Julie Parker Smith sat idly tracing patterns in the dust at her feet. She looked up, and smiled at Roger.

"I am so looking forward to a shower", she said.

They were sitting under a stunted olive tree, trying to take every advantage of the small patch of shade that it was able to offer.

Roger sipped from a can of Coca Cola. Julie was half way down a plastic bottle of water.

"How much further have we got to go", he said. "I'm a car dealer. Car dealers don't do walking".

Julie screwed the cap back on to her water bottle.

"About another five miles", she said. "About an hour and a half. John and Peter timed it so that we should arrive in the early evening".

Roger sighed

"This has got to be the craziest thing I've ever done", he said.

Julie looked long and thoughtfully at her companion.

"But it's your only chance to get her back", she said ."He is the only person in all of human history that can help you".

Roger shook his head.

"But I'm going to ask Him to break the rules .... simply because I want them broken".

"He's broken those rules before", said Julie.

Roger nodded.

"I know", he said. "But will He break them for me".

"I think that you have to ask", said Julie."And by doing that .... you'll know that you have done absolutely everything you possibly could to get her back .... more than you could ever have thought possible".

Again .... Roger nodded.

"Are you still feeling OK about being involved in this", he said.

"Roger", said Julie. "I promise you .... I'm absolutely fine with it. I have met Him before, remember".

Roger stared at Julie. He still found it difficult to accept that this young woman had actually met the man they were going to see. She had helped rescue Him from execution. She had helped to tend His wounds. And she had been the communication between Him and the rest of her team.

And that, of course, Roger reflected, was why Miss Julie Parker Smith was sitting there drawing patterns in the dust at her feet. Because Julie spoke many languages. But what counted above everthing else .... she spoke the language of The Holy Land in the first century. She spoke Aramaic.

Roger reached into the folds of his long robe. There was a pocket in there somewhere. He produced a bar of fruit and nut chocolate.

"Chocolate......", he asked Julie.

"Wow", said Julie. "You remembered to bring chocolate".

 She reached for the bar.

"So what is it with girls and Chocolate", he asked Julie.

"Do you want the scientific answer .... or the emotional answer", she laughed.

"Give me both", said Roger.

Julie snapped the bar in two, and passed half back to Roger.

"A woman's hormone levels vary a lot through the course of her month", explained Julie. Chocolate helps us to produce Serotonin, which is the "happiness hormone". So there are times of the month when we just crave chocolate".

"And the emotional answer", said Roger.

Julie chewed her first piece of fruit and nut reflectively.

"It's just absolutely gorgeous", she said. "Almost better than sex".

"But not as good as sex with Mark", said Roger.

Julie raised her eyebrows in mock disapproval.

"Mr Davies", she said."Your conversation borders upon the inappropriate".

Then she laughed.

"No", she said. "Not even the best Belgian chocolate is as good as sex with my man".

"I liked him a lot when we had that meeting", said Roger. "Is it true that he's Italian".

"His Father is Italian", said Julie, "but his mother is English .... and he grew up in England".

"You make a great couple", said Roger.

"Thank you", said Julie. "I fell for him the very first moment we met. I feel absolutely loved, and safe, and protected when I'm with him. And he is always so gentle with me".

Roger watched the love in her expression as she spoke.

"And yet", said Julie. "I watched him kill four men in as many seconds .... and it appeared to have no emotional effect on him whatsoever".

They both fell silent. Roger stared at the dusty ground. He had seen a person killed. The girl he loved most in all the World. The girl he had asked to marry him. The Girl who had said Yes.

Julie saw his mood.

"Roger", she said, "It's time we got moving again".

They stood .... and stretched ....and made their way back to the road. They turned to the south-east and took up the easy, but steady pace, that Mark had taught them.

"So how safe are we here", asked Roger.

"What .... in the first century Holy Land you mean", said Julie. "Fairly safe actually. The Romans are in charge of law and order .... and believe me .... there are some very nasty punishments waiting for anybody who steps out of line.

I suppose I wouldn't want to walk a jouney of this length on my own. But with a man, who people would assume is my husband, yes we're quite safe".

She reached into her robes .... and to Roger's astonishment .... brought out an automatic pistol.

"Besides", she said. "Mark gave me this nice little Walther PPK .... and that will dissuade anyone from bothering us".

She saw Roger's nervous expression.

"Don't worry", she said. "I had an afternoon on the range with it .... and Mark .... of course. I know how to be safe with it".

"May I look at it", said Roger.

"No .... you may not", said Julie. "You'd get it all dirty".

Roger sighed. They walked on steadily.

"Roger", said Julie, eventually. "I never understood how you knew about this .... I mean, how you knew what we're doing is possible. John and Peter are very very secretive about it. How did you find out about their operation".

There was a long silence. Julie glanced at Roger, but waited patiently for him to speak.

"It was Debbie's duffle coat", he said.

Julie waited.

The first few days after Debbie died were bad", said Roger. "Very very bad.

Doctor Samuels wanted to give me a course of sedatives. She said they would help me get through the first few days. But I wouldn't let her do it. I told her that I knew I would have to go through Hell itself .... but that I would go through it. And I would get out the other side. And the sooner I opened the door, and went in, then the sooner I could get through .... and out the other side again".

Roger's voice choked.

Julie looked at him. She had thought that her man Mark was brave .... but she began to see that Roger was brave too ..... but in a quite different way to Mark.

"So Doctor Samuels made me agree to something", said Roger. "She made me agree that Isobel would be with me all the time. With me night and day .... until she herself .... Doctor Samuels, that is .... agreed that I was through the worst of it".

Julie had glanced quickly at Roger when he mentioned Isobel's name. A few days ago she had seen Isobel and Roger together....and she had spotted something. It was so very obvious. At least .... it was obvious to Julie. She wondered if it was quite so obvious to Roger. She suspected that it wasn't.

Roger had gone silent again.

"The duffle coat", prompted Julie.

"You sort of stop living when something like that happens", said Roger. "You exist .... and most of the time you wish you could stop existing because of the never ending pain of it.

Your mind tracks through the event over and over again .... and you wish that you had run just that little bit faster .... or that you had shouted a warning just that little bit earlier .... or that you had arrived in the street just that little bit later. At the moment when the girls were coming out of the hair salon .... because if you had ....".

Julie took Roger's hand into her own.

After a while .... he began again.

"But Isobel was there through every moment of that Hell", said Roger. "When I cried .... Isobel cried with me. And when Isobel cried .... then I cried with her. We did it a day at a time. And if we couldn't do it a day at a time .... then we did it an hour at a time .... and if we couldn't do it an hour at a time .... then we did it a minute at a time. And she never left me. She sat on the edge of my bed .... and she would hold my hand till I fell asleep. And the moment I woke in the mornings .... and that was worse of all .... she was right there to hold my hand again".

"Did you see Doctor Samuels", asked Julie.

"Yes", said Roger. "She .... or Helen Lloyd .... would visit every other day. In fact it was every day at first .... for the first ten days or so. They were both fantastic. Helen Lloyd was very clever at suggesting these little tiny things that sort of helped to ease your mind away from the pain .... and from the endless replay of the events".

"What about John and Lorraine", asked Julie. "Did you see them much".

"Things weren't quite so bad for John", said Roger. "Or .... at least .... I thought they weren't. Lorraine was recovering well. John hardly ever left the Hospital. I found out later that they did have a scare with her condition. Her temperature suddenly shot up two days after the stabbing .... and they suspected an infection. But she responded to the anti-biotics .... and she came through. I didn't know there were problems with John. Not until Lorraine herself phoned me about ten days after the attack. She told me that John was scared to see me. He blamed himself for not being quick enough to save the girls .... and he felt a great sense of guilt that his fiancee had survived .... but Debbie had died. Lorraine asked me to go and see him. He was still in the Hotel that the Police put us in that first night".

"You went", asked Julie.

"I had to ... the moment I knew the score", said Roger. "Isobel went with me. It got pretty emotional. John has a lot of French blood in his veins .... so he can be very un-english in that respect. And, of course, he hadn't had Isobel's support in the way I had. Isobel saw that she hadn't been there for John as much as she could have .... and she got upset. It wasn't a meeting I would ever want to go through again".

"How did you work it out", said Julie.

"We all went to visit Lorraine in the Hospital", said Roger. "And this was the amazing thing.....it was Lorraine who sort of pulled the team together again. She said we could never ever get over what had happened to us all .... but that we would have to find a way to live with it. That's what we should work together on .... to find a way to live again .... even though we had to live with Debbie's loss".

I remember her saying one last thing before the nurse threw us out .... it was past Lorraine's bed time.

She told me that she and John would delay their wedding day .... until I could join them in making it a double event.

I didn't know what she meant. Still don't.............".

Julie glanced quickly at Roger again.

"So where on Earth does a duffle coat come into all this", she said.

Roger smiled.

"Debbie's Father is into classic cars", he said. "He has a 1959 Buick ragtop .... a convertible. The first time I saw the car, it had Debbie's duffle coat laying on the rear seat".

Julie looked puzzled.

"I don't see ......", she said.

"After that meeting in Lorraine's hospital room", said Roger. "It was like things started to get a little bit easier. It was like the really sharp edge of the pain had gone. It was still bad .... but not like it had been. I began to sleep through the night again. I had been waking up in the middle of the night sobbing .... and Isobel would calm me down .... and do her best to get me off to sleep again. And it was rough on her .... because I knew that she was feeling Debbie's loss just as much as I was. But women are tough in that way. They create life .... and they know damn well that life has to find a way to go on .... whatever happens".

Julie nodded.

"John Steinbeck says that in "The Grapes of Wrath", she said.

"So Isobel and I had a whole nights sleep …. for the first time", said Roger. "But I had a dream. Not a complicated one. It was just that I was looking at Debbie's duffle coat laying on the rear seat of Lord Wintersham's Buick convertible. And in the dream I was puzzled. It was like what I was looking at was a puzzle …. or a riddle …. and it was my job to solve the puzzle. I had that same dream every night for the next ten days".

"Did you tell Isobel about the dream", said Julie.

"Yeah", said Roger. "We talked about it a lot …. but Isobel thought it was my puzzle to solve. And on the eleventh morning, I woke up …. and I had it. It wasn't the duffle coat I was meant to be questioning. It was the car seat it was laying on".

"How could the seat be the answer", said Julie.

"It's a 1959 Buick", said Roger. "Which means the car is fifty eight years old. But the rear seat was virtually as new. The colours weren't faded. The material was unmarked and soft".

"Re - upholstered", asked Julie.

"Nope", said Roger. "Couldn't be done …. not in coloured leather like the original. You just cannot buy material like that anymore".

"Then what ……", said Julie.

"I phoned Lord Wintersham …. and I can tell you that I was pretty excited …. because if I was right ……………

I asked him how old his Buick was".

"Roger", he said. "It's a 1959 Buick …. you know that".

"Lord Wintersham", I said. "I know it's a 1959 Buick. I'm asking you how old the car is".

There was a very long silence on the other end of the phone. A very long silence.

"Lord Wintersham", I said. "Please please tell me how old your car is".

I heard him take a deep breath.

"It's three years old", he said.

Julie stared at Roger. She smiled.

"And if a car that was built fifty eight years ago, is just three years old", she said. "There is only one possible solution".

Roger smiled at her, and nodded.

"Time travel", he said.

"I get it", said Julie. "And you realised that if it is possible to travel back to 1959 .... then it must be just as possible to travel to other points in time".

"That's what I got so excited about", said Roger. "And I was right".

"And here we are", said Julie.

"Crazy isn't it", said Roger.

TWO

"In actual fact", said Roger. "I didn't have what we are doing as part of my plan. My idea was much more direct. I would simply ask to be sent back to that street in Bracknell an hour before the attack".

"And how would you have handled things if you could have done that", asked Julie.

"There were lots of ways I could have handled things". said Roger. "I had one or two ideas .... but it never got that far because John and Peter wouldn't do it for me".

Julie nodded.

"It's the "Time line" problem", she said.

"I know", said Roger. "Peter pointed out that although I could, in theory, stop the girls from leaving the salon ..... that would leave their assailants facing little more than possible charges for carrying offensive weapons in the car. Without any previous records of terrorist activity .... they would probably have been released with a caution. And that's if I could persuade the Police to come and investigate in the first place".

"And leave them free to strike again wherever they chose", said Julie. "That's the problem. You can't arrest somebody for something they haven't done. Until they commit the atrocity .... they are just as innocent as the rest of us".

"There was no doubt in our minds", said Roger, "that they would plan another attack .... and if they did, there might not be a Sue Witherspoon there to limit their activities. There's no doubt that Sue saved at least two lives that afternoon .... possibly more".

"What happened to Sue Witherspoon", asked Julie.

"She was suspended from duty, but on full pay, pending the investigation. But her Boss had instructions to accept her resignation from the force .... non negotiable. Sue was wanted elsewhere. Three days later she was interviewed for a post with another organisation. They had a letter of introduction from John Haines on the table. She got the job".

"What does that organisation do", said Julie.

"They do their best to make sure incidents like Keeling Street don't happen", said Roger. "If you'd been there that afternoon .... you would have seen Sue Witherspoon in action. She had a lid on the situation almost from the word go. She just didn't quite manage to save Debbie ....".

Have you seen Sue since that afternoon", asked Julie.

"Yes", said Roger. "She had promised to tell Isobel what happened .... but she had to get John Haines' permission to do that".

"And she got permission ....",

"Yes", said Roger. "So Sue spent a couple of hours with Isobel at my place. I didn't want to sit in on that .... and I didn't ever tell Isobel what I saw. Couldn't bring myself to face it".

Roger fell silent again.

The road stretched out ahead of them. Their shadows grew longer as the afternoon lengthened. The heat began to ease a little. In three hours of walking they hadn't seen another living thing.

"We are sure about being on the right road.....", said Roger.

"Sure as we can be", said Julie. "We've followed Peter's instructions to the letter. We should see the house in another twenty minutes or so".

"And Peter is certain He'll be there ....", said Roger.

"Yes", said Julie. "But don't ask me how he knows".

"So if He is there", said Roger, "this will be the second time you have met Him .... but the first time He has met you".

"Confusing, isn't it", said Julie.

They walked on.

Roger considered his situation.

He was walking along a road in the first century Holy Land, and in about thirty minutes, he would knock on a door, and ask to speak with a young man called Jesus of Nazareth. He would ask that young man for a favour. That Roger's Fiancee, Miss Deborah Wintersham, be brought back from the dead.

Not much to ask then.

Roger would have thought the idea to be completely crazy .... but to his continuing astonishment, the team, of whom Julie was a member, didn't seem to find it astonishing at all.

As Peter, their technical guru, had said.

"Roger .... there has only ever been one man who can do this for you. And we have the means to allow you to meet Him .... and to ask the question.

And remember .... He has done it for others .... at least three times that we know about".

Peter had looked up from his computer screen. He was designing a Church.

"What colour cushions should I have on the chairs", he asked Roger.

"Blue", said Roger. "I like blue".

"Blue it is then", said Peter. He clicked on blue.

"Quantity .... ", he pondered. "Well .... two hundred should do the job".

He clicked on two hundred, confirmed the delivery address, clicked on PAY, waited for confirmation of his order, and closed his laptop. He sat back in his chair.

"Churches'R'us", he smiled. "Great company to deal with. Everything you need to put a Church together".

....

The house stood fifty metres back from the road. The buildings were surrounded by a high wall. It was a dwelling that spoke of some prosperity. The roofs were tiled rather than thatched. The arched entrance way, set centrally into the outer wall, was closed by a pair of decorated wooden doors. The metal hinges were fashioned as vine tendrils, snaking across the sun bleached wood, the bunches of grapes formed in relief by skilful carving of the doors themselves. From the doors, two paths ran, at angles, to meet the roadway. One to the left, and one to the right. The triangle of ground between them was planted with an olive tree. It was the only tree visible in either direction, and stood as a sentinel for the premises. There was a table set beneath its branches, with two benches, all much weathered, but sound, and well made, by somebody with an eye for proportion.

One of the doors in the outer wall opened. There was a pause .... and then a large colourfully dressed black lady emerged into the evening sun. She was carrying a large tray which bore three cups, and three platters. There were olives in a wooden bowl, a large piece of cheese, a loaf of bread, and another bowl containing figs.

She paused, and examined the tray, as though checking her wares. Seemingly satisfied, she carried the tray to the table, set it down, and returned to the entrance. She went back inside, but emerged again almost immediately, with a corked pottery flagon. It's porous sides glistened with beads of condensation. She set the wine, for such it was, on the table, then stood with her hand to her brow, looking up the road to the place where it topped a slight rise in the ground. She shook her head thoughtfully, and sat down, as though to wait. She uncorked the flagon, and poured herself a cup of the wine. She recorked, then moved the wine carefully out of the sun, so that it should remain cool. She sat, sipping the wine, and smiling, and watching the road away to her left.

Ten minutes later, her patience was rewarded. Two figures came up over the rise, walking steadily. As they drew closer, she nodded to herself, and smiled. She could see a young man, and a young woman.

She sat patiently, until the couple approached. They slowed a little in the last few paces, but, after a word to her companion, the young woman stepped forward confidently. She smiled.

"I am sorry to disturb your meal", she said, "But I wish you a good evening, and wonder if you might tell me whose dwelling we have come upon".

The black lady rose, and came around the table.

"May the Lord be praised", she said. "And I do declare to the Lord that you have the prettiest intonation of Aramaic that I have had the pleasure to hear".

She laughed.

"So will you come to Mama Kath for a hug, Miss Julie Parker Smith", she said, "And you in your turn, Mr Roger Davies. And you are welcome in the sight of the Lord, and you truly are a great pleasure for Mama Kath to behold".

Julie stepped forward into Mama Kath's outstretched arms. They embraced.

"You speak English ....", said Julie in astonishment.

Mama Kath laughed .... and held Julie at arm's length, beaming at her.

"Well praise be to The Lord, that He has seen fit in His wisdom, to grant old Mama Kath The Gift of Tongues", she said. "And it is a gift that has it's uses in the service of The Lord, and I count it at His Blessing".

Roger stood waiting. Mama Kath turned to him.

"And now you Mr Roger", she said. She took him into her arms, then pressed his head against her shoulder, and held him there.

"You have come with a great sorrow", she said. "As many come with great sorrow. But they come with hope .... and that hope is well met".

And Mama Kath laughed, and held Roger at arm's length, as she had done with Julie, and she looked Roger up and down, and she shook her head and smiled.

"Because there ain't nothing in the world The Lord can't do if The Lord have a mind to", she said. "But He likes to be asked .... and here you are to ask him .... and His will be done".

"He is within", she said, "but He is a might busy at this moment. Will you take a cup of wine with Mama Kath, and rest your legs .... and here is food after your journey".

"We would love to try the wine", said Julie.

Mama Kath poured two more cups and passed them to her guests .... Julie first. They all sat. Julie sipped from her cup, and smiled at Mama Kath.

"This is a very good wine", she said. "It's a ruby cabernet isn't it".

"Well", said Mama Kath, sipping from her own cup, "I believe it's well enough .... even if it is scarce twenty minutes since He changed it from water in a pail".

Roger and Julie stared at her in astonisment.

Mama Kath looked to the sky and laughed, and shook her head.

"Oh Glory be to the Lord .... Glory be to the Lord", she said "Oh the expression on your faces when I told you that. Oh it was a picture to be seen .... and a picture welcome in the sight of The Lord".

She laughed .... placing her wine on the table lest she spill it.

"Oh" she said. "Water into wine" isn't by any means the least of the Gifts. Even if .... may the lord preserve us ...., that young Mark saw fit to leave it out of the list at the end of his Gospel .... and I do wonder if he did it of a purpose .... headstrong that he is".

Roger and Julie stared at her. They wondered if Mark was here .... just a few yards away.

 "No", said Mama Kath, "It is by no means the least of the Gifts .... paticularly when you have guests upon you, and the nearest supermarket is two thousand years away".

She laughed at her joke, then passed around the platters, and they helped themselves to cheese and olives and bread and the figs.

"This is wonderful cheese", said Roger.

"Ah .... and you are a man who appreciates a good cheese", said Mama Kath. "Mary from Magdala has a skilled hand at matters in the dairy. She is a blessing to us all in so many ways".

Julie looked up.

"Is Mary of Magdala here at the moment then", she asked.

"Not just at this moment", said Mama Kath. "She and the other Mary have returned to Magdala for a few days. The other women have gone with them. So it's very much a "lads weekend" in the house at the moment .... with the exception of Mama Kath, of course .... to keep an eye on them all".

They ate quietly for a while .... and seeing that they seemed content .... Mama Kath set down her cup, and turned to Roger.

"Mr Davies", she said. "You could perform me a small service if you were willing".

"Happy to oblige", said Roger.

"If you look across the road there", said Mama Kath. "You will see a path that runs directly away from the house. Follow it for two hundred yards or so, as it drops gently down hill. At the bottom of the slope you will find a well. There is a windlass, and wooden pails, ready for use. Would you draw a pail of water from the well, and bring it back for us".

"Happy to", said Roger. He stood, took two more olives, and a scrap of cheese, and started on his errand.

"Roger", Mama Kath called. "Perhaps you might rest at the well for ten minutes before you start back".

She glanced at Julie.

"Men are a Blessing from the Lord, and that cannot be denied .... but we Sisters in the Lord's Grace have matters to discuss that are not for the ears of men .... though the Lord will hear them, non the less".

"Give us fifteen minutes Roger", Julie called to him.

Roger nodded, and turned back to the path. Julie and Mama Kath watched him go. He raised a hand in salute before they lost sight of him into the lower ground.

"That is a fine young man in the sight of the Lord", said Mama Kath .... by way of opening the conversation.

"I believe he is", said Julie. "He has a good reputation amongst those who know him".

Mama Kath nodded.

"But he suffers much grief", said Mama Kath. "And what happened was a great vexation to the Lord. A very great vexation. And the Lord heard the prayers for Deborah, and He took Deborah into His care .... and I promise you, Miss julie Parker Smith, that Deborah sits at this moment safe in the care of the Lord .... and always will".

"That is good to hear", said Julie.

"But what I have to tell you now", said Mama Kath ,"is that the Lord heard another prayer. A prayer from a young lady named Isobel".

Julie looked at Mama Kath. They held each other's eyes for a few moments.

"I have met Isobel", said Julie.

"And she is a sweet child in the sight of the Lord", said Mama Kath, "And I have been blessed to meet Isobel ... and blessed again .... in that I was able to offer her some assistance as she suffered, as we sisters in the Lord must suffer on occasion".

Julie winced.

"Isobel looked after Roger in the days following Debbie's death", she said. "The Doctor, who was called in to council Roger, asked Isobel to be with him".

Mama Kath nodded.

"That sweet child was told long ago that she would be asked .... but that she could refuse".

"I don't think that Isobel would refuse to help someone .... not if it was in her power to do so", said Julie.

"No", said Mama Kath. "We know that she would do anything to help Roger get through his grief. And she has prayed to the Lord .... and the Lord is troubled".

"What has she prayed", said Julie. Then her cheeks coloured ....

"I'm so sorry", she said. "I shouldn't have asked that".

Mama Kath reached for Julie's hand.

"And strictly speaking", she said. "I shouldn't have told you .... but the Lord is sorely troubled. Sorely troubled indeed".

Julie sat quietly. She wasn't sure what to say. She was still fairly new to praying herself .... and she was far from certain about the protocols associated with it.

"Well .... if I can help in any way ....", she said, eventually.

Mama Kath smiled at Julie.

"Isobel offered to surrender her own life to the Lord .... if the Lord would restore Deborah to Roger", said Mama Kath.

Julie stared at her. There was a long silence.

"To offer up your own life .... for someone else .... is a very serious prayer. A very serious prayer indeed", said Mama Kath. "It's not a prayer that the Lord can take lightly. And the Lord is much troubled".

"So if Roger's request is granted", said Julie. "Would the Lord require Isobel to fulfil her promise".

Mama Kath looked at Julie long and thoughtfully.

"Isobel has prayed to the Lord", she said. "And the Lord must answer that prayer. It was for this purpose that mankind was taught to pray".

"But Roger must know of this", said Julie.

"He must not know of it", said Mama Kath. "Isobel went into her closet and she prayed in secret. Isobel's prayers must remain between her and her God".

"But you have told me", said Julie.

"I have told you", said Mama Kath. "Why do you think that I have told you Julie".

They sat there in silence. Julie's hand still held gently in Mama Kath's.

"Julie", said Mama Kath. "I think you may have something that could help us. You are a perceptive young woman..............".

Julie stared down at the table Her eyes traced the grain of the weather bleached wood. She was well aware that her cheeks had coloured. She sat thinking .... then she looked up .... into Mama Kath's eyes.

"Isobel is in love with Roger", said Julie.

Mama Kath nodded.

"But she was a friend to Debbie. She loved Debbie very much .... like a sister".

"Yes .... I believe so", said Julie.

Mama Kath sighed.

"It was neccessary for the Lord to create love", she said. "That a man should leave his mother and father .... and that he should bond to his wife".

Julie smiled. She recognised the piece of scripture.

"Yes", said Mama Kath. "And the Lord saw fit to make it the strongest of the Human emotions".

Julie nodded.

"So", said Mama Kath, "Does Roger know that Isobel is in love with him".

Julie shook her head.

"No", she said. "I really think he doesn't know .... and I think that he hasn't spotted it because he is still totally absolutely completely in love with Debbie".

Mama Kath smiled at her.

"Ah", she said. "The difference between men and women is a Glory to the Lord. The woman will see a thousand men .... even ten thousand men .... and only one will suit her for her partner. That one and only that one .... and it is by the Lord's will for it to be so .... because she must bear that man's children".

"But a man is different", said Julie.

"He is", said Mama Kath. "His mother had dark hair, so he thinks that he could only love a dark haired girl. But along comes a young woman with fair hair, and she sets her sights upon that young man .... and she makes herself pleasant in his company. And after a while that young man begins to think, "Well this fair haired girl is pleasant company. She is making herself pleasant to me. Perhaps I could love this young woman, though she is not dark haired in my sight".

And that same young man. His mother had a slender figure, and he thinks to only love a girl with a slender figure. But along comes a young woman with a fuller figure, and she sets her sights upon that young man .... and she makes herself pleasant in his company. And after a while that young man says to himself: "Well I thought only to love a slender figured girl .... but this young lady of fuller figure is making herself pleasant in my company. She is making herself pleasant to me. Perhaps I could love this woman ... though she is not slender in my site".

And before that young man knows where he is .... he is married to that fair haired girl, with the fuller figure .... and he loves her, and extols her virtues in his mind".

Julie laughed at Mama Kath's description of a man's ability to adapt to circumstance.

"Ain't love grand", she said.

"Designed by the Lord Himself .... in all His wisdom .... said Mama Kath.

Roger came up over the rise carrying a pail of water.

"What's going to happen about Isobel", asked Julie.

Mama Kath smiled.

"The Lord can work in mysterious ways", she said. "And the Lord will have a plan. He always has a plan".

THREE

Roger placed the pail of water carefully by the tree. He sat down again with Mama Kath, and Julie.

"So how did the "Girl Talk" go then", he asked them.

Julie laughed.

"It went well", she said.

"So do men do "Girl talk", asked Julie.

"No", said Roger. "We never say anything to each other that we wouldn't say in front of our ladies".

He gazed at the sky .... a smile flickering on his lips.

"Ooooooh", said Julie. " You are such a fibber Roger. I don't believe that for a moment".

"True enough", said Roger, continuing to direct his gaze to the sky.

Julie looked to Mama Kath for help.

"I do declare in the presence of the Lord", said Mama Kath, "that men have greater virtue than women in this respect .... although, I do confess, it is hard to believe".

Roger smirked at Julie.

She made a face in return. They laughed.

"Well", said Mama Kath, beginning to rise. "It's time for you both to go and break up the "lad's weekend" if you've a mind to".

As she finished saying this, the entrance doors to the house flew open, and a young woman came out, in a flurry of robes. She hurried away on the path to their left. When she reached the road .... she turned to smile at them .... and then broke into a run. They watched her disappear in a small cloud of sunlit dust.

"Let me guess", said Julie. "Her daughter was possessed by demons".

"And Somebody has just been taught a lesson", said Mama Kath.

"Come then", she said. "It's time to meet the Master of this house".

They gathered up the remains of the meal. Mama Kath took the tray, leaving the wine flagon for Roger. He picked up the pail of water. She led them through the open doors into the inner courtyard, and then to another pair of doors into the house proper. Here she stopped.

"Just knock .... and enter", she said. "You are expected. I have the blessing of employment in this house, and I must away to the rear quarters to tend to the children. I must see that they take to their beds with clean hands, clean faces, and prayers said".

"That was the routine in our house when I was a little girl", said Julie. "Things don't change much do they".

"They cannot change", said Mama Kath. "It is the responsibility of all parents to bring up their children to be a pleasure in the sight of the Lord".

She laughed.

"Or at least to try", she added.

Roger offered her the flagon .... now more than half emptied .... but she told him to leave it by the door.

"Put the flagon of wine into the pail", she said, "and it will remain cool".

Roger and Julie stood at the doors. They took a deep breath. Julie knocked. They heard a voice call a greeting. Roger pulled the latch cord. The door swung open.

Julie entered first, Roger immediately behind her. It was a large room .... wider than it was deep .... and very nicely proportioned, with good natural light. A cooking fire smouldered on a hearth. There were several tables, and many chairs, scattered around the room .... mostly occupied by a group of young men who talked and laughed and argued and ate and drank. The buffet style meal appeared to be nearly over .... although there was still food in plenty on a side table.

The young men looked up as Roger and Julie entered .... but perceiving that their business was with their Master .... they returned to their conversations.

Julie walked straight to the young man who sat against the rear wall .... a little apart from His companions. He seemed lost in thought .... but would occasionally glance up at His friends .... enjoying their presence .... but content to sit quietly and observe them.

As Julie approached, the young man stood up, and smiled at them.

Without any hesitation, Julie went down onto her knees before Him, then pressed her forehead to His bare feet. Roger was a little taken aback by this .... but he also knelt .... and bowed his head.

The young man laughed .... and spoke gently to them.

"He says we may rise", said Julie. "He says that the Blessing of His Father is upon us .... and that we may speak freely in His presence".

Jesus of Nazareth (for it was He) beckoned that two chairs be brought for them. They all sat.

Jesus turned to July. He looked quietly at her .... then began to speak. He paused to allow Julie to translate.

"He knows why you are here", Julie explained to Roger. "But He must hear your request from your own lips .... and He promises that "He that hath ears to hear .... let Him hear".

"Oh .... and He said that last bit because He thought you would like it", added Julie.

While Julie had translated for Roger .... Jesus had requested that wine be brought for His guests.

A very young man .... barely more than a boy .... appeared with two cups of white wine.

Jesus spoke to Julie again .... apparently introducing the young man to them.

Julie Blushed. She turned to Roger.

"This is Mark", she said. "And yes .... it is the Mark who will write the earliest Gospel".

Roger reached a hand forward. The young man took it .... he bowed to Julie, and then retired.

Jesus looked to Roger.

"He's waiting to be asked", said Julie.

"In English ....", said Roger.

"I'll translate when you've finished", said Julie.

Roger took a deep breath. It seemed as though he would start to speak .... but then he changed his mind. He stood, moved the chair aside, and knelt at Jesus feet. But this time he looked up into His face.

"I kneel before you", he said, "to honour your Father .... and to honour you. I have come here because I believe a great wrong was done to me. You are the only person in all of history who has the power to right this wrong. I have come to ask that you restore life to my Fiancee, Miss Deborah Wintersham".

Roger bowed his head while Julie translated. She finished. There was a long silence.

Jesus of Nazareth sighed. He spoke again to Julie.

"He says that what you ask for is a Miracle", she said. "He says that your time is not a time of Miracles. He says that science must explain everything in your world. How will you explain such a Miracle in a world that loves science and it's explanations".

Roger closed his eyes, and thought.

"Tell Him", he said. "that there are many Miracles in my world. But that science can only explain how a Miracle is performed .... how God does what He does. Not why. Tell Him that we do recognise Miracles in our

scientific world. Tell Him that science has explained many Miracles ....
many of the Works of the Father. But science recognises that it can not
explain all Miracles. But it still recognises them for what they are .... and it
works endlessly to understand .... because man has a mind that must quest
for knowledge".

Julie translated carefully, stopping occasionally to check a point with Roger.

Roger looked up at Jesus again. His eyes were closed. He seemed lost in
thought.

They waited.

Eventually Jesus opened his eyes, and smiled at Roger. Julie spoke to Him
in Aramaic. He nodded .... and responded..................

"He says that what you desire is beyond His power to grant", said
Julie."That He is a man .... and this is beyond the power of man to grant".

Jesus interupted............

"But He would remind you", said Julie. "That His Father does have that
power. And He would also remind you .... that with His Father .... all
things are possible".

Jesus lowered His head .... as though in prayer.

"I think we should leave now", said Julie.

She went to rise, but Jesus indicated that He would like her to kneel next to
Roger. She moved her chair and knelt.

Jesus placed His hands on their foreheads .... and it seemed as though He
sang to them. It wasn't quite a song .... but then it was more than simple
speech. Julie didn't recognise the language .... but she guessed it to be
ancient Hebrew.

Mark came to them .... and they followed him to the door. They looked
back at Jesus .... but He had left the room.

They stood in the evening sun, and looked around them.

"We left something on the table", said Julie. They walked across and found a small bundle of food, and a flagon of wine. There was something written on the table top in charcoal. Julie bent to translate it.

"It's for us", she said. "For the journey .... from Mama Kath".

"That's a very nice thing for her to do", said Roger.

They picked up the food and the wine .... and started back along the road.

Julie felt just a little guilty. Guilty because she knew that Roger couldn't read Aramaic. She had translated what it said on the table .... but she hadn't translated quite all that it said. Because the second part was for Julie only. The second part was"Girl talk". Very definitely "Girl talk".

FOUR

William Feswick (Fezzy to his friends), was sea fishing. Beach fishing, to be specific. He was fishing for flounders from Sandbanks beach in Dorset. It was just after midnight, on an early Spring morning, and Will was fishing at the Chain Ferry end of the beach. In fact from where he sat he had been able to watch the ferry making it's crossing to and from Shell Bay, until it moored for the night, at about eleven thirty. It had been back and forth many times while he had been sitting with his rods. He had arrived at seven thirty, having had an early supper. He was alone on this section of the beach. The other beach fishermen tended to avoid it, because they thought that the noise from the ferry scared away the fish. Will, however, didn't agree. He had been very successful over the years, fishing this short section of shelving sand and shingle. It was his opinion that the ferry had been operating for so many years, that the fish no longer saw it as anything other than a natural feature of the area. And , of course, this section had not been "over fished", which must help to some degree.

It was a most unusual evening on the beach, in that the water was dead flat calm. The moon was up, and almost full, and the water stretched out in front of Will like a great flat mirror. Not a breath of wind rustled in the fir trees behind him. Each ferry crossing had generated a set of tiny ripples in the water .... but he was some three hundred yards from the ferry just here .... and the ripples quickly faded.

He had two long rods on their stands. Two small gas lanterns, to draw the fish in, stood on the sand below the rods. Will had erected a windbreak .... although it was not needed .... and was sitting comfortably ensconced in his favourite folding chair. If he looked away to his left he could see the beach lanterns of other fishermen curving around the bay .... but the closest of them was nearly half a mile away. Will was sure of a peaceful session.

He had enjoyed sitting here with his rods. Nothing to disturb his thoughts. He had even left his mobile phone in the car .... which was parked in the ferry car park.

It had been a remarkably peaceful night, very peaceful indeed .... and he hadn't caught a single flounder .... which had surprised him.

He glanced at his watch, and decided to call it a night at about 3am. Another three hours. He would have had enough by then. He stood up, and stretched .... he wasn't sure that he hadn't fallen asleep for a while. He reached down into his bag and pulled out a large tartan patterned Thermos flask. It had been his Fathers. Will unscrewed the lid .... which also served as a cup, and poured himself a hot chocolate. As he tucked the flask back into his bag, the bell on the tip of one of his rods began to jingle. Will had a bite.

"And about time too", he said .... out loud .... to no one in particular.

He put his cup of hot chocolate carefully down by his chair, and went to his left hand rod. The bell was ringing a tune that was music to Will's ears. From experience, he knew that he had a good sized flounder on the line. He began the gentle process of reeling it in. Flounders tended to put up a fight when they found themselves in the shallows, and Will readied himself to release some line, if the fish were to make a break for deeper water.

In fact this fish seemed uninterested in any sort of resistance. Will wondered if it was an older weaker fish. Anyway, he would soon see. He continued to reel in, and went down the sand, until the toes of his boots were at the very edge of the water.

He thought afterwards that had he not been concentrating so entirely on the fish (his first of the night) .... well, he might have payed a little more attention to the water lapping at his boots. But he didn't.

Will gently eased the fish from the water. He got his thumbs into it's gills, and held it up to the moonlight. It was a good large flounder. As good as he had ever caught in this spot. And then Will gasped in surprise as he turned his flounder into the light. It was bright red. He was so surprised that he nearly dropped the fish back into the sea. But he held on .... and got it up the beach to one of his gas lamps. He put the fish on the sand. It seemed to have expired quickly .... at least it made no movement. Will knelt to examine it, bringing the lantern in closer.

The flounder was bright red because it was soaked in blood. Or at least

Will thought it was blood. He wiped part of the fish with his glove. It was flounder colour under the blood. Will examined the red liquid. He sniffed it. He wondered if there had been a chemical spill .... but there was no chemical smell of any sort.

Will removed his glove, and touched the bloodied flounder with his finger tips. He rubbed his finger tips together. He was sure this was blood. But how ....

Leaving the fish laying where it was, Will returned to the waters edge. He held up his lantern. It didn't throw the light very far, but it threw it far enough for Will to see that he was looking out upon a sea of blood. The water was red. He found a piece of driftwood near at hand, and dipped one end into the sea. It came out bright red.

"I wonder how far this goes", he said to himself.

He took the lantern and walked fifty yards to the left along the waters edge. He stopped, and finding another scrap of wood, he dipped it. It came out bright red.

Will had a strong feeling that somebody in Authority should be told about this as soon as possible. The Coastguard, he thought.

Will walked back to his rods, and began to take down his gear. Then he remembered his hot chocolate. It was cold. He threw it away, poured another, and sat down to enjoy the hot drink. It was a tricky thing to make really good hot chocolate .... but Will was a professional chef. He knew how to make hot chocolate. He reached into his bag for his biscuits (home made, of course). He had barely seated himself, when there was a cough from behind him. Will sprang up and turned. He dropped the cup .... and the biscuit .... and he stared in amazement.

Standing just within the glow of his lantern was a young woman. She was completely naked .... and even more alarming .... her whole body, her face, every part of her glistened with blood. She was bright red from top to toe. Her hair straggled down to her breasts. It too was soaked in blood.

She smiled at Will.

"I'm so sorry to have disturbed your fishing", she said, "But my name is Miss Deborah Wintersham, and I believe that I am in some need of assistance".

She smiled weakly. Her eyes closed .... and she collapsed onto the sand at Wills feet.

Will stood glued to the spot. He was terrified. He wanted to run away .... but a young woman with an awfully posh accent had just very politely asked for assistance.

Will couldn't begin to think what it must cost you to ask a fisherman for assistance when you are a young woman standing naked on the beach in the moonlight at 12.30, in the first hour of the morning .... and soaked from head to foot with blood.

He sort of panicked because she was naked. Will had never had a girlfriend. He had seen pictures of naked girls .... but he hadn't realised that he would find the presence of a real live naked girl quite so disconcerting. He did however feel a strong urge to cover her from the cold, and to offer her such protection as he could.

He felt uneasy about looking at her .... and a great deal more uneasy about actually touching her. But there was only himself to assist her .... so he thought he'd better get some sort of plan into action.

He didn't doubt that she had come out of the sea. But what was she doing swimming naked at midnight at this time of the year ....

Will took his coat off. He moved the girl gently into the recovery position. He remembered being taught this in a first aid class. He checked her pulse, which seemed pretty good, then held his ear to her mouth. She was breathing, which was a huge relief to Will. But she was clearly unconscious, and Will began to worry about Hypothermia. He had no idea how long she had spent in the water. He held his hand to her neck. She felt very cold.

He needed to get her somewhere warm as quickly as possible. He would have used his phone to summon assistance .... but it was in his car. He didn't want to leave her un attended while he went for the phone .... and in any case .... if he was going back to the car, he might as well take her with him.

Even if he had to carry her. Which looked highly likely at the moment.

Will remembered his chocolate. There would still be one cup left in the flask. He found the cup, wiped it free of sand, and filled it for the third time.

"Third time lucky", he said to himself.

He knelt by the girl's head, and lifted it gently with one arm. He poured a little of the hot chocolate between her lips .... having taken a sip himself first, to check that it would not scald her.

The girl spluttered, swallowed, and opened her eyes.

"Oh what super specially delicious chocolate", she said. "You are so kind .... and I'm so sorry that I must appear to be in the most wretched mess".

"We need to get you somewhere warm" said Will.

There was no response .... she had lapsed into unconsciousness again.

"Oh well", thought Will. "Best get on with it".

He finished the hot chocolate, threw the cup aside, and knelt by Miss Deborah Wintersham. He slipped his arms beneath her, pulled her to his chest, and rose slowly to a standing postion. He was relieved to find that he would be able to carry her to the car. He looked at his fishing gear .... but there were more important things to worry about. It would be safe enough here ....

Will set off up the beach, at what he judged to be a steady and sustainable pace.

FIVE

Jesus of Nazareth sat with Mama Kath at the table beneath the olive tree. They were watching the sunset. It was spectacular this evening. A far off dust storm had created a fuzzy pink and orange light display that varied in colour from moment to moment.

Mama Kath topped up their cups from the wine flagon that stood between them on the table. There would be just fifteen minutes of twilight before another night was upon them. They both loved this part of the day.

They sat and watched the sunset until the colours faded.

"So are you going to do something for that couple", said Mama Kath.

Jesus shook his head.

"It's not within my power", he said.

"But your Father has that power", said Mama Kath. "You told them as much yourself".

Jesus turned to face her.

"In their Holy Scripture", he said "In their "New Testament", as they call it ....I raise three people from the dead. And their scientists look at these three cases and say:

"Ah .... well yes. He raised these three people from their death beds. But were they clinically dead. Deciding when somebody was truly dead wasn't the exact science that it is now".

And so the faithful can believe the stories as written .... and the scientifically minded have a plausible explanation .... because, of course, they are the really clever ones .... and they know, without any doubt, that you cannot raise people from the dead".

Mama Kath nodded.

"But with God .... all things are possible", she said.

"Yes", said Jesus. "With my Father .... all things are indeed possible".

"The real problem with this case", said Jesus, "Is that Roger is not going to be able to claim that Deborah wasn't clinically dead. If Deborah's life is restored to her .... then it will be a Miracle that is completely beyond any plausible explanation".

Mama Kath smiled at Jesus.

"Does there always have to be a plausible explanation", she asked.

"Well", said Jesus. "Even with smaller prayers .... the ones we can answer .... we do always make sure that an alternative explanation is available .... to keep the un-believers happy".

"And the Faithful happy in their Faith", added Mama Kath.

"Exactly", said Jesus.

There was a long silence. They sipped the last of the wine, and made to return to the house.

As they walked, Mama Kath put her arm around Jesus' shoulders.

"Do you know", she said. "I think there is a way to do this...........".

Jesus turned to her, and took her hands. They stood, facing each other, their eyes catching the last moments of the evening light.

"Show me a way", He said. "Show me a way .... and My Father's Will shall be done .... on Earth as it is in Heaven".

"That's rather nice". she said. "Where is that from".

"The Lord's Prayer", He said. "I wrote it yesterday afternoon. The lads wanted to know how to pray".

"Do you write very often", she asked Him.

"Not often", he said. "I usually leave it to the others to record my teachings".

"We should go into the house", saids Mama Kath.

They turned to the doors.

"Do you know", said Jesus. "I spend three years walking around here, teaching anyone who will listen. Three years. And then, after my death, the scribes spent three hundred years writing about my life".

"I know", said Mama Kath.

"But do you know how much of my teaching is included in their Holy Scripture .... their "New Testament", he asked her".

Mama Kath stayed silent .... waiting for the answer.

"Two hours", He said. "Just two hours".

"And they think they know You", she said.

"Yes", He said. "And they think they know me ....".

....

Will was relieved to reach his car. Although his burden was not heavy, she did have a disconcerting habit of sagging in the middle, which made walking difficult. He considered changing to a "firemans lift" style of carrying his charge .... but as it would mean handling her in ways that Will didn't feel very comfortable with .... he continued as he was.

It was also very awkward when Will's coat slipped off .... beacause he had no choice other than to lay her gently down, place the coat back over her unconscious form, and then pick her up again. It was quite a short coat .... Will's black duffle .... and it didn't cover quite as much of her feminine form as Will would have liked.

"But then", he thought to himself, "I didn't apply for this job".

Vaguely remembering that the human body loses a great deal of heat from the scalp, Will had taken his own woolly bobble hat off, and pulled it well down over the young woman's head. Her ears felt horribly cold, and Will managed to tuck them inside the hat.

It did occur to him, that should a Police patrol car come along .... then it could hardly fail to display some interest in the proceedings. They might want to know why Will was walking along this deserted road to the ferry, in the early hours of the morning, carrying a completely naked young woman, whose body was covered in blood.

Will could explain .... but would anybody in their right mind believe a word of it. He was uncertain.

In fact, Will saw nobody. The ferry had stopped running at about eleven thirty, so there was no traffic, and when Will reached the car park, his was the only car there.

He thought for one panic stricken moment that he had left his car keys in his fishing bag .... but, after a moment's thought, he retrieved them from his jacket pocket. He unlocked the car, and with less difficulty than he had expected, he managed to slide his charge onto the rear seat. He tucked the coat around her, and noticed that the blood on her arms and legs was drying. He hoped this might be a sign that she was still producing at least some body heat, but he wasn't sure.

Will started the engine, turned the car, and headed for the Hospital.

In all of this, Will had been encouraged by the knowledge that he did have one thing on his side. His sister, Elizabeth, was a nurse at the Hospital .... in A&E .... and he knew she was on duty tonight. He knew .... because he had telephoned her that afternoon to tell her he was going fishing.

Will had been allowed to fish on his own since he was thirteen .... but his Father had insisted upon one condition. He must always tell them where he was going .... and when he intended to return. Then .... if he had a mishap .... the alarm could be raised.

Will was thirty five now .... both his parents gone .... but old habits die hard .... and Will had phoned Elizabeth that afternoon.

The drive to the Hospital was uneventful. Will kept the speed strictly to thirty. He didn't want to be pulled over.

To his astonishment, he was able to park virtually outside the doors of the

A&E department. He opened the rear door of the car, and eased the girl out, until he could lift her in his arms. He pushed the car door closed with his knee, and headed for the entrance.

As Will pushed through the double doors, the coat slipped from the girl for the last time. Will wasn't about to retrieve it. He adjusted his burden so that her modesty was preserved as much as was practical, and headed for reception.

There are times when it seems as though things are being directed from above .... and this was one of those occasions.

Will's sister, Elizabeth, was behind the desk. She and a receptionist were discussing something displayed on one of the computer screens.

"Hi Elizabeth", said Will. "I've brought you a patient".

Elizabeth, and the receptionist, looked up as Will reached the desk. They stared transfixed at his burden.

Will didn't give them a chance to speak.

"I was beach fishing at Sandbanks", he said. "I think she must have been swimming in the sea. She came out of the water, asked for my help, and then collapsed in front of me. She is horribly cold. I'm worried that she has hypothermia".

"This is my brother Will", said Elizabeth, hastily. She had spotted the receptionist's hand reaching towards the telephone.

"She's covered in blood Will", said Elizabeth. "Is she injured".

"I don't think so", said Will. "The water down there is bright red tonight. I pulled out a flounder that was as red as she is. I thought it was some kind of chemical spill .... but I actually think it is blood. I'm going to tell the Coastguard".

Elizabeth rested her palm on the girl's cheek.

"She's far too cold", she said to the receptionist. "I'll get a trolly and some blankets. Are you OK to hold her for a few more moments Will".

Will nodded.

"Try not to be too long", he said.

Elizabeth hurried away .... and Will and the receptionist stood staring at each other.

"She was covered with my coat", said Will. "It slipped off as we came through the doors".

"I'll fetch it", said the receptionist, who seemed relieved to have something practical to do.

She returned with Will's coat, and tucked it around the girl's still unconscious form.

"It's not quite long enough", said Will. He smiled wanly at the receptionist.

Elizabeth returned with a trolly, blankets .... and a young doctor. She looked frighteningly efficient. She summed up the situation in one glance, applied her stethescope, layed her palm on the girl's brow, and turned to Elizabeth.

"Get Veronica to help you", she said. "Get her into a hot shower .... not too hot initially .... but gradually increase the temperature. Check her for injuries .... but I don't think this is her blood. Get her dry, and into a warm bed. I have a feeling that she'll have come round by then. If she hasn't .... we'll start more checks. But her breathing is OK, and her pulse is fine .... so I'm hoping we'll be talking to her in twenty minutes or so".

Elizabeth hurried away with the trolly, and the doctor turned to Will.

"Under normal circumstances", she said, "I would call the Police .... but Elizabeth tells me that you are her Brother".

Will nodded.

"So Elizabeth knows how to contact you".

Will nodded again.

"I only live at Parkstone", he said.

"In that case", said the Doctor. "I'll wait until I have talked to the young lady. Did she mention her name at all".

"She was only conscious for a few moments", said Will. "But I think she said her name was Deborah. I didn't catch her second name .... sorry".

"Well wait here Will", said the Doctor. "You can get a tea or a coffee from the machine in the corridor".

"Look", said Will. "Is there any chance I can go back to Sandbanks and collect my fishing gear. I left it all on the beach, because I wanted to get her here as quickly as possible".

The Doctor looked at Will .... as though trying to reach a decision.

"OK", she said."But can you come back here afterwards. We may have more questions".

"I'll be back in an hour", said Will. "Elizabeth has my mobile number if you need me before then".

He reached out a hand to the Doctor. They shook.

Will hurried away.

SIX

Isobel was shopping. Tesco's shopping. She had been living at Roger's home at Christchurch for some weeks now. Roger was away at the moment. He was in the Holy Land. The first century Holy Land. Isobel knew why he had gone. He wanted Debbie back. There was only one person he could ask.

Isobel was troubled by the concept .... but she had made her own prayers. She remembered what Mama Kath had said to her that afternoon.

"Isobel .... there ain't nothing in the world the Lord can't do .... if the Lord has a mind to do it".

Isobel paid for her shopping using Roger's card. She pushed the trolly to her Golf, unlocked the tail gate, and transferred her groceries to the car boot. She returned the trolly to the front of the store.

It was cold in the car park. She was missing Roger's company. She looked up at the long avenue of Beech trees that divided the car park into two. The trees were skeletal against the grey sky. Isobel longed for the Spring. She longed to see Roger happy again. And she longed for ....

She shrugged. She would have a cappuccino .... and a lemon zesty tart. She went back into the store, turned to the right, and went up the stairs to the Costa Coffee shop. There was no queue and within a few moments Isobel was carrying her coffee and lemon tart to a table. She sat down. There was a young woman, with a baby in a carry seat, on the next table. Isobel glanced at the baby. It looked very new.

She had just taken the first sip of her coffee, when the girl on the next table spoke.

"Excuse me", she said. "You're Isobel aren't you. Do you remember me. We used to sit next to each other at school".

Isobel turned. She was puzzled for a few moments .... then her face lit up.

"Samantha", she said. "Wow ....it's been ages .... how are you".

They stood .... embraced .... and then Samantha turned to the carry seat.

"And this is little Maisie", she said. "Maisie is just three weeks old …. aren't you sweetheart".

Samantha tickled her daughter under the chin.

"Oh she is adorable", said Isobel. "Is she your first".

"And my last", laughed Samantha. "You just cannot believe how long nine months can be Isobel".

The girls sat down again, and Samantha turned the carry seat so Isobel could admire little Maisie. Maisie gurgled, waved her arms, and blew bubbles at Isobel.

Isobel reached over and took one of Maisie's tiny hands between her fingers.

"Oh, she is just so cute", she said.

"Would you like to hold her", said Samantha.

"Oh could I", said Isobel. "That would be wonderful".

Samantha undid the retaining straps, eased Maisie out of her seat, and passed her to Isobel. Isobel held the child to her breast, and instictively began to rock her gently back and forth.

Samantha smiled at her.

"So have you any children yet Isobel", she asked.

"I'm not even married yet", said Isobel.

"You're in a relationship though………..", said Samantha.

Isobel coloured.

"Not really", she said."Not yet……………".

Samantha glanced at the screen on her phone. She grimaced.

"We've got to dash Isobel", she said. "I've got a hair dressing appointment in fifteen minutes".

Samantha was puzzled to see a shadow cross Isobel's face.

"Are you OK Isobel", she said.

Isobel nodded.

"I'm OK", she said "Look .... you had better take Maisie back .... or I'll be wanting to take her home with me".

Samantha took her daughter back from Isobel, and carefully secured her in her carry seat. She stood up.

"Let's swap phone numbers", she said. "Then we can catch up over a coffee when we have more time".

The girls swapped numbers. They embraced. Samantha picked up Maisie's seat by it's carry handle.

"Phone me then", she said.

"I will, I promise", said Isobel.

She watched Samantha through the window, as she walked to her car .... swinging her child gently back and forth in the carry seat.

Isobel sat down, and cut her lemon zesty tart into four. She stirred her coffee thoughtfully .... and lowered her head.

The first tears began to form in the corners of her eyes.

"Awesome God ....", she began.

"Are you Ok".

Isobel looked up. The Barista was clearing Samantha's cup and plate .... wiping the table. She smiled at Isobel.

"That was such a sweet Baby", she said. "I wanted to take her home with me.............".

Isobel smiled.

"I guess I did too", she said.

The Barista picked up Samantha's cup and plate. She put her hand on Isobel's shoulder.

"Then let your hair down", she whispered.

Isobel looked up in surprise .... but the Barista had gone.

....

Jesus of Nazareth sat with Mama Kath in her room at the rear of the house. Mama Kath had checked on the children .... two girls and a boy. They were all asleep.

"How are your charges", asked Jesus.

"Clean and sweet in the site of the Lord", she said.

Jesus smiled at her.

"You had a plan ....", he said.

Mama Kath nodded.

"Deborah's Father is one of a group of seven people who have keys to a door", she said.

Jesus looked puzzled.

"One of the doors between Worlds", said Mama Kath.

"But they were all closed by My Father at the beginning", Jesus said.

"Well .... it must have suited the Lord to leave one open", said Mama Kath.

"How long have these people known about the door", asked Jesus.

"At least five hundred years", said Mama Kath.

"Five hundred years ....".

"Yes", said Mama Kath, "And it has been used regularly for all of that time".

Jesus shook his head in disbelief.

"And nothing has happened ....", he said.

"They have been very careful", said Mama Kath.

"It has to be closed", said Jesus. "They cannot realise the danger".

Mama Kath nodded.

"I thought you would say that", she said.

Mama Kath stared at Jesus.

He stared back.

"Has Deborah existed in both of the Worlds", he asked.

"She has", said Mama Kath.

"Was she killed in the World to which she belongs", said Jesus.

"No", said Mama Kath. "In the other".

Jesus sat staring at her. Then he stood, and pulled Mama Kath to her feet.
He hugged her .... and kissed her on both cheeks.

"Where there's a Will .... there's a Way", said Mama Kath.

Jesus left the room. He was in a hurry.

"Ladies and Gentlemen", said Mama Kath. "Jesus has left the building".

....

Back at Sandbanks, Will had saved some time by being able to leave his car
on the double yellow lines at the head of the footpath leading to the beach.
There was a Police patrol car standing there. Will pulled in behind it. He
made a dash for the beach. Two police officers, a man and a woman, were
examining his fishing gear.

"It's mine", Will called to them.

They turned towards him.

"It's your gear, is it Sir", said the officer. "A local resident informed us that there was fishing equipment here .... but nobody in sight. He was worried that you were in the water".

"No", said Will. "I'm fine. I had to dash off and take a friend to hospital".

"By the way", he added. "Have you seen the water".

"The water Sir", said the officer, glancing towards the sea.

"Yes", said Will. "The water is bright red. I think there might have been a chemical spill. I think we should tell the Coastguard".

"Bright red Sir", said the officer.

The WPC treated Will to a long and appraising glance.

"Perhaps we'd better have a look then Sir", said the Officer.

Will picked up one of his gas lanterns, which were still glowing brightly, and they walked to the water's edge. The tide had gone out some yards since Will had left.

Will held the lantern up, and they all looked out over a grey/green sea. The gentle swell created tiny waves that broke at their feet.

"Well the sea looks quite normal to me Sir", said the Police officer.

Will nodded in agreement.

"It's OK now", he said, "But an hour ago it was bright red. In fact, I landed a flounder that was bright red .... like it had been dipped in red ink. I'll show it to you".

They walked back up to Will's rods, but there was no sign of the flounder.

"I expect a dog found it", said Will.

"Yes Sir .... very probably Sir", said the officer.

"And I dipped a piece of driftwood into the water, and that came out bright red as well", said Will. "It should be here somewhere".

He cast about with his lantern, but was unable to find the driftwood".

"I expect the dog took it Sir", said the Officer.

"Must have done", said Will.

"So are you going to continue fishing tonight Sir", said the WPC.

"No" said Will. "I'm going to collect my gear, and go back to the Hospital to check on the friend".

"Would you like our help to carry your fishing gear", asked the WPC.

"That would be very kind of you", said Will. "We'll only need one trip back to the car".

They gathered the equipment together, sharing the load between them, and set off up the beach.

Back on the road, the police officers watched Will load his car.

"Well …. we shall wish you a very good morning then Sir", said the WPC.

"Thank you", said Will. "And I wish you the same".

They turned away.

"The water really was bright red earlier", Will called after them.

The WPC turned back. She smiled.

"I'm sure it was Sir", she said. "By the way Sir …. please be careful about parking on double yellow lines in future Sir".

"Sorry" said Will.

The police car moved away. They gave him a split second of their flashing blue lights as a farewell.

Will raised his arm, and waved goodbye.

He started his car, and headed back to the Hospital.

SEVEN

Will walked back into the A&E reception just a few minutes over the hour. Elizabeth was on the desk.

"How is she", asked Will.

"There's been a big improvement since you left", said his Sister. "She's sitting up in bed, and able to talk now".

"Is she injured at all", asked Will.

"Not in any way we could find", said Elizabeth. "She had just got very very cold .... and very very hungry".

"Can I see her", said Will.

"Well the Doctor is with her at the moment", said Elizabeth. "I'll let her know that you're back".

The receptionist appeared. She smiled at Will.

"So was your fishing equipment still there", she asked.

"It was", said Will. "In fact it had the Police guarding it when I arrived".

"Was the water still red", asked the receptionist.

Will looked puzzled.

"No", he said. "It was the normal grey green colour".

"Whatever it was must have cleared then", said the receptionist.

Will nodded.

Elizabeth came back with the Doctor.

"Thank you for coming back", she said to Will.

"The news is good, I'm pleased to tell you. Deborah is sitting up, she is eating some supper, and she wants to thank you for saving her life".

"Saving her life ....", said Will.

"Almost certainly", said the Doctor. "Her core temperature was way below what it should be. Another half an hour could have had very serious consequences".

Will went to speak .... then found he couldn't.

"Would you like to see her", said the Doctor.

Will looked to his Sister.

"Go and see her Will", said Elizabeth.

The Doctor led the way along a corridor, and stopped ouside a door.

"We call this our "warm room"", she said. "You may want to take your sweater off. We use it to warm people up. It's pretty hot in there".

She looked at Will.

"There is one odd thing", she said. "The young lady has a very visible white scar running right around her neck. It is very noticeable. Perhaps it's better not to mention it. She seems quite sensitive about it".

The Doctor knocked. A nurse opened the door, and stood aside for Will to enter.

The girl sitting up in the bed seemed to Will to bear no resemblance to the girl he had carried into A&E a little over an hour ago. In fact he turned to the nurse to ask if there had been some mistake.

"Hello Will", said the girl. "I'm Deborah .... and I want to thank you for saving my life".

Will stared at her. He was speechless. She was stunningly gorgeous, with a pale complexion, and a mass of blonde ringlets that fell to her shoulders.

The girl laughed at his expression.

"It really is me Will", she said. "I scrub up quite well don't I".

Will blushed red.

"You look very lovely", he said.

The girl swallowed the last spoonful of the beef stew that she had been eating.

She passed her plate to the nurse.

"Tell Chef it was super specially delicious", she said.

"I'll make sure and tell him", said the nurse. She smiled at Will.

"You can have just five minutes", she said. "Then I want to tuck her in for the night".

Taking the supper tray, she slipped quietly from the room.

"Five minutes, remember", she said, as she pulled the door closed behind her.

Deborah pointed Will to the chair beside the bed.

"Everybody has been so kind", she said. "The nurses have even searched their lockers and put some clothes together for me".

She pointed to a neatly folded pile of clothing on her bedside cabinet.

"How did you get in the sea", said Will.

"I really don't know", said the girl. "I remember a terrible stinging pain on my neck .... and then the world went all topsy turvy .... and then I was just so horribly cold for ages and ages .... and then I was here. I just don't seem to be able to remember how I got into the water".

She looked stricken .... and Will thought he could see tears beginning to form in the corners of her eyes.

He stood up, took her hand, and kissed her on the cheek.

She smiled at him.

"Will", she said. "You've never had a girlfriend .... have you".

Will blushed again.

Deborah began to look drowsy. She yawned.

"Oh .... I'm so sorry to yawn Will" she said. "But I'm beginning to feel very sleepy. Perhaps you could ask the nurse to tuck me in".

Will nodded.

"Kiss me goodnight then"

Will kissed her on the cheek again.

Her eyes began to close.

"Will", she said. I'm going to talk to a friend of mine .... and we are going to send you a super specially delicious girlfriend .... I promise".

Will went to reply .... but he saw that she was asleep.

He slipped quietly from the room.

....

Jesus came to Debbie at 4am. He stood looking down at her for a few moments, then gently touched her cheek. She woke up, and stretched.

"Hi", she said.

He smiled at her.

"We have to go", He said. "We have things to do, and we haven't much time".

Debbie scratched her neck.

"This scar really itches", she said.

"Sorry", said Jesus. "We really were working at the edge of the envelope with you".

"Up you get then", He said.

He moved the bedside chair to the corner of the room, and sat down.

Debbie pulled the duvet cover up to her chin.

"Well excuse me", she said. "I do have to get dressed you know".

Jesus rolled His eyes skyward.

"Debbie", he said. "I created you .... every tiny part of you".

"Yes I know you did", she said. "But it doesn't mean you'll be watching me get dressed .... thank you very much. Out you go, and you can wait in the corridor".

She glared at Him.

"I can't wait in the corridor like this", said Jesus.

He was wearing his best white robes. They glowed with incandescent light.

"Nobody will take any notice", said Debbie.

"They won't ....", said Jesus.

"No", said Debbie. We're in a Hospital. People are always seeing Jesus in Hospitals. It's in the news papers all the time".

"They are", said Jesus.

"Promise you", said Debbie.

"What shall I do if somebody comes along", said Jesus.

Debbie laughed.

"Look spiritual .... and definitely do not smile for the camera", she said.

"The camera", said Jesus.

"Yes", said Debbie. "Everybody has a camera on their mobile phone now".

"But there would be a picture of me ....", said Jesus.

"Don't worry about it", said Debbie. "People will just say its a Photoshop job".

Jesus sighed. He stood, opened the door, glanced up and down the corridor, and left the room, pulling the door gently closed behind him.

Debbie watched Him go.

"He's such a sweetie", she said. "But He really shouldn't be allowed out on His own".

She got out of bed. She pulled her night dress over her head, glanced down, and grimaced. She flicked back her sheets .....

"Oh that's just wonderful", she said. She glared at the wall, as though looking at a film crew and the director.

"Nigel", she said. "This book is positively awash with blood already. Do I really have to be on another period".

The wall glared back .... but remained silent.

Debbie shrugged.

"Now what am I going to do", she said.

She turned to the bedside cabinet in desperation, and pulled open the top drawer. The drawer contained a small box of tissues .... and a pack of Kotex towels.

She glared at the wall again.

"Well thank you for small mercies", she said.

She opened the packet and pulled out a towel.

She waved it at the wall.

"You do know it's not real blood don't you", she said.

The wall remained silent.

Debbie attended to this latest emergency. She pulled on the underwear and tights, and dressed herself in the black skirt, and red polo neck sweater, that Elizabeth had lent her. The shoes were a touch on the "sensible" side for Debbie's taste, but they were the right size, so she slipped them on, and did up the laces.

She looked at the sheets again and sighed.

"Sorry", she said.

She went to the door, and turned for a final glance around the room. It wasn't likely that she had forgotten anything .... because she had arrived naked ...., but she took another couple of Kotex towels from the packet .... and tucked them into the waist band of her tights. As she turned to the door again, she spotted the small mirror on the side of the wardrobe. She stared at her image .... then moved in for a closer look. She had orange eyes.

Debbie went for the door. Jesus was waiting outside.

"You've been ages", he said.

"I'm a girl", said Debbie. "We always take ages .... it's what girls do. We keep you waiting for ages so you appreciate us more when you see us".

Jesus sighed.

"Now", said Debbie. "Lets talk about my eyes shall we. What's with them being orange".

"Technical difficulties", said Jesus.

"Technical difficulties", said Debbie. "But you are the Creator".

"I like the orange", said Jesus. "Will didn't seem to have a problem with it".

"Oh dear", said Debbie. "I think Will has fallen for me".

"Does everybody fall for you", said Jesus.

"I should absolutely jolly well think they would", said Debbie. "I am a Little Angel of Girly Loveliness".

She giggled

Jesus smiled at her.

"Before we go", said Debbie. "There's a little girl in the children's ward

............".

"Done it already", said Jesus. "I heard the conversation".

Debbie reached up and kissed Him.

"Thank you", she said.

They headed for the A&E reception. Jesus fired up the computer systems, and deleted the records of Debbie's stay".

"They might have back up", said Debbie.

"They have", said Jesus. "Cloud storage .... I found it".

....

There was a taxi waiting outside A&E. The driver jumped out to open the rear door for them.

"Hey", he said. "You must be Jesus .... great outfit man .... how do you get the robes to glow like that".

"It's a new type of cloth", said Jesus. "Glows in the dark".

"Wow" said the driver. "Respect due man .... is the beard real".

"Yes", said Jesus. "The beard is real".

Debbie giggled.

Jesus gave the driver the address and postcode.

He popped it into his sat. nav.

"Christchurch", he said "About a twenty minute run .... might be a little bit less. The traffic will be light at this time".

In fact the run to Roger's place took them nearly half an hour. There was a road closure .... with a diversion.

The driver said something suitable about night time road closures.

"Can't do anything about night time road closures for me, I suppose", he said, glancing back at Jesus.

"In respect of night time road closures .... you will, in future, be greatly blessed", said Jesus.

"Thanks", said the driver. "Hey .... respect due man ....".

EIGHT

Julie and Roger sat in a hollow in the ground, a hundred yards or so off the road. A camp fire burned brightly in it's circle of stones. They had intended to walk back to their "transport" that same evening .... but by midnight they had run out of energy. They agreed to stop for the night, and finish their journey in the morning.

A clump of trees on the edge of the hollow had provided all the wood they could wish for .... and they sat by their fire enjoying the supper that Mama Kath had provided.

"How are you feeling about things", Julie asked Roger.

Roger looked up at her and smiled.

"He is an amazing man", he said.

Julie nodded.

"The courage He shows when He waits to be arrested, in that garden, with His Disciples asleep around Him, is incredible", said Julie.

Roger looked straight at Julie.

"I have a lady I know who thinks He made the wrong decision by staying", said Roger.

"He didn't", said Julie.

Roger looked thoughtfully at her.

"But you tried to rescue Him", he said.

"We did rescue Him", she said. "But He went back".

They fell into silence.

"Roger", said Julie. "Are you glad that you asked Him".

"Yes", said Roger. "I do feel some sort of contentment that I have done everything I possibly could to get her back".

Julie nodded. She added more wood to the fire.

"Roger .... do you think you can ever love again", she said.

There was a long silence. Roger stared at the ground.

"I am going to have to find a way", he said.

Julie looked closely at his face.

"Is there anybody else that you think you could love", she asked.

Roger looked quickly away .... but Julie was sure that she had seen his cheeks colour.

"Is there", she asked again.

Roger turned to face her again. Julie sensed a different tone in his voice .... frustration .... sadness.

"There is somebody I admire very much", he said. "But she's quite a lot younger .... and a lot more sophisticated than I am. But she really is a lovely person. Totally different to Debbie. But I think we could ....".

"You should ask her", said Julie.

Roger laughed.

"She's way out of my league", he said. "She should marry a Lawyer, or a Doctor. She wouldn't want a car dealer".

"You think so ....", said Julie".

"I know so", said Roger.

"Love is a strange thing", said Julie.

"I know", said Roger.

"A girl will change her whole life to be with the man she loves", said Julie. "I did that for Mark remember".

"I couldn't ask that of her", said Roger.

"But you had the courage to ask Jesus of Nazareth to give Debbie back to you", said Julie.

"Doesn't take courage when there's only one way", said Roger.

"No", said Julie. "I wonder if Jesus of Nazareth felt the same".

They sat, lost in their thoughts, watching the flames.

"I'm going to turn in now", said Roger. He built up the fire, and made to lay down.

"One last thing Roger", said Julie.

He looked up at her. The firelight flickered across her face.

He waited for her to speak.

"Isobel is in love with you", she said. "She is waiting for you".

Roger stared at her.

Julie stood. She went around the fire and kissed him.

"Roger", she said. "Isobel is yours .... if you can find a way to let Debbie go".

....

Isobel carried her shopping from the car into Roger's kitchen. John's Dog Tyson, watched her impassively from the top of the wide steps.

"He's due back this evening, Tyson", Isobel said.

Tyson raised his ears .... and let them fall back again. Tyson knew very well that the Boss was grieving.

"I expect you'll be pleased to see him", said Isobel. "It's been quiet here without him hasn't it".

Isobel dropped a packet of peas into the chest freezer, and went over to

Tyson. He had left his vantage point on the porch, and returned to his basket in the kitchen.

Isobel cupped her hand under his chin, and looked fondly at him.

"Cheer up Tyson", she said. "Isobel has a plan".

Tyson made a soft grunting noise, and settled into the basket. Isobel had washed his blanket yesterday. Tyson wasn't at all sure that his blanket had needed washing.

Isobel, however, had thought differently.

"Isobel is your Mistress while I'm away Tyson", Roger had said to him, just before he left. "You look after her for John and I".

Tyson liked Isobel. She was obviously quite at home with a dog in the house, and she was very punctual with Tyson's dinner .... which he appreciated.

Tyson had been watching Isobel and Roger for nearly a month now .... and one thing perplexed him. Why on earth were they sleeping in separate baskets.

"I'm just popping out again for a while Tyson", said Isobel. "I have some girl shopping to do".

Tyson left his basket to see Isobel to the door. She ruffled the fur between his ears.

"See you soon", she said.

He went to the kitchen window, and stood with his front paws on the edge of the sink, to watch her drive away.

He grunted softly again, and returned to his basket .... and his freshly washed blanket. He snuggled down .... and sneezed.

....

Isobel drove to the large "out of town" Marks and Spencers, on the edge of Christchurch. She needed some new under wear .... but she also intended to buy herself a present.

"Well …. I suppose it's for me", she thought to herself.

The afternoon light had long gone by the time Isobel had found a slot for her car. A damp and chilly wind blew across the car park.

The store, as always, was pleasantly warm, and brightly lit.

Isobel selected two new bras, and a multipack of briefs fairly quickly. Nothing fancy …. just good quality every day wear.

She looked around the store.

"Excuse me", she said to an assistant, a girl in a Marks and Spencers tunic.

"Can you tell me where the night wear is please.".

The girl smiled.

"It's all on the rear wall", she said. "Sensible stuff to the left …………….".

She looked at Isobel.

"…………….but if you want something more romantic, it's on the rails on the other side of the aisle".

Isobel blushed.

"Would you like any help", asked the girl.

Isobel was about to say no. But she looked at the girl's smile …. and changed her mind.

"Perhaps you might help me", she said.

"Pleased to", said the girl. "So are we doing "Sensible" or are we looking for "Romantic".

Isobel blushed again.

"Romantic", she said.

"Wow", said the girl. "Most of our customers want "Sensible"".

She shot a shy smile at Isobel. The two of them laughed.

"Right", said the assistant. "Romantic" here we come".

She led Isobel to the aisle .... and waved her arm along the rail.

"I'll tell you what", she said. "We had a new line come in this morning. It's not cheap .... but I think it's really lovely".

She led Isobel along the rails, nearly to the end. She ran her hand along the hooks and lifted out a nightdress for Isobel to see.

"Pretty isn't it", she said.

Isobel nodded. She had never remotely imagined herself wearing something like this .... but deep down .... well .... it was quite appealing.

"It's gorgeous", she said.

The white material was beatifully soft. The bust had minute rouching.

"The top part is stretchy", said the assistant. .... and it's cut just right ..... so you don't show too much too soon"

Isobel looked at her, and raised her eyebrows. They both laughed.

"The skirt part is really lovely", said the girl. She draped it over her arm, and held it up for Isobel's inspection.

The soft material was gathered under the bust, and fell in folds to a bottom freize .... which was embroidered all round, with a garden of flowers, in reds, yellows, and purples all interspersed with green foilage.

"The embroidery is so pretty isn't it", said the assistant.

Isobel nodded in agreement.

"And it comes with matching briefs", said the assistant.

She held them up for Isobel to see.

Isobel blushed again. The briefs were of the same soft white material, gathered a little at the hems. Two blue butterflies danced below the tiny bow on the front panel. One larger, one smaller.

The Marks and Spencers assistant allowed Isobel a few moments to make up her mind.

"Is it for your honeymoon", she asked.

Isobel smiled.

"Yes", she said. "It's for my honeymoon".

"Congratulations", said the girl.

Isobel smiled at her.

"Thank you for helping", she said." You've made things much easier for me".

....

Roger settled himself into the rear seat of the hire car. He put the window down, and smiled at Julie.

"Thanks for everything Julie", he said.

She reached in, and kissed him on the cheek.

"You look exhausted", she said. "Is that the furthest you've ever walked".

"I have never walked even a quarter of that distance before", he said.

She stood back. Roger closed the window.

"About an hour and ten minutes", said the driver. We're going to be into some rush hour traffic".

"No rush", said Roger. "Do the best you can".

The driver glanced back at him.

"Blimey mate", he said. "You do look whacked".

"I've been abroad", said Roger. "No cars there, so I had to walk everywhere".

"No cars", said the driver. "Where did you go".

"Tyre and Sidon", said Roger.

"Bit backward out there is it", said the driver.

"At the moment", said Roger. "But they'll catch up".

The driver negotiated the motorway junction, and they slipped down the ramp onto the west bound carriageway. Roger layed his head back on the seat, and studied the head lining. What Julie had told him, by their campfire last night, had given him a lot to think about. He closed his eyes. The driver put the radio on softly.

....

"Phone a friend mate", said the driver.

Roger started.

"You were talking in your sleep", said the driver. "You were asking what you should do............".

"Sorry", said Roger.

"No worries", said the driver. "Phone a friend" .... like on that TV program "Who wants to be a Millionaire". "Phone a friend". That's what I always do".

"Do you know", said Roger. "I'm going to do just that. Thank you".

"No worries", said the driver. "Glad to help".

....

Roger pulled his mobile phone from his pocket, and scrolled for a number. He pushed dial, and sat back, the phone to his ear.

"Recovery", said a voice.

It was Nigel .... an old friend of Rogers.

"Are you still answering the phone like that, Nigel", said Roger. "It's been months and months since you retired".

Nigel laughed.

"Sorry Roger", he said. "Force of habit, I suppose".

"So how is the book doing", asked Roger.

"It's going well", said Nigel. " I've finished the writing, and the photographer is shooting the picture for the cover tomorrow .... well she's doing some light tests .... to be exact."

There was a pause.

"Look .... Roger", said Nigel. "We know what happened. I'm dreadfully sorry Roger .... I wish we could have met her".

"You'd have loved her", said Roger. "She was such a character .... right up your street".

"Roger", said Nigel. "We made a decision not to phone you. Mary wasn't so sure, but I knew from John and Peter that you were getting some really expert help .... and that you had somebody with you all the time".

"Nigel, it's alright", said Roger. "I always knew you were on this number .... twenty four hours .... if I needed you".

"If you need me now .... I'm yours", said Nigel.

"I have a question for you", said Roger. "Is Mary with you at the moment".

"She is ", said Nigel. "We're just getting ready to go down for dinner".

"Hi Roger", a voice called.

It was Mary.

"Hello Mary", said Roger."I'm glad you're there. You might want to help Nigel on this one ....".

"Nigel", he said. "I've just got back. You know where I've been".

"I know", said Nigel. "Julie phoned me to get my feelings on the idea".

"What were they", said Roger.

"That you had to do it", said Nigel. "I would do the same. You would have to .... and you would know that whatever decision He made would be the right one".

Roger thought. He hadn't seen it quite like that.

"Nigel", he said". "You went through a long grieving process many years ago .... you lived in the past for ages and ages".

Roger heard Nigel take a deep breath.

"Yeah .... that's true enough", he said

"And then you met Mary".

"Yes", said Nigel. "And then I met Mary".

"But did it work out with Mary because you had already stopped living in the past, before you met her .... or did it work out with Mary, because you stopped living in the past at the moment you met her".

"Wow", said Nigel.

Roger heard Mary say something to Nigel.

"Roger", said Nigel. "You've met Mary often enough .... I stopped living in the past at the moment I met her. She doesn't do the past. Mary is always about the present .... and the immediate future. And if you are with her .... that's the way you live .... you live in the "Right here, Right now".

"And if you do that", said Roger. "The past doesn't hurt as much".

"It can't touch you", said Nigel. "I live with Mary for the moment. I think it's like that with the right person".

There was a long silence.

"Have we helped you Roger", Mary said. "I hope we have".

"Yes", you've helped", said Roger. "You've helped a lot, thanks".

"We'll get our supper now Roger", said Nigel. "Stay in touch .... anytime remember".

"Roger", said Mary. "If you can .... go for it.....................".

The hire car went under a motorway bridge. The signal failed.

Roger returned the phone to his pocket.

"I phoned a friend", he said to the driver.

"No worries mate", said the driver. "No worries".

NINE

It was nearly eight by the time Isobel let herself into Roger's bungalow. Tyson greeted her at the door. She went to a tin in the kitchen cupboard, and found him a dog biscuit.

Tyson retired to his basket. He chewed thoughtfully, and watched Isobel.

It had become a very cold evening. The damp and chilly breeze of late afternoon, had been replaced by a steady, and icy cold wind that was doing it's best to turn Roger's domicile into a cold store.

Isobel stepped up the central heating, and put a match to the fire, that she had laid earlier, in the woodburning stove.

Tyson waited in his basket .... then .... judging the optimum moment, he moved to the living room, to lie in front of the fire.

Isobel went to the bathroom and switched on the supplementary heating .... an oil filled radiator. She glanced around. The bathroom was spotless, and she remembered that Thursday was Roger's "cleaning ladies" day.

When Isobel had first arrived at Roger's home, she had been rather expecting a "batchelor" establishment. Dirty clothes everywhere .... a kitchen sink full of unwashed crockery .... a fridge full of beer.

But not a bit of it. Roger had a cleaning company come in once a week.

"And I have to keep the place tidy for them", he had joked.

And .... as Isobel had discovered .... Roger would not allow alcohol in the house.

"Start of a slippery slope, Isobel", he had said.

Isobel went to her room to sort her new purchases. She unpacked her new "undies" and stored them in a top drawer. The nightdress, which had been quite horribly expensive, she laid out on the bed. She sat on the edge of the coverlet, and examined the embroidered butterflies. They were so pretty, she thought.

Tyson padded in, sat, and looked at Isobel hopefully.

She checked her watch.

"You're right Tyson", she said. "It's your supper time".

She fed him in the kitchen .... and added another biscuit to the side of his bowl. Tyson grunted.

He wasn't a fast eater. In fact Tyson didn't do anything very quickly. He was, however, very robust, very imposing, and not a little alarming. Alarming .... if you didn't know that Tyson had been taught to play a part for John and Roger. He enjoyed playing this part. There was a particular low frequency growl that he could maintain almost indefinitely .... without appearing to draw breath.

Isobel watched him eat for a few moments, then went to the front door, and checked that it was locked.

She returned to her room, undressed, found a large towel, and headed for the bathroom.

For the next hour Isobel showered, washed her hair, and generally attended to a myriad of matters pertaining to feminine grooming. Nine o'clock saw her sitting on her bed, in a pair of new pants, painting her toe nails.

Isobel was expecting Roger at ten pm. He had sent her a text message.

At a quarter to ten she pulled on her faded blue jeans, and a white T shirt. It wasn't quite warm enough to just stay with the T shirt .... which was a shame because her new bras were really rather good....................

So she pulled on a red sweater, checked her toe nails, and put on a pair of white socks and trainers.

She went through to the lounge, and found Tyson sitting by the front door, which, Isobel knew, meant that Roger was nearly home.

"How do dogs do that", she thought to herself.

A few minutes later she saw a car pull up outside the gates. She heard the gates open, the outside light came on automatically, and Roger came walking up to his front door. Isobel let Tyson out to meet him.

He came up the front steps, put his bag down for a moment, and embraced Isobel.

"Honey, I'm home", he said. "Wow, Isobel .... nice perfume".

"How did it go", she asked.

Roger looked at Isobel thoughtfully.

"There's a lot to tell you about", he said.

....

Isobel brought tea through to the lounge. Roger was flat out on the sofa.

"You look tired out", she said.

"We had to walk about a hundred miles", said Roger.

"It wasn't anything like that distance", said Isobel. "You're just not used to walking".

"We should have taken a Landrover with us", said Roger.

Isobel laughed.

"Wonder what the locals would have made of that", she said.

"Satan and all his works, I suppose", said Roger.

He sat sipping his tea.

"Shall I fetch the biscuits", said Isobel

"No .... I'm fine", said Roger. "Julie and I had a meal before I left".

"So how did you get on with Julie", asked Isobel .... carefully pouring herself another cup of tea.

"We got on fine", said Roger. "Mark is a lucky man".

He glanced at Isobel, but she was busily tidying the tea tray.

"Actually Isobel", he said. "I think I might jump in the shower, and go straight to bed. Do you mind if I tell you all about it in the morning".

She smiled at him.

"That's fine", she said. "But just one question .... did you manage to ask Him".

Roger put his cup back on the tray, and stood.

Isobel sat waiting for his reply.

"Yes", he said. "I asked Him .... I've done everything that I can Isobel. Absolutely everything that I can".

He headed for the shower.

Isobel watched him go. She missed Debbie so much .... but she had never been entirely comfortable with what Roger had wanted to do.

Tyson watched Isobel from his basket.

She returned the tray to the kitchen.

....

Roger came out of the bathroom. Isobel was on the sofa reading her Bible.

"Which bit are you reading", asked Roger.

"Mark's Gospel", she said.

Roger laughed.

"We met Mark", he said.

"You actually met the Mark who wrote this Gospel ....".

"Tell you tomorrow", said Roger.

Isobel stood up and gave him a "good night" peck on the cheek.

"Sleep tight", she said.

"See you in the .... ".

.... And they were plunged into darkness as the power failed. The only light was from the stove.

"Oh dear", said Roger. "I didn't hear the circuit breaker click .... so I think it's a power cut. Sit tight. I'll check the breaker".

Isobel sat down. Roger pulled his mobile phone from his pocket, and lit up the screen. It would give him enough light to find the power switches. He went through to the hall.

"No", Isobel heard him call. "It's not the circuit breaker .... I'll get the candles".

He came back from the kitchen with two old fashioned enamel candle holders, one pink, one blue .... and a new packet of candles. Isobel watched him pull the old stumps from the holders, fit new white candles, and light them. He passed her the pink one.

"Pink for a girl .... blue for a boy", he said. "Right .... bedtime .... see you in the morning".

Roger disappeared into his room.

Isobel smiled. She looked thoughfully at the candle .... then she looked towards the ceiling.

"Was that You", she said."............Thank You...........".

....

Isobel went to her room.

Tyson had watched them say goodnight to each other. He grunted................

Isobel took off her jeans and sweater, and slipped under the duvet. She lay there, staring at the ceiling, in the candle light. There was no risk of her falling asleep. The strong cup of coffee she had drunk before Roger arrived would see to that.

After an hour, she rose, took off her remaining clothes, and changed into her new nightdress. She let her hair loose from it's tie, allowing it to fall over her shoulders. She brushed it carefully, then opened the wardrobe door to check her apperance in the full length mirror.

Isobel had once watched a fascinating TV program where electronic head bands had been placed on a group of young men and women who were to meet each other for the first time in a restaurant. The headbands supposedly monitored their "brain activity". In reality the headbands had a concealed miniature camera. This camera allowed the researchers to monitor exactly what a young persons eyes do look at, when they meet an attractive member of the opposite sex. Would it be the face .... the legs .... the eyes .... the hair ....

No .... the cameras showed that it wasn't any of those ....

Isobel looked in the mirror, and immediately suspected that the designers of this night dress must have seen the very same documentary. Her feminine form was displayed to perfection. She saw that the butterflies were carefully positioned to draw the eye.,

Isobel took a very deep breath. Her heart seemed to be beating quite loudly.

She picked up her candle stick, let herself out of her room, crossed the lounge, and stood at Roger's door.

Tyson watched with interest from his position by the stove.

Isobel gently opened Roger's door and slipped quietly into his room. She stood there looking down at him. His candle was still alight on the bedside table.

"Roger", said Isobel. She touched him gently on the shoulder.

He stirred, opened his eyes, lay quite still for a moment, then pulled himself up in the bed. He sat there looking at Isobel.

"Roger", she said. "Please don't speak .... just listen to what I have to say first".

He nodded.

Isobel did just wonder where his eyes might be looking. She remembered the documentary .... and the butterflies.

She blushed.

"Roger", she said. "I've always seen myself as a very modern and independent young woman. I've never had any desire to get involved in a relationship with the opposite sex. In fact I've looked at the girls I know .... and seen them with their boyfriends .... and thought that what they were doing was as much out of a desire to conform, as it was anything else. I thought they were "role playing". I thought their behaviour was largely "affectation".

And then I saw you with Debbie .... and I saw John with Lorraine"

Isobel paused. She was near to tears.

"And then .... outside "Thai Sing Can" .... you put your arms around me. And something happened that I never expected .... and that I didn't know was possible".

She faltered ....

"And this afternoon .... in Costa's .... I met an old schoolfriend. She had a new baby with her, and she let me hold her little daughter ....

And I realised that, although I might think myself "sophisticated", and "intelligent", and "independent" .... well it's all really just an act .... and what I really am, underneath it all, is a young woman who wants a husband to love me, and hold me .... and I want to stand by his side .... and I want to hold our baby in my arms ....".

She paused for breath. She smiled bravely at Roger.

"Roger", she said. "I have come to you to ask you .... will you accept me as your wife".

Roger pushed the covers aside. He stood, and came to Isobel, and put his arms gently round her. They stood like that for a long time. Roger gently allowing Isobel to become used to the sensation. He felt her slowly relax .... her head rest against his shoulder ....

And when he thought there had been time enough .... he picked her up .... and layed her gently in his bed .... and he joined her there ....

And now Isobel began to cry .... and Roger held her .... and soothed her.

And Awesome God looked down, and watched Isobel cry.

But this time .... it perhaps wasn't quite so bad .... being Awesome God .... and watching people cry ....

TEN

Tyson watched Isobel enter Roger's room. He went and stood guard outside the door.

All seemed peaceful. Tyson looked thoughtfully across the room, to where Isobel and Roger's mobile phones were laying on the coffee table. He went over, and carefully picked them up, one at a time, and carried them to his basket. He layed them on his blanket .... and covered them with a cushion from the sofa.

He ensured the landline would remain silent by the simple expedient of lifting the receiver from it's base, and laying it to one side.

He grunted softly to himself. He wanted the Boss and Isobel to have a peaceful night. He returned to his position by the bedroom door, and settled down to wait.

....

The fire in the woodstove burned very low, until just the slightest flickering of flame remained, to cast strange shadows around the lounge.

There comes a time in any house .... in the early hours .... when all becomes silent. And when sleep reachest it's deepest point.

And at that time .... Tyson stirred. He stood .... and pressed his nose against Roger's door. It swung open. Tyson had long known that the latch was broken. The door stayed closed, simply because it was a tight fit in the frame.

This domestic defect was on Roger's list of "things to do".

Tyson entered the room. He turned, and pushed the door closed behind him. He looked at Roger .... and at Isobel .... and then he went and layed down in the corner. The room seemed filled with contentment, and peaceful happiness.

Tyson watched over them .... his eyes bright in the candle flames. He sat .... until the candles expired .... first one, and then the other. And Tyson watched over Roger and Isobel. And he watched the smoke from the candle wicks rising to the ceiling .... and .... as it gathered there .... he saw the first tiny point of golden light appear.

It seemed to play in the smoke .... shooting from one side of the room to the other. And then it shot down to Isobel, and circled around her brow, as she lay asleep on the pillow.

Tyson stood .... and growled softly. His ears went back .... but the tiny light came to him .... and settled on his nose .... and Tyson looked at it .... and his ears relaxed .... and he settled down to watch.

The light .... the tiniest of tiny golden stars .... returned to the ceiling. It seemed to hover .... almost stationary for a moment ....before beginning a steady circular motion. It was soon joined by another .... just like it .... and then another .... and another .... and by more .... and more .... and more .... until there were thousands of tiny pinpoints of golden light swirling in unison below the ceiling.

The circular mass shimmered, and swirled .... and then it began to elongate .... and to take on a human form. A human shape of dazzling golden brightness .... shifting .... and undulating .... in the haze of smoke from the candles.

And then .... in a moment .... it fell. It fell upon Isobel .... and for the briefest of moments her form glowed with golden light, as she lay beneath the coverlet.

And then the light was gone. And the last traces of red embers died on the candle wicks .... and Tyson lay down to sleep.

He dreamed about a golden star .... a golden star that had perched on his nose .... and he dreamed about what it had said to him ....

....

They asked the taxi driver if he would wait ....

He agreed.

"Not likely to get another fare at this time in the morning", he said.

Jesus rested his palm against Roger's entrance gates for a moment .... and then gently pushed them open.

"How do you do that", said Debbie. "She had been studying the security lock keypad on the left hand gate post.

"I've always been good with locks", said Jesus. "..................except when people lock me out of their hearts ....".

Debbie rolled her eyes skyward.

They went up the steps to the front door. Again Jesus rested his palm against it. He applied a gentle pressure, and it opened noiselessly.

They walked across the lounge, the glow from Jesus' robes giving them sufficent light to negotiate the furniture. They stood in front of Roger's bedroom door.

"You can do this one", Jesus said to Debbie.

She placed her palm on the door, and pushed.

It opened.

"Wow", said Debbie.

Jesus smiled.

They went into the room .... and stood looking at the sleeping forms in the bed.

"So how do you feel about what you see", Jesus asked.

Debbie turned to Him.

"It's not like I thought it would be", she said. "They look so peaceful and happy together".

Jesus nodded.

"You must talk to Isobel", he said. "Roger will not wake".

He placed his hand on Isobel's forehead .... and she stirred .... and opened her eyes. Jesus looked to Debbie. He went to the corner of the room, and knelt, and whispered gently to Tyson.

"Isobel", said Debbie. "Don't be alarmed .... its me .... Debbie".

Isobel looked sleepily at her. She reached her hand out to Debbie .... and Debbie took it between her own.

"Am I dreaming", Isobel said.

"You're not dreaming Isobel", said Debbie. "I really am here".

Isobel came wide awake .... and sat up. She looked at Debbie .... and then she looked at Roger. She blushed .... her eyes fell.

"Debbie", she said. "I'm just so awfully ....".

Debbie put her arms around Isobel and held her close.

"Isobel", she said. "It's OK .... it's really OK. There is absolutely nothing to be sorry about .... I promise you".

Isobel drew back and stared into Debbie's eyes.

"Debbie", she said, looking puzzled. "You have orange eyes".

"I know", said Debbie. "Technical difficulties apparently".

She cast a withering glance behind her, but Jesus was still talking to Tyson.

"So Roger's request was granted", said Isobel. "You really are alive again..............".

She looked down at Roger.

"He won't wake up", said Debbie .... helpfully.

Isobel had become very thoughtful.

"Do you know that I prayed to Awesome God", she said.

"I know", said Debbie.

Isobel looked at Debbie .... and at Roger .... and back to Debbie".

"But how is this all ....".

Debbie embraced her again.

"Isobel, you are going to have to trust me", she said. "You are really really going to have to trust me. Please say you will .... and it will all work out .... I promise you".

Isobel stared at Debbie.

"I'm scared", she said.

At that moment .... Jesus was there.

Isobel looked in awe at Him.

She looked at Debbie. Debbie saw the question forming ......

"Yes, Isobel", she said. "It really is Him".

Jesus reached down and kissed Isobel on the forehead.

"You will need courage Isobel", He said. "You will need your greatest courage when it appears that all is lost to you".

"Isobel", said Debbie. "In a moment He will touch you on your brow .... and you will fall asleep again .... but before that happens .... we have to ask you to do something for us".

Isobel nodded. She was staring at Jesus.

"Isobel", He said. "You must bring Roger to the doors between the Worlds at noon tomorrow".

"He means the corridor in my block of flats", said Debbie.

Isobel nodded.

"At noon tomorrow", she said.

"Isobel", said Jesus. "You have always been known in my Father's house. Trust .... and all will be well".

He touched Isobel on the forehead. She closed her eyes .... laid back onto her pillow .... and was asleep.

Jesus looked to Debbie.

"Let's not keep the taxi waiting", he said. "Breakfast at your flat young lady".

"Honeycomb and broiled fish", said Debbie.

Jesus grimaced.

"I was hoping for scrambled eggs on toast", he said.

Debbie laughed.

"We'll have to find a "One Stop" on the way", she said.

....

The taxi driver was waiting. He had dozed off.

"Southampton .... just off Bassett Avenue please", said Debbie.

The driver looked at his fares. They were not going to believe a word of this back at the rank.

He sighed.

"Southampton then", he said.

....

By noon of that day Debbie's block of flats in Southampton lay bathed in bright spring sunshine.

Debbie, and Jesus of Nazareth, sat in the garden at Lord Wintersham's end of the block.

"A great deal rests on this young man's decision today", said Jesus.

He held out his hand .... and a pair of Bluetits came and perched on his fingers. He carried them over to a stone bird bath .... and left them splashing in the water .... creating tiny rainbows of colour in the sunlight.

"Are you going to try to influence what he does", said Debbie".

Jesus shook his head.

"He has to make the decision himself", he said. "Once made .... there can be no turning back.

This doorway between two worlds is a very special one. These doors were closed long ago .... but this was left open. It was left open because there was no other way for a prayer to be answered. A prayer not dissimilar to Isobel's ....

Two people met. They should not have met .... but their meeting each other resulted in ....well .... there was no other way. The door was left open".

"But now it has to be closed", said Debbie.

Jesus sighed.

"Yes", he said. "Now it must be closed because it is dangerous to both worlds. Two worlds were created so that one might remain if the other suffered calamity. But with the doorway in place .... each of these worlds presents a potential threat to the other. They are separate .... but they are joined. And in that connection .... lies their vulnerability".

They sat in the sun. The Bluetits finished their bathe, and flew up into a tree.

Debbie looked at her watch.

"It's five minutes to twelve", she said.

They stood. Jesus had changed his robes for a more subdued effect. He was dressed in tones of grey and brown. Debbie retained the red sweater and black skirt that had been loaned to her in the Hospital.

They walked towards the flats.

"At the risk of sounding dramatic", said Jesus. "That door was left open for love. And only love can close it".

He held open the door into the block for Debbie, and they walked along the corridor. They stood silently .... each lost in thought.

Debbie checked her watch.

"It's time", she said.

Jesus nodded.

Debbie unlocked the door. She hesitated. She turned to Jesus.

"Do I look OK", she asked.

Jesus looked up to Heaven. He sighed.

"Apart from a large white scar that runs right around your neck .... and your having bright orange eyes .... you are quite perfect in every way", he said.

"My hair is nice is it", said Debbie. She shook her mass of golden curls.

"Quite perfect", said Jesus. He looked towards Heaven again .... as though seeking Divine Patience.

Debbie opened the left hand door.

Roger and Isobel were standing on the other side.

Roger's eyes opened in astonishment.

"Debbie ....", he said.

He seemed almost incapable of taking in what he saw. But then he rushed forwards and took Debbie in his arms, and crushed her to his chest.

"Hi Roger", said Debbie. "I'm back .... and I hope you have been very good while I've been away".

She felt him flinch .... and then tighten his hold on her.

She pulled away and held him at arm's length. She looked into his eyes, and smiled.

"It's okay Roger, I know about you and Isobel", she said.

Roger glanced round .

Isobel nodded.

Debbie thought how beautiful she looked. And as Isobel saw Debbie looking at her, she cast her eyes downward. She was trying very hard not to cry.

Roger held Debbie. His Fiancee. The Fiancee he had seen murdered in front of him. The Fiancee for whom he had travelled two thousand years back in time .... And the Fiancee for whom he had asked that the natural laws be broken.

He held her very tight.

"Debbie", he said. "I love you more than you could ever imagine".

Over Roger's shoulder, Debbie saw Isobel begin to turn away.

"I love you too Roger", Debbie said.

She raised a hand to the back of his neck, and pulled him closer. She realised that she wanted him very much ....

Roger released his hold on Debbie. She let him go .... reluctantly.

He stepped back through the doorway. He caught Isobel just as she was about to walk away. He embraced her.

"Isobel", he said.

Isobel layed her head on Roger's shoulder. She wasn't ashamed to be crying.

"Roger", she said. "Awesome God answered your prayer. Your Fiancee is waiting for you. You are the most fortunate man in the whole world. I love you so much Roger .... but I could never keep you from Debbie".

She kissed Roger .... and turned to Debbie.

"Love him for you", she said, ".... and love him for me too".

She turned .... and walked away, along the corridor.

Roger looked at Debbie.

"Were we really married", he said.

"We were", said Debbie. "Married according to the rules of my world. Married till death us do part".

Roger looked long into her eyes. He looked with the purest love .... and she returned his gaze with the purest love.

And Roger kissed her for the last time .... and he released her from his embrace .... and he smiled at her .... and he stepped back through the doors .... and the doors slowly closed behind him.

Isobel was halfway to the exit. She heard the doors close. She turned for one last look . Roger was running towards her. She stood nonplussed for a moment .... and then she saw that Roger was truly hers .... and she started to run towards him ....

....

On the other side of the doors Debbie and Jesus looked at each other .... and they looked at the doors.

"Wow", said Jesus, "I really didn't know which way that was going to go".

Debbie smiled at Him. There were tears on her cheeks.

"I felt so sorry for Isobel", she said. "She looked heart broken. It must have been so difficult for her .... just waiting for Roger to make the right decision".

"Do you think he did make the right decision", said Jesus.

Debbie wiped the tears from her eyes.

"Of course he did", she said.

"Are you still in love with him".

"Of course I am", she said.

And as she said it .... the doors vanished. Jesus and Debbie were looking along an empty corridor.

"I've still got the key", said Debbie.

She held it in the palm of her hand .... and as she held it .... they saw it vanish away.

"It belonged to the other world", said Jesus.

They turned and walked towards the entrance .... towards the doors that would take them back into the garden.

"Isobel is pregnant, isn't she", said Debbie.

Jesus turned to her in astonishment.

"Is it Roger's baby", asked Debbie.

Jesus smiled.

"It might be", he said.

Debbie looked at Him.

"Will Roger ever be able to see that necklace of tiny golden stars around Isobel's neck", she said.

Jesus embraced Debbie.

"He will only see the necklace of stars when Isobel chooses to give it to her first daughter .... but I will have spoken with Roger long before that day will come to pass".

They went out into the garden.

But Debbie opened the door again .... and looked back down the corridor.

She smiled brightly ....

"Nigel", she said. "I have seriously promised myself that I am never working with you again .... period".

Nigel winced.

Debbie closed the door.

"Oh bother ....", she said.

Jesus stood waiting for her.

"Debbie", he said. "Are you OK ....really".

Debbie came to Him .... and slipped her hand into his.

"How could I not be OK", she said. "I have you, don't I .... and you will be with me always ....".

She stood and looked at Jesus .... and smiled .... and she began to cry.

And Awesome God looked down and watched.

And sometimes it's not quite so awful .... being Awesome God .... and watching people cry.

WILL

It had been a really beautiful evening at Sandbanks. Will was sitting on the beach, in his usual spot, watching the last of the evening sun reflecting on the water.

He had started to come here more regularly as soon as the weather had improved. Sometimes he brought his rods. He'd brought them this evening .... but they lay unused on the sand.

Will preferred to sit .... and watch the water .... and to think about that extraordiary evening, just three months ago. The evening the sea had turned red.

It had been nearly six am that night .... well, that morning .... before Will had made it to his bed.

Elizabeth had phoned him just after nine o'clock to tell him that the girl had gone.

The hospital had been searched .... but they could find no trace of her.

"And there's been a problem with the computers", said Elizabeth. "Her records have vanished .... even from the back-up systems".

Will was disappointed. He had been looking forward to visiting her again very much indeed.

So Will watched the sea .... and remembered.

His eye was drawn to a young lady walking along the beach, along the water's edge. She had a dog with her. She paused, and looked over at Will. To his surprise, she turned in his direction. Will stood up as she approached.

She had a figure that was "to die for". Skin tight blue jeans. A white short sleeved blouse. Bare feet .... she was carrying her shoes. Will smiled a welcome.

"Excuse me", she said. "Is it much further to the ferry".

"No", said Will. "It's only another three hundred yards from here .... but you can't get to it along the beach, because there are buildings that come right to the water".

The dog sat by his mistress' feet, and gazed happily up at Will.

"How do I get to the ferry then", said the girl.

"You have to go up the footpath, between the houses, just behind us, and then turn left along the road".

He turned and pointed to the path, where it came down onto the sand.

"Hey .... thanks", said the girl. She glanced down at Will's rods.

"Aren't you fishing tonight then".

"Not tonight", said Will. "Sometimes I like to just sit here, on the beach, and think ....".

" .... and sometimes you just like to sit".

The girl finished the saying. They both laughed.

"Hey", she said, looking down at Will's bag. "Is there any chance you have some coffee in that flask there .... I am dying for a coffee".

Will smiled.

"Hot chocolate any good", said Will. "I make it myself. I'm a chef".

"Sounds good to me", said the girl. "I'm Nettie, by the way".

"And I'm Will", said Will. "And who is this............".

Will bent down and rubbed the dog between his ears.

"This is Nobby the Dog", said Nettie. "He sort of adopted me when I moved into a little house in Bracknell last month. He'd been living in an old water tank on some waste ground at the end of the street .... but I moved in to number thirty three .... and Nobby moved right in with me ....didn't you Nobby", she said, tickling his ears.

Will laughed at Nobby's expression.

"I've never seen a dog with such a cheerful expression", he said.

Nettie laughed.

"He's always such a cheerful dog", she said.

"OK", said Will. "Hot chocolate then".

He pulled the tartan flask from his bag, unscrewed the lid, and poured a hot chocolate for Nettie.

She stepped towards him as he held out the cup. She smiled happily.

Will looked into her eyes...................

They were bright orange.

Will started.

The girl laughed.

"Don't panic", she said. "I haven't really got orange eyes. They're contact lenses. I'm a model. I came down from Bracknell to do a photo shoot for a book cover today .... and for some reason, I had to have orange eyes .... weird isn't it................".

"Actually .... I think it suits you", said Will.

"I might keep them in then ....".

She laughed.

So what is the book called", asked Will.

Nettie screwed up her face .... as though trying to remember.

"Watching People Cry", she said. "There's a girl in the book with orange eyes".

Nettie sipped her hot chocolate.

"Will", she said. "This is amazing hot chocolate .... it's just super specially delicious Will .... Super Specially Delicious ....".

Will looked at her, thoughtfully.

"May I walk with you to the ferry", he said.

THE END

AND FINALLY

It seemed as though we had lived in tents all that summer.

Isobel joined us when we moved to Dorset. It was the early morning .... of her third day.

We sat .... two mugs of tea steaming gently on the table beside us. I looked expectantly at her .... but she shook her head.

"It's your turn today", she said

I was embarassed .... but she waited .... quietly.

I took a deep breath ....

"How do I start", I said.

She looked at me and smiled .... and sipped her tea.

"Just say : Good morning Awesome God ....".

....

Isobel .... Thank you.

Also By Nigel White

"get Him out"

A prequel to " . . . . watching people cry".

A Soldier ... a Doctor ... a Linguist ... an Empath.

John Forbes, and Peter White have assembled a team of specialists. They are going to send their team back two thousand years .... to rescue the most famous man who ever lived.

They are going to rescue Jesus of Nazareth from the crucifixion.

But there are implications ..... can the team achieve their objective, without altering the course of human history .... and what might they learn about themselves, on their journey to the foot of the cross.

Over two billion people on this planet believe that "Jesus was crucified for my sins".

In his first novel, Nigel White explores that most extraordinary of all dilemmas:

"If you had the ability to rescue the Greatest Teacher who ever Lived .... from the most barbaric means of execution ever devised .... would you do it".

You are invited to join John and Peter, as they recruit their team, and plan the greatest rescue mission of all time.